WHAT A

Life

Emmanuel Igwaro Odongo-Aginya

What A Life by Emmanuel Igwaro Odongo-Aginya

ISBN 978-1-955136-30-3 (Paperback)
ISBN 978-1-955136-31-0 (Hardback)
ISBN 978-1-955136-32-7 (eBook)

This book is written to provide information and motivation to readers. Its purpose is not to render any type of psychological, legal, or professional advice of any kind. The content is the sole opinion and expression of the author, and not necessarily that of the publisher.

Printed in the United States of America.

New Leaf Media, LLC
175 S. 3rd Street, Suite 200
Columbus, OH 43215
www.thenewleafmedia.com

Foreword

This is s remarkable fast moving tragic story of a young man, Peter Opiyo, dogged by misfortunes after a very successful career rising from a Graduate Teacher to a Permanent Secretary in the Ministry of Education during the military regime in Uganda. The story begins when Peter is already a Permanent Secretary, happily married to Rose, a Matron at Mulago Hospital even though they did not have children as Rose was unable to bear them. Tragedy hits the family when Robert Opiyo, Peter's father is shot to death by robbers in Nairobi where he was the Regional Manager of Trans Ocean, Uganda Limited with its main Headquarters in Kampala, Uganda. Robert Opiyo's murder was planned from Uganda with apparently the involvement of the Government State Research Bureau, the secret service arm of the Government at that time. Robert Opiyo's death sparked off Peter's misfortune. While in Gulu for the burial of his father, Peter's house is burgled and swept clean except for the bookshelf with all the books intact and the house telephone. What surprised Peter and his friends, is that Peter's house is sandwiched between two Senior Army Officers, in Princess Anne Avenue, in Kololo. None of the Peter's neighbours heard any noise of the breakage or noise of the lorry that carried off his whole household items. As if this was not enough misfortune, on their way back from Gulu, Peter and Rose in shock, drove back to Kampala and just as they approached Bombo Town, where a military barracks is located, a military lorry appeared out of nowhere heading towards Gulu and drove straight into the path of their car. To avoid a head of collusion, Peter swerved off the road and the car rolled several times into the valley before bursting into flames. During the fall, Peter was thrown out of the car and sustained multiple fractures but Rose, strapped in her seat belt, was burnt to ashes. After semi recovery, Peter took the remains of Rose and buried her next tohis father's grave. Peter was completely broken, constantly thinking and weeping for Rose as they were very close not just as husband and wife but friends.

Coupled with the loss of his wife and father, was the loss of their property. Peter's inadequate salary as Permanent Secretary and with no access or benefits from his employment began to feel the pinch of poverty. His standard of living dropped and his only clothes which survived the robbery because he had them in Gulu began to wear out. The former smart PS was now a pitiful site but continued to be a dedicated Civil Servant. Peter's childhood friends, Andrew and Walter became his sole-mates supporting him not only during his family loss but also financially. To bail himself out the financial challenges, Peter tried his hands at various 'smuggling businesses' which was trending at the time but, all ended in failures draining his meager savings and pilingup debts with his childhood friends and relatives. The only glimpse of hope was in the ivory tusks which 'nearly succeeded' and would have relieved Peter from financial challenges but in the last minute, they were out-smarted by a disloyal friend of Walter who sold the tusks and he disappeared into thin air with the two million shillings. Peter's heart broke and he gave up trying any other 'illegal' business but because he had met a lady in Gulu who looked like his dead wife Rose, he fell in love with her and proposed marriage after a one night-stand. She visited the PS to'check out his social and financial status' before making up her mine 'to or not to be' his wife. The abject poverty she found her PS living in put her off. Peter did not know her decision. To win her, Peter once again was lured into another attempt and this time in 'gold trade' smuggled from Zaire and sold in Kampala. His fortune ran out again and this time, he called it quits. The rich young man of Nebbi who had tried his best to help him, even loaning the cash to procure the gold, felt so sorry for Peter as the attempt didn't work. Peter gave up but prayed a blessing on young Simon Ucamgiu who told him to keep the money he had loaned him as a gift. Peter decided to come back to Kampala and continue with his job as PS but after ascertaining from Rosemary whether or not she was still betrothed to him. On his arrival in Gulu from Pakwach on the train and with two hours to spare, Peter went to Wilobo Inn to meet Rosemary face to face only to find that she off duty attending her introduction ceremony. He met the prospective 'husband'. To console himself, he emptied a bottle of the local brew he had bought in Pakwach to 'kill his boredom 'on the long twenty-four train trip to Kampala,' In semi drunkenness, he decided to walk to the Railway Station in Gulu but his life was cut short. A military truck coming from the Kampala side to Gulu knocked him dead. His only living sister collapsed and died in Nairobi where she was buried as she had no known relatives. Peter's faithful friends organised his burial in Gulu cemetery as his village home had been so neglected during his struggle to break out of poverty.

The mystery as to who was behind Peter's misfortunes is never revealed but the reader is given clues throughout the novel, *what a life*. It is a compelling novel, historical and fictional. Insightful of the military coups rule with its state apparatus in full grip of the economic power through privatization of state institutions which enriched those highly placed in Government and their cohorts of smugglers. Dedicated Civil Servants like Peter bore the brunt or were killed off like flies. The novel is a must read as its flashbacks keep the reader glued to the text. Stronglyrecommended reading for literary and historical scholars.

By Associate Professor of Literary and Cultural Studies Charles Okumu
Gulu University, P.O.Box 166, GULU.Uganda.
Dept: Languages and Literature
Email. add: c.n.okumu@gu.ac.ug/ charles.okumu52@gmail.com
Phone contact: +256-772-961-256

Chapter One

Tu – T. Tu – T. Tu – T.

"Darling, someone is ringing."Mrs. Rose Lapyem aroused the husband.

"Umm what is it?" Lapyem retorted

"The telephone is ringing."

"A-s-h let it ring. Whocould be ringing so late in the night? I am drunk. It could be one of those sugar mammies or sugar daddies ringing."

"What an idiot you are, it can't be. It must be a friend ringing the house trying to find out something important or delivering an important message."

"Well attend to the caller then. I am unable to lift my head up. But do not get the shock if you hear I am going to be given a date."

"I have heard that many times and tonight is not going to be the first you rascal."Rose said and lifted herself up and sat on the bed.

"So you know?"

"Of course I do." Rose said threw the blanket from her body swung her legs out of the bed and switched on the bed side light before she walked and picked up the receiver of the telephone.

"Hello Mr. Lapyem's house". Can I help you?

"Hello Rose nice to hear your voice in the night. How are you dear?"

"I am fine. Who is speaking?"

"You should know my voice by now Rose. I am Christine Ange."

"Oh-oh-oh Christine! Is that you? How is Nairobi City? Your voice is a little changed, you sound as if you have a heavy flue. How is Daddy and everyone there?" Rose allowed her questions to flow with great excitement.

"We are still fine in Nairobi, and how is Peter?"

"Peter is here drunk. He was unable to attend to the phone. He was teasing me that the caller could be a sugar daddy or a sugar mammy but I told him that it could not be, because it is too late for such characters if ever they exist to ring at night knowing well that we are both in."

'Ha-Ha what a funny drunkard he is."I hope he is not failing to go on duty after all the heavy drinking."

"Oh no. That is the good side of it. He always wakes up smart without any hang over. He believes, the brand of the Local alcohol they drink does not cause any hang over.

"What is that Brand."

"The alcohol is made locally here mainly by ladies from the north especially those from Lira and that is why the alcohol is called Lira-Lira. It's supposed to be the strongest local distilled alcohol around. A tea spoonful could make you get drunk if you are a teetotaler like some of us. But, you find Peter taking a liter of the stuff every evening and you know he gets up sober in the morning. That is why Peter likes it and he calls it an appetizer for him. Indeed it's true with him, whenever he comes home drunk, he eats like a starved pig but when he is sober his appetite is very poor."

"Oh well if the drinking does him some good then there is no problem. By the way Rose I rang late in the night to keep you aware that tomorrow Daddy will be flying home using Uganda Airlines he should be arriving at EntebbeAirport at 10 am. The plane leaves

Nairobi that is of course Jomo Kenyatta International Airport at 9.15 am and by about 10 a.m they should be landing at Entebbe. So tell the drunk or you yourself should be there to meet Daddy. Will that be alright Rose?"

"Sure. Why not Christine?" I will go there myself. I will make it a surprise to him. I am going to prepare everything to welcome Daddy home in the morning and at 9.15 I will go and wait for Daddy. And he will only be surprised to see Daddy home at table at lunch hour."

"That means you are not going to tell him about our telephone conversation in the morning when he asks who called?"

"Of course not if I am to give Peter the surprise. I will keep Daddy out of sight from him until lunch."

"Oh well Rose, amuse yourself tomorrow. From me tonight, have a good night."

"The same to you Christine and say hello to Daddy." She said and hung up.

Rose walked back to her bed, and as she walked passed in front of their dressing mirror and saw her nude image in the mirror, she glanced at her slender body. She stopped to admire her own shapely body before she switched off the light and walked to the bed and entered under the blanket.

Lapyem, because of drunkenness, lay naked in bed on his stomach. The warmth generated by the alcohol plus that from the blanket was too much for him so he kicked the blanket away and turned on his back and continued to snore with open mouth. Rose slid in bed and pulled on the blanket over her head and soon was also snoring beside her drunken husband.

"We can't cross this river darling. Can't you see how swollen the water is? We must return to town take in more fuel and take the Eastern road to the airpot. It has a better bridge."

"If we go right back to town, and start again through the Eastern Bridge we won't be able to reach the airport in time. Beside you said we do not have enough fuel we shall be too late and we will keep Daddy waiting."

"Better be late than drawn in the river. I will drive fast and I am sure we shall make it."

"That road over that bridge is too bad Peter, the maximum speed you can drive at on that road is perhaps 10 miles per hour and now it is 9.45 a.m. I am sure the plane is due to touch down in fifteen minutes from now. If we transverse this body of water which is a few yards only we shall be at list five minutes in time at the air field. Oh come on Peter, take courage and let's drive through. Daddy will be waiting!"

"I can't go through this body of water. It's flowing fast and the surface of the bridge must be too slippery. We might skid there and the fast flowing current will just sweep us in the river."

"Cowards."

"They live long."

"Let me drive if you think you can't manage it."

'Well here is the steering wheel. I am not coming with you. You go and pick up Daddy through this road. I will walk home and wait for you at home."Peter said and got out of the car. Rose move from the passenger's seat to the driver seat behind the steering wheel and started the engine. She eased the brake and sifted the car in gear number one and set the car into motion moving at a crawling speed. She had gone nearly half way through in the water almost smiling in her dream that she was going to transverse the water when suddenly something happened. The engine of the car stalled and went dead. She ignited the engine but it wouldn't

fire. It only made groaning sound and went dead. *She rolled in the glass window on her side and screamed for help as the water rushed in the car washing it away in the fast flowing river.*

It was then that she woke up.

Rose found herself sweating. She was panting with fright. Her heart was slamming against her rib nearly bursting her chest. Oh dear she sigh as she found out that it was a dream. Peter drunkenness had reduced he had heard his wife groan in her sleep like a dogbarking in its sleep. He knew she was dreaming but did want to disturb her. It was until she screamed that he held her by the hand.

"What is it honey?"

She sighed and said, "Peter dear, I am so happy it's a dream."

"What is it all about?"

"Let me rest darling I'll tell you all when I am alright."

"Okay". Peter said and was soon fast asleep.

Rose was relieved that Peter fell asleep before she had time to reveal to him her dream which was going to make the surprise she intended for him less exciting.

Oh God it is nice he is sleeping, but why the dream? What is the meaning? Rose kept thinking as Peter snored next to her with open mouth. The smell of Lira-Lira alcohol issuing from him was strong enough to repel mosquitoes away. It was not until dawn that Rose Mary fell asleep again.

The beam of the early sun rise piercing through the glass window and the oriental curtains they had in their bed room fell on her sleeping face. Rose woke up and with the excitement of receiving Daddy home that morning went to the kitchen to prepare their breakfast the routine she did every morning before her husband woke up to prepare for his duty. That morning she did not wake Peter as she always did. She did this because she wanted him to wake up too late so that he would not have time to ask her about her dream nor the telephone conversation she had with Christine.

It was only thirty minutes to eight, Time to be in office. Rose went and awoke Peter up.

"Umm" Peter moaned and stirred in his bed.

"Get up honey you are too late today."

Peter yawned and rubbed his face. "Ha-a, I had a drop too much last night. Why did you not wake me up early enough was it because of your night mere you had last night? What was it all about?"

"Come on Peter, you are late it's only thirty minutes for you to be in office. And you know you must wash, dress, eat your breakfast and drive to office. Thirty minutes is not much. Get going honey." Rose insisted ignoring his quest into her dream.

"Oh well if you want to send me out without your dream then keep it until tonight."

"I prefer it that way Peter." Rose agreed and walked out of the bedroom.

It was not until Peter left the house that Christine got through to Rose.

"Hello good morning." This is Peter house, can I help you? "Rose answered

"Rose". She heard a dull voice calling her almost in a whisper. Before long, the voice went on. R-o-s-e this- is- Christine, morning?"

"Good morning Christine. What is wrong? Are you alright? Is daddy preparing to come?" Rose said in a mixed feeling wondering why Christine voice sounded strange.

"Please Rose I know you won't believe it."Christine said and broken down crying bitterly in the phone and continued to talk in voice of a dying person as she cried.

"What is this you are trying to say? Rose asked expectantly.

"Robbers"------Christine said as she continued to cry bitterly in the phone.

"What is it Christine? Tell me please?" Rose demanded and felt weak. She felt like crying without knowing the reason why Christine was crying.

"Daddy-daddy has been murdered by robbers who broke into his apartment last night after, I had telephoned you. I tried to get through to you in the night but failed.

"Oh – no – Christine that can't be, it is impossible, it is untrue I don't believe you.

Rose said and broke down crying bitterly jumping up and down with the telephone receiver glued on her ear. It just can't be- no-no I had prepared everything to welcome him now, today. Why? Why? Why? Did I not have a strange dream about him last night? Oh Lord why did you do this to us? Why? Why? Lord?" We lost our mother only a year ago and now Daddy is gone? I still don't believe it is true. I won't before I see his dead body. I want his body here then I will believe you Christine." Rose continued to wail banging the table on which the telephone set sat while bunching up and down on the floor.

Peter Lapyem, a swarthy stocky man with bald head was the Permanent Secretary in the Ministry of Education. He looked like a twin brother of his father by right of his birth. Before his final promotion to the rank of Permanent Secretary, Peter Lapyem worked in various posts in the Ministry of Education. His wedlock wife Rose was a Nursing Sister in Mulago Hospital.

Robert Opiyo, the father of Peter Lapyem worked as the General Manager of Trans-Ocean Uganda Limited based in Nairobi. He had lost his wife Helen Opiyo after laparotomy in Mulago Hospital in 1960. Helen left the widower Robert with two children Peter

Lapyem and Christine Ange. After Helen's death, Robert lived with his two children and never married again.

Christine after her Secondary education joined Stenography Course at Uganda College of Commerce which she successfully completed and was absorbed in the Trans-Ocean Uganda Limited as the Personal Secretary to General Manager Nairobi branch, being head by Kylihabandi John Moses an elderly Uganda working on contract with the Company at that time. Because of his ill health Moses was transferred back home in Kampala and Robert who was the Assistant Manager in Kampala was posted to Nairobi on promotion as the General Manager Nairobi Headquarter where his daughter Christine was already serving as the secretary to the General Manager.

He was happy to join his daughter in Nairobi who was to work for him as his Personnel Secretary. Christine was even happier to receive her father in the higher post of the General Manager, Nairobi Office.

When Peter got to his office that morning he found that he was feeling drowsy, a feeling he never had after his Lira-Lira boozes. *What is happening today? He asked himself. Is it the alcohol I drank yesterday or what? I usually feel like this when I mix drinks. But last night I drank nothing but Lira-Lira only.* He thought and yawn covering his mouth with the back of his hand. He was stretching his hand up when his secretary came in with some files and put them in the tray marked "IN".

"Good morning Sir". She greeted him "Good morning Beatrice. You look gorgeous this morning". Lapyem commented her.

"Thank you for the complement Sir."Beatrice had put on one of the latest dresses in the women fashion. A dark red almost see through frock with a white collar. She had been to the hair salon and done her hair in the latest style too, what they called the "*wet look*". The excess cream she applied on the face, and the red lip stick she applied with the care of someone who knows the job, made her look a girl of that year. The flat heeled shoes she had on made very little noise to worry anyone. However, the smart scent she wore told people that a charming girl was around.

"What are these files for now?" Peter asked lazily as he bent forward and opened the cover of the file on top without taking it.

"They are for those students whom you said should report today."

"Which students are these? I am dealing with so many of them this week."

"I think they are those supposed to be leaving for Moscow next week."

"I see, I will deal with them now. But I don't feel well today."

"Sorry to hear that". Beatrice remarked.

"Thanks, but I think I will be alright may be with a cup of coffee at 10 a.m." as they talked the telephone on the Secretary's desk rang.

"Excuse me" Beatrice said and jumped to her office. She lifted the receiver from the cradle and put it on her ear and said

"Permanent Secretary Ministry of Education office can I help you". Beatrice was shocked to hear a sobbing voice of a lady on the line.

"Yes please the sobbing voice said. May I talk to Peter? I am his wife".

"Oh. Sure, why not?" She said and switched the button on the secretarial set and immediately the telephone on Peter's desk became alive Tu – T. Tu – T. Tu – T."

With a trembling hand he reluctantly took the receiver and mumbled in it.

"Hello."

"Hold on the line for Mrs. Lapyem." Beatrice briskly said and put down her receiver on the set which went dead except the glowing red light indicating that it is being used. Beatrice slowly went to her chair perturbed. *Why is she crying?* Beatrice thought as she sat down on the chair. *Well I will know shortly, if it's not personnel he will let me know. I am not going to openly ask him. I know he knows I must have heard the wife crying.* Beatrice continued thinking.

"What is wrong honey?" Peter inquired in the mouthpiece when he heard his wife sobbing on the line. The tremor, the lousiness and the drowsiness he was experiencing before, all disappeared and were replaced with excitements and anxieties to know what was happening at home.

"Peter" she began; we have bad-bad news at hand dear. I have just received a telephone call from Christine now telling me that Daddy is dead."She said and broke down crying bitterly.

"What? What are you saying? Daddy is what? Dead? You mean Robert Opiyo our Daddy is dead? What happened? Did she give you the details?"Peter yelled trembling and sweating.

"Yes. She said robbers broke in his house last night after she had put a call to us informing us that Daddy would be arriving home today at 10a.m. by Uganda Airlines."

"Christine rang yesterday?"

"Yes the call which came in when we were in bed".

"So that was her."

"Yes."

"You didn't tell me that this morning. That bit of the news."

"I know I didn't. I am sorry about that but I just wanted to have fun with you. I wanted to give you a surprise by bringing Daddy at table when you were not expecting him." Rose said in a drawling voice and went through the whole story for him.

"Is Daddy dead, really? I don't believe it. I must book a flight to Nairobi straight away now. Meanwhile I want to find out from their Head Office here in Kampala if they already know about it." Peter put in curtly with tears slopping from his eyes.

"Just too terrible I can't imagine it to be true. No wonder I had that night mare last night. I never had such terrible dreams before". Rose commented

"I know you never scream in dreams but I was awoken by your scream last night. No wonder I was also feeling strange this morning. Anyway we must find out what happened and do what is right. I would suggest you put call to Christine asked her what is going on there. Meanwhile I will go to their Head Office here and confirm that father is dead and if so what arrangement they are making to bring the body home. If I do that I will go and book my flight to Nairobi now."

"Peter". Rose called him.

"Yes honey".

"Control yourself. I know it is true Daddy is dead. Christine can't joke with us that way. It is always difficult to accept such news of sudden death of love one like Daddy. It has happened. We can't do much about it now all we can do is to bring his body back home."

"I will be alright honey. Don't worry about me. I won't do anything silly to myself."

"That is good darling" Rose said and cradled the receiver.

Peter sat quietly at his desk with his elbows pinned on the desk supporting his face in his palms. He found himself swooning as tears oozed quietly form his eyes. He felt a lump in his throat, an angry lump which was strangling him. After sometimes he relaxed sat back on the chair and sighed, pulled a handkerchief from his pocket to wipe out tears from his face when the telephone on his desk buzzed again. He looked at it disdainful and picked it up after it has rung for three times.

"Hello." Peter answered without interest.

"Hold on the line for Trans Ocean Head Office." Beatrice said and connected them.

Peter nearly threw the receiver down and walked away. He knew for certain then that his father has been killed. How he wished he could get at the killers. He would castrate all of them before burning them with the strongest acid there is in the world.

"Hello, Peter here." He said with a thick voice of a patient suffering from heavy flu.

"Hey young Man this is Andrew here." Andrew was a pal of Peter. They were class mates at school for many years in both primary and secondary. They only separated when they both join Makerere University. Andrew went to do Commerce in the University while Peter took Education. Andrew was then working as Administrative Chief Accountant with Trans-Ocean Head Office in Kampala.

"Andrew, how are you there?" Peter said trying to sound normal

"We are here man pulling life around. "Andrew replied

"I have not seen you for a while. I was in our club yesterday. I drank lira-lira too much and it seems I have the hangovers with the staff for the first time." Peter struggle with the conversation.

"That's excellent stuff. It does not give any hangovers. May be you mixed with other staff last night". Andrew retorted

"No I didn't. May be I am catching malaria or something." Peter said with a shrug of his shoulders. He was impatiently waiting for Andrew to change the topic and tell him that his father is dead. *May be he is not yet got the news and this telephone call was nothing to do with the death of his father*. Peter thought and waited anxiously for the bomb shell to blast soon from Andrew. Peter last statement to Andrew indicated that he was expecting some sad news. So he thought there was no need to beat around the bush any more. There was a pause between them and Andrew said.

"Peter."Andrew said and paused. "I don't know where to start from Peter. I know it's painful but as a man"… Andrew paused again and swallowed saliva down his throat trying to get the best way of putting the sad news about the death of Peter father to him. Well Peter I received a telephone call from our Head Office in Nairobi this morning at about six a.m." He said and paused again and swallowed saliva the gabble sound it made in the throat was clearly transmitted online to Peter. "It was by the Personnel Secretary of the General Manager who happened to be your sister Christine "Andrew said and went on. The new was a sad one Peter. I don't know if she… she has communicated the same news to you already. Some armed thugs broke in the house of your father last night as he was preparing to come home for a one-week holiday. I am sure the thug must have been aware of his visit. They shot him at close range on the head and he died instantly. They took away all the money in cash plus other portable goods including his car. The police are informed and they are handling the matter. Peter, I can reassure you that all is being done by the Kenya Police to bring the culprits to book. And the culprits will never escape it. When the Kenya Police have finished with their parts, we shall bring the body of your dad back home ourselves so do not panic Peter. I have been told that the home and the entire surroundings are being guarded by the police and so is your sister, since at the moment, the motive of the killing is not yet known. And in that case I would not like you to go and plunge yourself into trouble there. Wait until the dust settles down and we shall go together. Is that okay with you Peter?" Andrew said.

Peter cleared his throat and sighed. "As a matter of fact my wife has just telephoned me about twenty minutes ago telling me that Christine rang us up giving the news that Daddy is dead. And yet she rang yesterday when we had just gone to bed telling us that Daddy was coming home today at 10 a.m. I didn't attend the call myself. I was too drunk to even sit up to talk in the receiver. In fact I wanted the phone to go on ringing until the caller gave up. I remember making a joke over it when I told Rose that it could be some sugar daddy or sugar mammy ringing. To which she replied that no sane sugar mammy or sugar Daddy could ring the house knowing well that we were together then.

Anyway she attended the call as for me after that joke I slept only to be awoken by her scream in the early morning. She had a night mare which I think is connected to this incident. I fell asleep again just before dawn and slept until late when I woke up. I had to rush through my routine before I left for duty. She deliberately refused to tell me that Christine rang because she wanted to make it a surprise to me. She wanted to go and pick Daddy secretly from the airport and bring him home and confine him in a room and let him out when we would be eating our lunch. And now we hear that Daddy is dead. I am shock beyond doubt but I am sure Rose is even worse. At least for me I wasn't expecting him but Rose. As you said Andrew there is nothing we can do at the moment I was going to ring you up all the same if you didn't. I wanted to find out the truth from your office and book a flight to Nairobi straight away. I wanted to go this afternoon on the two o'clock flight. I thought Christine was handling the situation alone there and as you have explained now, I think I will follow your advice. We shall wait until we hear that all is okay then we shall fly to Nairobi. Thank you very much Andrew. Keep me inform about all the new developments, meanwhile I will also try to ring up Christine now.

"I do not know if it is possible to talk to her if she is being taken care of by the police in her house or somewhere in the police station? I think the police want to know whoever is talking to her each time she gets a call to ascertain if the murder was political or a grudge or even the City thugs with lust to kill. Therefore if the suspected assassins think that Christine has some information which might be useful to the police to track them down, they could or may try to block it getting to the police by eliminating her. I think that is why the police are giving Christine that protection." Andrew said.

"You could be right Andrew, but it also depends on the state in which she is in at the moment. The sock she had needs someone around her."

"I hadn't thought of that." Andrew said

"Nevertheless that couldn't stop me from calling her. I know as Christine is the next of kin of Daddy in Nairobi the police will share whatever information they will find with her and the Head Office in Uganda. Beside she is in contact with Rose and I am sure she will call her if there are more to this." Peter remarked, thanked Andrew and added "I must go home and see her in case she has received more information as you said."

"I will also ring you up should I receive anything news from our Head Office there." Andrew said.

"That is fine Andrew." Peter said and hung up. Peter sighed and got up from his chair. With both hands in the pockets he walked towards the window and stood staring emptily in space, as Beatrice entered the office with her arms folded over her breasts. She walked in sorrowfully slowly and stood near Peter's desk, with both thighs touching the edge of the desk."Is there something wrong Sir?" She asked. Peter wheeled round and saw Beatrice standing behind him.

"Oh Beatrice, I got sad news that my father is dead. He was shot dead in his house in Nairobi last night. The motive of the killing is being investigated by the Kenya Police."

"Oh dear. I am sorry Peter. It is very sad Peter." Beatrice consoled Peter while she broke down wiping tears from her eyes with her well perfumed handkerchief. That triggered again Peter's emotion and he lowered himself on his chair and resting his head on the back of his folded arms resting on the desk and openly wept bitterly.

Beatrice walked around the desk and came and stood near him, put her hand on his solder and said "Peter, it has happened, there is nothing any human being can do to bring him back. We need to pray for soul only." With that tender touch, and the fragrant scent of the perfume near his head, Peter lifted his head and with both hands, he held on the back of Beatrice hand resting on his solder pressing down on it lightly. He raised his tear-redden eyes and looked at Beatrice and said. "I - I agree with you Beatrice I am sorry.

After a spell there was silence between them and Beatrice broke the silence and asked "Have they arrested those who shot him?"

"Not yet but Andrew believes that they won't go for long before they are apprehended."

"I am sorry Peter to hear that. Please except my heart fell condolences. I was really moved when I heard Rose sobbing on the phone. I knew something must be seriously wrong somewhere."

"Well that is it Beatrice" Peter said wiping his tears. "I am sorry Beatrice I---I" Peter said and paused.

"I know what it means". Beatrice said and walked slowly back to her office in tears also.

Because of that Peter decided to leave the office and go back home. He found that Rose was home and her friends from the hospital whom she had informed about the death of her father-in-law with her to keep her company.

The early morning news on Radio Uganda broadcasting the death of Robert Opiyo the father of Peter was sad news in the morning in the Ministry of Education Peter's workplace; in Mulago Hospital the work place of Rose and in the Trans Ocean Head Office in Kampala so that their friends and relatives who heard the news immediate came to console them. While those who could give him a ring did so that the Secretary was kept busy receiving and remitting the condolence calls to their house number every minute. In the evening their home was thronged to capacity with sympathizers' that came to console them.

Rose tried to contact Christine in her house in Nairobi before and when Peter returned home but there was no reply. What happened was, When Christine delivered the message to Rose and Andrew in the morning she fainted at the sight of her father lying in his night dress in the pool of his clotted blood. It was fortunate that the police ambulance was at site when she collapsed. She was rushed to Kenyatta Hospital in the Police ambulance which was at the scene. Therefore, although Rose got through to her house several times there were no replies. That alone caused Rose some concern as to what might have happened to her. It was not until Andrew enquired through their Head Office in Nairobi, his news source about Christine that they told him she was recovering from shock in Kenyatta Hospital.

The following day at mid-day there was not much news from Andrew. The only information he got was that the body of Robert had been removed from his house by the police to the police mortuary.

And the autopsy report said that he died from the gunshot on the head which scattered his brain out of his skull.

Christine had recovered from the shock she had and was still resting in the bed in the hospital. But later at 2 p.m. Andrew rang again and informed him that the motorcar of Robert, robbed from the garage, a Mercedes Benz model 280 Registration number KUM 305 cream in colour was arrested at a road block mounted at Gilgil by the Kenya police. The motorcar was believed to be heading to Uganda and that there was a fierce exchange of gun fire between the police and the well-armed robbers in which two of the robbers were shot dead, two arrested, and one police man was also shot on the arm and he is admitted in Nakuru Hospital in Kenya. Four AK 47 guns were recovered from the armed robbers. The two robbers killed were identified as Ugandans because of the identity cards of the notorious State Research Bureau in Uganda found on them. The arrested robbers, a Kenyan a well-trained ex-Mau Mau fighter and a driver, employed by Trans Ocean Kenya Limited, was arrested together with his Ugandan friend, an ex-Uganda police constable employed as a watchman. All the properties robbed from Robert were recovered in the car at Gilgil by the police. The two survivors revealed that the murder of Robert Opiyo was organized in Uganda. The two murderer killed were dispatched from Uganda to go and meet the guides one Ugandan and a Kenyan working with the Trans Ocean in Nairobi. These two were to take the murderers to the site of crime to avoid mistakes of home identity. They were supposed to walk in the house pretending that they had gone to say fare well to their boss and furthermore the Ugandan was to deliver messages to his home in Uganda through him. Then the two gun men would bust in, order, everyone to lie down and demand for the keys of the Mercedes Benz first and shoot to kill Robert Opiyo.

The Kenya police reports were compiled and submitted to Trans Ocean East Africa Based in Nairobi. It was then deemed that the heirs of Robert's properties should report to the Head office, for arrangement for compensation and burial arrangements.

Peter flew to Nairobi accompanied by his friend Andrew to go and join Christine to receive the body of his Daddy and return it home for burial. They were welcomed in Nairobi Central police station by the officer in-charge of the station who expressed sympathy and regret for the barbaric act committed against innocent Robert Opiyo on Republic of Kenya soil. Peter thanked the Kenya police for their vigilance which led to the arrest of Robert's murderers. He regretted the death of the other two robbers who were killed in the exchange of gun fire on humanitarian bases. He assured Peter and Christine that the arrested robbers will face the law of the land. "All the evil doers from the neighboring states if found guilty will be dealt with according to the law of Kenya." He said and added "for those people who have murdered Robert you leave them to us. I repeat, on behalf of Kenya Government, the people of Kenya and on my own behalf regret this barbarism very much. I hope nothing of this kind will happen again in Kenya." the Officer in-charge of Nairobi Central Police Station Superintendent George Kiruki concluded.

Peter thanked the Kenya police for their gallantry without which the culprits would have got away with their evil act. He praised Kenya police for the serves they are rendering to Kenya Government and all the citizens of Kenya and citizens of other states living in Kenya. Peter thanked the Kenya government for giving them facilities to return the corpse of their father home and most of all esteemed them for their loyalty to the people of Kenya and the entire African continent, which he described as excellent. He said, that was attributed to the good indiscriminative uncorrupt leadership in the country. In addition Peter said "good parents are known by the behaviors of their children in public places." That is to say if a child comes from a home where no politeness and gentility prevail that child reflects the same rudeness, roughness and inhuman behavior wherever he/she goes even if he becomes a leader. Because he will have never seen such virtues how will he practice? He needs to be introduced to them and that it takes time. A bent tree is straightened when it's still young because the moment it passed a certain age it cannot be straightened. So it is with us human beings. I am grateful to the entire Kenya police force and I call upon all of the men and women composing this body to keep up with their respect for the good names of the Government, and the people of Kenya and their own names." Peter said in his terse speech during the ceremony in which the body of their father was handed over to Uganda authorities to be flown home for burial.

The corpse of Robert Opiyo was flown home to Uganda on East Africa Airways by the Trans Ocean Company and it was welcomed at Entebbe International Airport where several mourners had gathered to wait the return of the body from Kenya. That same day in the evening the body of Robert was flown in a helicopter to his home Town in Tee Got in Acholi District where he was to be laid to rest.

Chapter Two

After the burial, Peter the only son of his parents, had to organize the last funeral rite of his father. Six months after, with the help of his wife Rose and Christine, Peter finished buying the essential requirements for the last funeral rite of their father according to the custom of the Acholi. It left them broke without a penny on their account. Being a kind popular man, men and women, relatives and friends, from all over the district came to attend the last funeral rite of Robert Opiyo. There were friends from the Trans Ocean the company in which he worked; Peter's friends from the Ministry of Education; Rose friends from the Ministry of Health; Christine's friends from Nairobi and within the country; destitute and freaks all assembled to attend the last funeral rite of Robert.

A week of prayers, eating, drinking and dancing passed by, the last funeral rite of Robert was accomplished according to the Acholi tradition. At the end of rite, Peter, Rose and Christine were then at peace with the spirit of their father Robert. The visitors who came began to disperse to their homes after having eaten and drunk every penny of Peter, Rose and Christine. The two didn't know how to go and start their lives again after going back to their respective duty stations. They had no money. As a result, instead of flying back to Nairobi Christine had to go by road using Akamba Bus through Busia to Nairobi.

Andrew was one of those who left earlier for Kampala as the Head office in Kampala was under his control. Peter had asked him to check on their home because he and Rose were going to be away until everyone else has gone. Andrew had no objection to that. When he got to Kampala he checked on the home of Peter. Everything was alright. He phoned him and told him his finding on the second day. In the evening Andrew went to check on Peters home again. He found that everything was alright. With those findings and the security of the area in Kololo Andrew did not think anyone would burgle into Peter's home in the highly secured place like Kololo.

I don't think anything wrong will happen to his home. Kololo is a safe area where thugs fear. Here we are mixed up. Some top officers in the army, police and prison officers are here and one must be isolated and identified before his house is robbed. And of course the fear that the next home could be that of an army officer renders this place free of these rascals." Andrew thought as he drove back home from Princess Anne Avenue where Peter's home was. When he got home he had a bath and supper before he went to sleep.

Convinced about the safety of Kololo residential areas, Andrew skipped two days without checking on Peter's home. On the third day, Andrew drove a friend who lived in lower Kololo along Kabaka Mutesa 1 Road which connects to Princess Anne Avenue where Peter lived. On his way back home he drove following Princess Anne Avenue with the intention of having a glance at Peter's home. On reaching Peter's home, he found the gate open. He braked and walked out of the car. *Has Peter come back? If so, then at what time? And why did he not let me know?* He thought as he walked to the gate. The bed sheet he met in the compound told him that there was something wrong in the home. *But I was here two nights ago and everything was alright. What are all these?* Andrew thought as he walked, almost running past the bed sheet lying in the compound to the main house. His heart pumping fast in his chest was almost making him breathless as he ran towards the house. The open door, the silence in the house, the emptiness of the sitting room and the dining room told him that some people were in that house illegally. The door heading to the corridor to the bed rooms was forced open. The door handle hang on the door frame on only one nail. The locks were unscrewed out and it was lying down on the floor below the door. Andrew without touching anything walked hurriedly into the bed rooms. All the doors to the built in wardrobes stood open looking at him sorrowfully with all their locks either unscrewed out or thrown on the floor or were force opened and remain hanging limply on the doors. Their contents were all removed. The spring beds stood without the sponge mattresses. The window curtains were all gone. A number of small items like Rose's lip sticks and cuties were scattered on the floor. Andrew walked back slowly to the dining hall. The door to the sideboard were Rose stored her cutleries stood open without anything. The entire executive set of plates, cup, spoons they had were all looted. The refrigerators, the cooker, were all gone. The sitting room was left with the book self with its content intact as the looter probably didn't know the value of the books otherwise the Grundy Radio Gram, the colour television set the oriental carpet the executive sofa set and the many deluxe Peter and Rose had in the living room were all gone. Andrew without a thought slowly walked out of the house and stood at the veranda with his hand folded on his chest. He was unable to think. He failed to reason as what to do. As he paced in the compound he saw the tyre marks left on the ground by the truck which was used for transferring Peter's goods in the night.

What is all this about? Has this got any connection to the murder of his father, Robert? It was proved that the origin plan of his father's death was done in Uganda. Is it a follow up? What would have happened to him if Peter was in? The two robbers who got killed in Kenya and they were the killer of Robert in Kenya were all Ugandans from the State Research Bureau. The two survivors' one was a Ugandan ex-police officer while the other is a Kenya, the former Mau Mau fighter. They have talked to the police and probable the Kenya police have now contacted their Uganda counterparts and investigation is now started as to who in Uganda are behind the plot to kill Robert. I am sure Peter would have been killed. And who could these people be. And why do they want his life anyway. I don't see why. Andrew thought as he moved around the house nearly weeping at the miserable house standing naked as if it wasn't luxuriously dressed by Peter and Rose. It looked gloomily at him only some metal on the roof snapped as if to tell him that "we have had a bad night last night". After he had gone all round the house Andrew came and stood at the gate and saw that the padlock used for locking the door was cut using a hack saw. Andrew walked out and stood at the door of his car undecided which way to go. At last he decided to drive to the Central Police station in the center of Kampala City to report the robbery. When his statement was written down by the police at the front desk, a truck full of a team of police experts were dispatched accompanied by Andrew back to the scene. As the Police with different expertise worked on the house, Andrew thought he should inform Peter of what is taking place at his home. He did not know how best he could deliver the message to him. *He is not yet about to begin recovering from the sudden death of his father and now he has lost all he own in the world.* Andrew thought as he walked to the telephone set at the corner of the living room. One of the few asserts that survived the robbery in the house. He booked a call to Peter in Gulu through the post office. After, he walked out and sat on a form in front of the house Peter had put under a mango tree in the compound. He was connected to Peter after one hour wait.

"Hello Peter this is Andrew in Kampala." Andrew said after he recognized the voice of Peter on the line.

"Hey boy how is the city?" Peter asked with excitement.

"The city is no good at the moment Peter."

"What has cropped up again in the city? Is it the usual gunshots you hear every night? I hate the boys. The way they keep me awake sometimes at night."

"It is not that Peter. I was in your home yesterday at about 10p.m. to check on the home." Andrew said.

"And what did you find? Someone broke into my house?" Peter said nervously. Andrew paused and swallowed saliva and said,

"Yes Peter."

"Oh dear, what is happening to us?" Peter lamented.

"I am really surprised Peter. As I was telling you I was in your home at 10 p.m. I put on the security lamp on the gate and those at the back and the front of the house then I closed the door locked the gate before I left. Now, this morning I first drove a friend to Lower Kololo along Kabaka Mutesa 1 Road before coming away through your Avenue I was surprised I found the gate open. I thought probably you came back in the night as you told me that you had another set of keys with you. But I wasn't sure. Just as I entered the gate I saw one bed sheet lying in the lawn. I knew at once that there was something wrong in the house. I ran to the house just to find the main door opened the lock was screwed out from the door. I walked in and….. Andrew paused to swallow saliva; Peter, the thing left are those which they do not know the value or too heavy to be taken out that time. All other things are stolen Peter."

"Oh God! What have I done to deserve all these, all our dresses stolen?"

"Yes Peter. Only your bookshelf and the books, the double beds and may be the wardrobes and the telephone set I am using now are the only things left."

Peter sighed and found it was difficult to think and to talk.

"Have you reported the matter to the police?"

"Yes I did Peter and I am here with them."

"Well Andrew I don't know what to say now. I don't know how Rose will receive the shocking news tonight. She has gone to town I am expecting her any time before noon."

"I am really sorry Peter."

"Well Andrew it has happened and I don't think the police will be of any use to recover any of my properties. Firstly, they have no time to spend on investigating about anything seriously these days. Secondly one must give a big bribe before they can do anything useful and now I am broke in the true sense of the words. I can't afford to part with any reasonable amount of money to make them work because I don't have any. Thirdly you know my home is sandwiched between the two Major Generals and it's very unlikely that ordinary thieves with a lorry could drive audaciously in my compound and spend the whole night empting my house completely dry without any fear nor scare that there could be someone in the neighbuoring homes hearing the noises. I......well anything is possible these days in Uganda. I won't like to discuss this on an open line like this. There is no security in Uganda today." Peter said emotionally.

"So you think your neighbuor should be in the know?" Andrew asked.

"I always hear clearly all loud noises from the two homes and it beats my understanding how security officers could fail to hear the unusual noise of that kind coming from the neighbuor. Beside they have guards at their homes." Peter commented

"Okay Peter. I get your points but let's wait and see what the police search will yield anyway. I will keep you informed if you are still staying long at home. But I would advise that you come here as soon as possible. The police may need your help in their investigations."

"As a matter of fact we were coming back to Kampala the day after tomorrow but as it stands now, if Rose comes back and I know the car is in a sound condition, we will come back tomorrow." Peter said

"We shall expect you then. You will come straight to our house. You will put up with us for some time before you organize yourselves. We have a spare room for you."

"That means forever is that it Andrew? I am saying this, because I do not see any future for us at the moment. To build up what we have lost in a night took us the entire years we started to work. And the same sum of money we spent for furnishing the entire house may just bring us a mattress today with the rocking prices of things in the country. Our earning put together is not much and how many months of service will that be for us to organize ourselves? It's just too terrible Andrew. I will come back and see what I can do. I accept your kind offer. When we come we will come straight to your home and be happy with your hospitality."

"Peter this is yet another death in a family so please hold yourself together and treat it as you have treated the death of our late father, Robert a week ago. I admired how you handled the situation, you did it with a lot of maturity and I am expecting you to handle this one similarly. "Andrew commended encouragingly.

"Andrew I am really getting drenched with the problems. Sooner or later I will reach my thresh hold and I might throw in my towel."

"Oh no Peter, you can't do such silly things I know you are a man of integrity and a good Catholic. You remember Job in the Bible. I understand your problem. If there is life in you, you will always succeed. Let us leave it at that Peter. I am expecting you tomorrow or the day after. Bye from now Peter."

"Bye Andrew." he said and cradled the receiver.

Peter sighed and fell back on his chair and stretched full length. He threw his head backwards on the chair and clasped his fingers together at the back of the head. He closed his eyes and begun to meditate over his problems. *My father was murdered in a cold blood by uncouth murderers. This murder was organized in Uganda and the murder squad was dispatched from Uganda to go and kill him in Nairobi. His properties were looted but were recovered by the Kenya Police. We brought his body home and we buried him. We have spent all our money to organize his last funeral rite. Now when we are penniless these house breakers loot our house dry. Is this a follow up of Daddy case? Were they after me, if so, then for what reason?" I don't see anything wrong I did to anyone. Well, maybe there is no connection. But no house has even been burgled into in Kololo and mine is the first to be meddled with. There must be a reason for it.* Peter thought. He normally slept in the afternoon but that day it was impossible for him to sleep. He was just sitting up in the chair when Rose drove in from town. Peter with heavy head, misty eyes struggled up from the chair to go and give traditional welcome to his wife. The transfiguration on his face was colossal. He tried to smile to his wife but it was like smiling with headache.

"Hello Darling". Rose said as she jumped out of the car. Normally Peter would have carried her shoulder high with a mouthful of kisses, light as she was. But that day he only shook hands with her and said "You are welcome back home. How was the town?" Peter asked with a voice foreign to Rose.

"You look sick honey what's wrong?"Rose asked ignoring his question. But Peter silently walked to the car and opened the boot.

"I am talking to you honey what is wrong are you sick?" Rose insisted.

"Yes I have a bad headache." Peter lied.

"Sorry honey Rose said and kissed him on the lips. Peter responded coldly and pulled her away from him slowly.

"We have some anti-malaria in the first aid box have you taken some."

"No I haven't I think I don't need them as yet. I will wait and see if it worsens in the evening then I might take some." Rose moved forward and put the back of her right hand on Peter's forehead.

"You don't feel very hot though."

"No. Just headache." Is the car in a sound condition?" Peter asked.

"Yes, I think so. You want to go somewhere now?"

"No. Not now but we are leaving for Kampala tomorrow."

"I thought you said we are leaving a day after tomorrow". Rose reminded him, and continued. "Why tomorrow?" Rose asked again.

Peter took Rose hands in his and said, "Darling, he sighed and went on, "We could be yet in another problem?"

"Problem?"What do you mean?

"Please take courage," Peter said and hugged her on his chest.

"What is wrong Peter, Darling?"

"I got a telephone call from Andrew at about 10 a.m. this morning. He said that thieves broke into our house and stole each and everything nothing is left beside the bookshelf with the books, telephone set in the corner of the living room and an empty double bed in our room. So think of anything we owned in that house, it is not there now. There we are honey we shall have to start again during the most difficult time. I don't see the solution to this problem now."Peter said as Rose wriggle herself from his arms and stood away glaring at him unbelievingly.

"Oh no--oh no, I just don't know what is happening". Rose said and collapsed on the car before she slid down on the ground sitting with stretched legs with the back of her head resting on the car with both hands clasped on top of head and began to cry.

"Honey I told you to take it easy. We are in for it up to our neck. Good enough we have no kids to worry us. Our misfortune in this line could be our fortune. No wonder we have no child."

"Please don't talk like that." You hurt me by talking carelessly like that."

"I am sorry Darling I think I am not normal in the head these days."

"You are Peter." Rose disagreed as Peter walked with the basket of food stuff Rose had brought into the house leaving Rose seated on the ground leaning her head on the car still weeping for her latest sad news, the loss of fashioned shoes, bags, necklaces, dresses and all her lady kits she had spent all their millions on.

After delivering the food basket in the kitchen, Peter returned to Rose and holding her by the arm, he lifted her up and walked her in the house as she continued crying.

"Take it easy darling God will help us and we shall be over it soon."

"I know darling He will, but that is not instantaneous, it will be done but that always take years on end and we need to work towards that."

"You are right darling all we need is faith." There was silence between them and the room was a quiet like a grave with each of them meditating on their past few days.

The sun was about to set. None had any interest in the raw food staff Rose had brought from the market. Rose turned her head wearily on the back rest of the sofa and looked at Peter who sat next to her. She put her hand on his and asked him, "Would you like to eat something?"

"No I am not hungry and I don't have appetite to eat."

"I have bought a lot for supper and I do not have strength to cook."

Don't worry. We shall keep them in refrigerator and we shall cook them at Andrew's house when we get there tomorrow."

"I wanted to make a special dice of pasted *Malakwang* with fish for you tonight."

"It's fine thank you we shall have it in Kampala. A cup of tea with some bread will do for tonight."

It was a sleepless night. Their double bed they always slept locked up in arms in the middle, that night each rolled away from the middle of the bed alone at the side of the bed after their tea. It was even worst for Peter who always slept well after his *Lira-Lira* booze. Without a tot that night he tried to sleep but no sleep came. He rolled in bed from side to side on his back, stomach but the sleep retreated further and further away.

Rose after having sobbed for most part of the evening was lulled to sleep. Peter heard her snoring softly in the sleep. He moved away from her and kept space between them so that his continuous rolling in bed from side to side should not wake her up.

The dawn reverted gradually into morning as the sun steadily crept up from behind the eastern horizon expelling the darkness away. Peter got up from the bed slowly to avoid waking up Rose who lay asleep with sad expression on her face the way she fell asleep. She looked less beautiful that morning than she always looked. Peter walked to the bath room and switched the water heater on. When the water was warmed, he came back to the bedroom and awoke Rose up. *We should be leaving for Kampala, by 9:00 am.* He thought as he walked back to the bedroom

"Honey, Honey, wake up." Peter said shaking his wife gently. She stirred, stretched and yawned.

"Umm." She said and coiled herself again under the blanket.

"Wake up honey we must be preparing to leave. The time is against us".

"What is the time now?" Rose asked and threw away the blanket from her head and sat on the bed inclining her weight on her left hand.

"It is 7.45am."

"How is your headache now?" She asked Peter ignoring the information about the time.

"Don't worry about that. Get up from the bed and start doing something."

"How can I not worry about it? How are we going to move if you are not alright."

"This is the trouble with nurses. Always asking how their patients have slept."

"I am much improved." Peter lied. As a matter of fact the intensive thinking he had it night worsening his headache so that he had to take some paracetamol and quinine at night in case the headache was malarial.

"That is nice to hear". Rose said and swung her slender legs out of the bed and got up. At the sight of her shapely body in the see through night dress, Peter would have heated up but that morning he need a glass of *lira-lira* to warm him up. He looked at her and managed a smile. He came and knelt at the side of the bed and put his head on her stomach as she cupped his head in her bosom and kissed it and walked away to the bath room.

She wanted to go and turn the water heater on but the glowing red indicator on the water heater told her that the water heater was already on.

"Did we leave the water heater on honey?" She asked.

"No I have just turned it on."

"You did."

"Yes. The water should be hot I bathed using it." Peter said. Rose turned the tap on and found the water hot.

"You bathe as I prepare breakfast."Peter said.

"Okay I will not take long." Rose soon walked out of the bath room and dressed.

After their breakfast they started to pack what they wanted to take with them to Kampala

"Honey I am thinking we should take this mattress and these beddings with us. We have the bed left for us there." Peter suggested.

"And most if not all of these cutleries Rose added."

"I never wanted to take whatever we have home here back to Kampala. If anything we should be bring more at home."Peter remarked with disenchantment.

"Are we going back in that house?" Rose asked

"What do you think? Peter answered rhetorically.

"I was thinking we move out of that house and find for ourselves another place to live in since, I still do not understand why that happened. I seem to think the people who killed Daddy are on our back. And why, I do not know. Daddy was not a politician and he never would want to be associated with any politician. I believe he was killed because of his job. Someone in Uganda must be interested in his job. In addition to that, the surviving assassins have revealed that the plot to murder Daddy hatched in Uganda, makes it more plausible to think he was killed for his job. Now they are suspicious that we are in the know and to tie all loose ends we must go and that also create more opportunities for jobs for their relatives yours and mine. You never know what would have happened to us if we were there. I am sure we would by now be all dead." Rose commented

"Well it would be a good idea to move out of the place but it might be difficult. You saw the difficulty we faced when the Ministry was trying to find for us that accommodation. Very few decent accommodations were left. What I think we could do is to repair the same house and bring back the government furniture we had returned last time. If really the thieves were after us, they could reach us anywhere even if we start living in caves or under water so long as we work in the same offices we have been working before they will still get at us. Don't be afraid honey? Let us put ourselves in the hand of God," Peter said assuring his wife and kissed her.

Everything was set by 9.25. Peter and Rose took with them whatever they wanted to take to Kampala. At 9: 30 Peter behind the steering wheel ignited the engine and soon set the car, a Peugeot 504 saloon registration UVS 360, in motion to Kampala. Peter wanted to make the 320 kilometers drive from Gulu to Kampala in two and half hours only. The highway from Gulu to Kampala was good and the traffic was light so one could drive at any speed he wanted. Determined to cover the 320 kilometers to Kampala by mid-day, after their prayers for safe journey they kissed and Peter set the Peugeot roaring down the road to Kampala, the speedometer flickering between 180 to 190 kilometers per hour. Rose apparently in approval of his speed sat mute in the co-driver seat with the window glass all rolled up. At 10.am they were crossing the bridge over the Nile at Karuma Falls.

"You are a good driver". Rose commented Peter for his speed. Karuma fall is about 80 kilometers from Gulu.

"I don't know if we shall make it. I want to be in Kampala by mid-day so that we could make some arrangement to have the repair on that house started by tomorrow. At least we can afford to stay with Andrew for only one or two days. No matter how terrible our house will look, those who know what have been happening to us will undoubtedly understand our position.

"You are right darling. I can't sit in someone's house indefinitely to be provided for with everything. There is a limit to such kindness. Beyond which you become bores."

Although she had slept for some few hours at night Rose still had some hang over which was soon activated by the warmth in the car and the speed at which they were travelling so that she adjusted herself and rested her head on therest head of the car and soon fell in a deep sleep. Peter saw her sleeping, he did not disturb her. He only shrugged and went on driving.

The time was 11.15 when they reached Luwero, about 84 kilometers to Kampala. *Well not a bad speed* Peter thought as he looked at his wrist watch and swept past the market at the road side and up the hill and down. It was then that Peter started feeling drowsy. Twice he dosed in the car nearly knocking his head on the steering wheel. *What is happening? I am becoming too tired and sleepy*

I wish she was awake she would have taken over the steering wheel for a while as I rest. Peter thought as he struggled with the sleep mounting up his head. They had reached Matugga Centre and the fuel gauge indicating empty. *I must refuel in the Agip Petrol station* ahead Peter thought branched in and switch off the engine. The petrol attendant, a young girl in a white dust coat, sprang out from the office and walked to Peter.

"Supper please." Peter said as he walked out of the car.

"How much?" the girl asked.

"Thirty liters." The girl set the amount on the pump and soon the filling pump was recording the number of liters and the cost at the side.

At thirty liters sharp the machine clicked and stopped. Peter paid her for the fuel and drove off. Rose had woken up briefly as the car rolled to a stop at the filing pump.

"Where are we now?" She asked as she stirred from her sleep.

"We are in Matugga." Can you drive? Peter asked. I was thinking you should remove the sleep by driving."

"No, I cannot I am weak beside the traffic is getting heavier as we near Kampala. Your speed is good you continue."Rose retorted.

Few kilometers later, Peter became sleepy again. He wanted to wake Rose up to drive while he rested but because of fear that she could even be worse than him as she has already indicated, he shrugged and continued to drive. As he descended a slop to bring them to Bombo, a military truck heading towards Gulu appeared on top of the slop coming towards them. Peter saw it and he became alert as sleep gave way. He drove on his lane living a wide gap enough for the truck but as he neared the truck, he observed that the truck was entering his lane. He wondered what the driver was up to. The truck continued to enter his lane as he drove. Seeing that the truck was heading for him, he swung his car off the road to avoid a head on collision with the truck, but the mid body of the truck got his car at the windscreen and threw the car in the valley below sending the car rolling about six times before it hit a rock and burst into flames. Peter was thrown out of the car a few meters away from the car. While Rose, who was strapped by the seat belt continued to roll with the car and was crushed by the metals of the car and burnt to death as the car hit the rock. She died sleeping. The truck driver did not stop but continued to dive away.

The kind on lookers who were at the scene saw how the truck driver deliberately entered Peter's lane and caused the fatal accident. They removed Peter's body from among the shrubs full of blood and rushed him to Mulago Hospital unconscious. Peter was admitted at the casualty department and was later transferred to Intensive Care wards for male patients in Mulago. The medical examination on him revealed fractures on the left leg, arm and two rib bones.

The sad news about the accident of Peter and the death of Rose was received again in the Ministry of Education Head office and Mulago Hospital with great shock and concern.

Why? They asked. Their Daddy's murder was the beginning of the tragedies. Their home was looted dry and now, this last nail on the coffin, Rose is dead Peter is in a critical condition in Intensive Care ward at Mulago. What does it mean? Someone must be behind this. It cannot be inadvertent occurrences.

The remains of Rose was collected from the wreckage of their car by the Mortuary staff of Mulago and put in the coffin donated by Mulago Hospital and brought to the cold room at the Mortuary waiting for the burial arrangement.

Christine, the sister of Peter had barely settled to start work with the new boss Moses Mushillaa Kikuyu from Kenya when Christine got telephone information from Andrew that Peter and Rose had a fatal motor accident as they returned from Gulu to Kampala in which Rose died and Peter is in Acute Care ward in Mulago. With tears Christine went and told Moses about the sad news. But Moses was already informed about the misfortune.

Moses had been the Deputy of Robert Opiyo, the father of Christine. He was one of those who escorted the body of Opiyo to Uganda for burial. When he returned to Nairobi he was automatically elevated to the rank of Managing Director of the company replacing Robert Opiyo. Moses had all along been a close family friend of Robert Opiyo. Because of that when Christine told him the unanticipated sad news, he automatically granted her permission to travel to Uganda by Uganda Air ways and some money for up keep when in Uganda and for burial as the contribution from Trans Oceans Company Nairobi Office.

Christine got to Entebbe and soon was in Mulago Hospital to see her brother. She was led to the Intensive Care Unit by the Nursing Sister in-charge of the ward. When she saw the bandages swathed on Peter's body and the medical gadgets on him. She broke down crying. But the Nursing Sister took her by the hand and led her out, since that room was to be noiseless. Later Christine was taken to the mortuary to see the coffin of Rose in the cold room.

Christine remained in Uganda living with Andrew before Peter gained his consciousness but he was not allowed to receive visitors. Two weeks after, Peter was allowed to see only close relatives and friends in the hospital. Nevertheless, he was unable to talk to anyone. He always sat on the bed mute. Whenever Andrew and Christine came to see him, Peter close his eyes and only tears oozed from the closed eye-lids streaking down his cheeks. No word of comfort was good enough for Peter lugubrious heart.

Peter and Rose used to talk about their first encounter in life when they met in train bound for Mbale, Rose's work station. Now that Rose was no more, for Peter the reminiscence of the episode was intense. This was what happened. Rose had booked a second class compartment No 2A to travel in from Kampala to Mbale a distance of about one hundred and fifty kilometers. A she walked along the train aisle to join her female flocks who were sharing the compartment with her, she walked pass the male apartment No1A were Peter was. She found Peter standing leaning at the window of the train looking outside the train. As she walked pass him, the baggage she was carrying in her hand, banged Peter on the thigh. Peter turned to see who had banged him. Rose saw him turn. She stopped and apologized. Peter accepted her apology with a smile which enchanted Rose. In return she gave Peter one which sent him looking for her everywhere. As they travelled Peter followed Rose to her apartment where she got her talking to two lady friends. When Rose saw Peter her heart leapt with excitement and desire for him. She didn't know why she reacted like that. She had never behaved like that at the sight of any man no matter how handsome. She glanced at him and he glanced at her too.

"Hello." Peter greeted her.

"Hello." She replied.

"How far?" Peter asked.

"Mbale."

"Oh I see I am also going there."

"You are."

"Yes." That was enough for that moment. At least Peter proved she was the talking type. Not those types of girls who find it hard to open their mouths in the company of men. Peter knew that with some luck he might meet her at her destination at Mbale and talk to her and may succeed. When they got to Mbale Rose disembarked out of the train as Peter did too. Peter met Rose seated on the bench in the waiting room. She was waiting for her sister to come and take her home.

After they had fully introduced themselves and exchanged addresses, Peter left for his hotel leaving Rose with her sister in the station. The following day the two met and Peter made a pass at Rose. It was quite a discussion which bore its fruit after a week. Then the two began to live together. The love between them grew with time as luck was also on their side with their jobs. Peter was promoted to the post of Permanent Secretary to Ministry of Education while Rose got her new appointment as the Matron of Mulago Hospital. The grand superlative wedding of Peter and Rose was organized by his father Robert Opiyo, his sister Christine and some friends coordinated by Andrew. Peter and Rose by virtue of their status got for themselves a house on Kololo hill overlooking the City of Kampala. This was an area for gentle people who matters, in the Republic of Uganda where even flies fear, because of persistent aerosol of insecticide in the air. Peter and Rose spent their happy days there.

When Rose died in the car accident Peter saw no need to live he never slept well to give rest to his brain. In order to sleep, Peter depended on sedative drugs administered to him in the ward. Nevertheless, Peter always slept for not more than one hour before he woke up and start thinking about Rose. He became thin and boney his deep set eyes engendered by the continuous use of spectacles were further sunk in their sockets so that he looked no better than a monkey with high eye brows bones.

Often Peter whispered to himself. *Oh dear, Rose are you really dead?* As tears poured out of his eyes.

Andrew, his friend, in spite the fact that Peter was not responding quickly to his consolations, come every day and sat with him for hours in the ward even if they talk very little. More often he came accompanied by Christine. If ever Peter accepted the truth of life that his dear wife Rose was dead, after she was burnt to death in the car, and the woman who has been lying in the cold room in the mortuary since the accident, was attributed to the effort of Andrew and Christine. At the end of the second month Peter was discharged from the hospital. Andrew came and took him home. It was at this moment that Christine asked Peter when he would like to bury the remains of Rose. At this Peter stared at Christine and said, "As soon as possible and it must be beside our parents at home. We have no money now. We will make a quiet one only her parents and a few of our friends will be informed."

"That's alright Peter." Christine agreed with Peter

After the burial of Rose, Christine flew back to Nairobi while Peter came back to Kampala and continued to stay with Andrews's family for about three months when he was recovering from the shock he got from the death of Rose. He virtually forgot about the death of his father, the loss of their properties including the car. But Rose never left his mind for long as a second. Whatever he did he did with a divided mind. The side of Rose was a constant but the variable side of his brain varied according to whatever he was doing. Peter tried to do many things to normalize his state of mind. He tried to walk on his catchers to go and watch games like tennis or went to the zoo at Entebbe to watch, games he used to go for together with Rose and now doing all these without her made Peter ever sicker in the brain. But what Peter refused was to fall in despondency. He struggled with the hardships.

Chapter Three

I t was a year after Peter lost his wife that he resumed work in the Ministry of Education. The fractures he had on the leg, ribs, and arms had healed though occasionally he felt some slight pains over the scars. The person who should have been nursing the pains was no more. The therapy in the private clinics was expensive. His income was limited to his salary only. In the end Peter found out that by sitting in the office day after day reading those scholarships application papers, clearing files and files in a day was not paying him much to cater for his health and other needs. He needed a car for himself. He also needed some furniture in his house at home. He needed many things and his salary as a Permanent Secretary was not enough to feed him in a month and buy essential requirements. He thought of how to go about this but could not immediately answer the questions. *Should I resigned and go into business? And what will the business be? Worst still I don't even have the capital to begin the business. The only money I have is the little serving we left in Kenya when we were there in exile and that is not enough to start any reasonable business. Perhaps I should talk to Christine for help. I am sure if I remain fixed at this desk I won't get anything for myself before I die. I must have extra source of income to earn me a better living. Our salaries combined solved most of our domestic requirements.* Peter thought as he cleared files of some applicants applying for government scholarships to go and study engineering in Italy.

Possessed by this thought, Peter with no immediate advisor, cheeked for help from his nephew Lanek, who was a dealer in general merchandise. Lanek has been doing cross but he occasionally did it between Uganda and Congo selling food commodities in exchange with lucrative items like gold and beautifully boarded fabric to be sold in Kenya at later date.

"Yes Uncle Peter your ideas are good." Lanek agreed with Peter when he called him and explained to him his desire to try out in the same business he was in.

"These days salary alone will not help you much. I know you have been through many problems which rob money away from you and you certainly need some additional source of income." Lanek agreed to help Peter starts a business.

"Thank you for accepting to help me. What do you suggest I start with?" Peter asked

"I think you need to start slow by trying to sell beans in Kenya especially at Busia boarder would not be a bad starting point." Lanek suggested.

"Where do I get the beans from? I have none." Peter retorted.

"We buy these beans from Owino Market in Kampala. Good beans of 100kilograms cost 50,000 thousand Uganda shillings and the same bag you will sell at 2500 thousand Kenya shillings. And you know the beauty of it. The exchange rate of Kenya shilling into Uganda shillings is 1Kenya shillings is 45Uganda shillings. Therefore, your 2500 Kenya shilling you will get 112,500 Uganda shillings. So from one bag sold in Kenya you may buy two bags considering transport, meals and accommodation. But these you don't have to worry I will take care of it for you until you are well established in the business." Lanek explained to Peter. Peter immediately gave in. He raised the fifty thousand shillings and gave it to Lanek.

The first trip was a success they got nearly one hundred percent profit. The second trip was not so bad but it showed declination in the profit due to the increase in the train fair and the competition in the market. The third trip was complete loss because many new faces with big capital came in the business and they dominated the beans business. They sold in tons not only in one or two bags like the Peter groups. Therefore, long waiting for the beans to be bought consumed all the profit. Peter was disappointed and he lost interest in the beans business. Peter was back in the office as the only source of his earning.

Six month passed by, smile Oyet working with Uganda Libya Arab bank as a custodian officer brought consignments of box files to the Ministry of Education head quarter. Beatrice received him and the items. After, she led Ismile to Peter to endorse the delivery paper. Peter waved Ismile to sit down as he scrutinized the document Beatrice had handed to him. After she handed the document to Peter, Beatrice walked back to her office where they had left the driver waiting.

On the wall of Peter's office, near the door to the secretary office, hang a Calendar with the pictures of Tilapia fish. Ismile could not hide his feeling about his love for the delicacy of the fish.

"Is it easy to find this fish here?" Ismile asked as he pointed at the picture on the Calendar.

"I think so, especially at the fishing villages along the lake shore like Lake Victoria at Entebbe." Peter replied as he continued turning the pages of papers in front of him.

"Do you know why I am asking you this question?" Ismile asked Peter

"I have no idea." Peter replied curtly.

"There is a lucrative business in fish in the Libya Arab Bank. There are some Libyans who are doing big business in fish at the bank. They buy mainly Tilapia to take to Libya. They cherish the delicacy of fish from Uganda fresh water." Ismile explained. Peter listened to him and found out that he was getting interested. Peter lifted head from the papers and put his pen down, folded his arms on the desk and asked Ismile,

"Is it easy to access the buyer?"

"Very easy. Those guys have a special room at the back of the bank were they conduct their business. When they get enough to export they pack and take them to Libya by air."Ismile explained. Peter kept quiet for a moment and asked Ismile, "At what price do they buy the fish?"

"It's depends on the type of fish and the condition in which they are being sold. Nile perch, both fresh and smoked are cheaper than the Tilapia. A kilogram of Nile perch fresh cost 5 US dollars while smoked cost half and Tilapia fresh cost 6 US dollars and smoked cost 4 US dollars. Ismile explain to Peter the procedure of the business. After his explanation Peter gave him the signed copies of the delivery papers while he put the Departments copies in the out tray for Beatrice. They exchange their contact and Peter wished Ismile well before he turned to work on the other paper at his table thinking. *This sounds a good business worth trying but if I am to go at it I will require two things. Firstly; the capital, which I have already exhausted, after the bean deal collapsed. Secondly; transport which I do not have. For transport I could use the Departmental Land Rover the only one working since nearly all other Land Rovers are grounded because of lack of spares. May be if my friend could join hand with me we could go to any of the fishing village up country and buy the first cheaply and sell them to the Libyans.*

Peter lifted the hand set of the Phone and he heard the voice Beatrice on the line.

"Yes Sir."

"Could you give me Charles Owiny at Trans Ocean transport Department?"

"Hold on the line please." He heard the telephone of Owiny ringing. In a minute he heard his voice on the line.

"This is Charles speaking at Trans Ocean Transport Department." Charles responded to the caller.

"Hello Charles. This is Peter here."

"Oh man, how are you doing?" Charles responded with excitement.

"It is the usual struggle for survival in Uganda." Peter answered and introduced to Charles the topic he had discussed with Ismile. All Peter's friends were very sympathetic to him and were ready to help him out his problems. After his explanation Charles Owiny agreed to use his office pick up and also to jointly go with Peter in the same business. They also agreed that they contribute fifty thousand Uganda shilling each to start with. When all were set the two friends left for Rwampanga a fishing village in Bulemezi District on Lake Kyoga. Luck was not with them. As they set off, on the way in trading center Namasangali, the carburetor of the pickup truck they were travelling in got burnt out. They tried to look for a garage which could help them repair their pickup but there was none and there was no shop which sold the spare of the carburetor in that town. Peter and Charles were left with no other alternative but to tow the vehicle back to Kampala using any truck which was travelling to Kampala. They were lucky at 4 pm a truck from Gulu to Kampala arrived. They waved to the driver to stop. The truck stopped and the driver jumped down to talk to them. Peter and Charles explained to the driver the troubles they were in. The driver agreed to tow their pickup truck back to Kampala at the cost of one hounded and ten thousand Uganda shillings which was ten thousand shillings more than their capital to start the fish business. Had it not been for Charles who had a friend in Namasangali from whom he borrowed the difference of ten thousand shillings it would have been difficult for them to return their pickup truck to Kampala.

With no more money left Peter gave up the fish business. Peter was disappointed he didn't know what to do. *It seems I am worsening my financial condition. Why? He asked himself. Am I just dull to plan for business or is there something wrong? I try the beans it flop and now this fish business too, ate all my capital and now I am left without a cent what am I going to?* Peter thought as he sat at his desk in the office without a cent in his pocket. *May be all I can do now is to try to develop my home in Tegot. I will plant some coffee, bananas, so that even if I don't get anything from them now, in futures, I might get something when I retired.* Peter thought and immediately embarked on this project. He transported seedlings of coffee and banana suckers to his home and planted two acres of each. But the rain failed him not a drop seeped on the ground for more than half of that year to maintain the coffee seedlings and banana suckers which need plenty of rain to established and maintain the young plants.

While at home planting the bananas and the coffee which wilted because of long drought, Peter met Lanek again. Lanek had heard that Peter was at home and he came to see him after their failed beans business. Lanek had also switched onto selling charcoal. Peter used to see many people at the railways good shed in Kampala selling charcoal they got from Opit forest. It had never occurred to Peter that he could get himself involved in that dirty job because of what he saw at the good shed where the charcoal was sold. He never thought he would withstand the charcoal dust. But when Lanek explained to him how lucrative the business was, although Peter wanted to try his luck in such business, the temptation of increasing his income after the failed banana and the coffee farming has eaten all his money, Peter gave into Lanek and took his last bit of his serving as his working capital for charcoal, which the people in the business dub *the black gold*.

"Let us give it a trial Uncle." Lanek said to Peter. "I am going to offer you four bags of charcoal for a start." Lanek said aware of Peter's financial constrain. I will transport them by train to Kampala and sell them for you." Lanek explained to Peter. Peter looked at Lanek unbelievingly and with uncertain voice asked Lanek, "How much will that be in monetary term?"

"It's about one hundred thousand shillings only Uncle" Lanek said. Peter suckled and shyly acknowledged the offer of Lanek.

"Thank you very much for the kind offer."

As usual the first trip was very successful one. Peter was encouraged to pursue the charcoal business because of the amount of money Lanek brought to him. Lanek doubled the capital he started with to buy the four bags of charcoal. That encouraged Peter and he asked Lanek to use all the money to buy more bags of charcoal.

Since the death of Rose, Peter decided to remain a widower. Without a wife and no child, Peter's rate of consumption *Lira Lira* alcohol went up from one liter gradually to two liters every night. This meant he needed more money but with only his salary it was hard to make ends meet. Lanek, his nephew was one of those who were sympathizing with Peter's condition, because of that, he always did exactly what Peter instructed and he always let Peter try any resourceful business.

"I will do that for you uncle." Lanek accepted to spend all the money he generated for Peter and bought ten bags of charcoal to be transported to Kampala by train. Nevertheless, before Lanek could bring the ten bags of charcoal he bought for Peter to Kampala, the Uganda Railway Corporation increased their fare by one hundred percent. Peter's money with his nephew was enough to pay for the transport charge in old rate, but with the new fare he was several thousands of shillings short. Peter heard the news about the fare increment with heart ache. Because of his frequent presence at the Railway station for trade in the charcoal, Lanek was a good friend of the station Master at Opit. He negotiated with the station master to allow him to transport the charcoal of Peter to Kampala in the old rate but pay the difference after he had sold the charcoal. The station master agreed and Peter charcoal came to the market in Kampala. It was sold, and the bill at Opit station was paid. The profit Peter realized was small. He didn't know why the moment he got involved in anything lucrative business which people have been at for years, something must go wrong in the same. The profit he got back after paying the debt at Opit station did not give him the encouragement to continue with the charcoal business. Beside the increase in the transport fees by the Railways Corporation there were many compulsory complications introduced for the charcoal sellers. The Railways Corporation authorities also introduced compulsory new tax on every bag transported to Kampala and the use of special heat resistance parking bags for the charcoal which were provided by the Corporation. Many people including Peter gave up the business because they thought it was not worth the effort. These demands by the railway authorities made the business very cumbersome and expensive.

That is life. Why always the case with me? Others are succeeding in all they do but in my case whatever I had have been destroyed and the attempts to get new ones are being frustrated from all corners. Is it a matter of timing, planning or am I just made that way. Surely all these attempt, nothing has stuck so far! Well, I will never give up. I will keep on trying. May be one-day luck will be with me. Peter thought as he got up from his bed.

However in spite of the scarcity of money, Peter was a honest man. He always paid credit and debts. He never embezzled government funds nor did he take any Government properties for his own use. That explained why before Rose died when they got a home in Upper Kololo, they removed all government furniture from their house and replaced them with their own. In spite of his alcoholism Peter went to Mbuya Church of Our Lady of Africa every Sunday and never missed Holy Communion each time he went for Mass. He was a little saint on earth everyone talked well about him.

Peter tried to make money in the honest way but he always failed. He never envied the majority of top Government officials who were living deceptive luxurious lives because they have misappropriated Government funds or properties. Peter never thought of doing the same, because he did not know how to begin. At worst he could have made use of their office vehicle for business. That was the first thing which came to his mind, if he was to practice such evils. Unfortunately, most of their vehicles were not in running condition. Otherwise he would have once in a while gone to do some business with the vehicles. He thought about the debts of people piling on him. He didn't know how to pay them. His salary was not enough to pay the electricity and water bills and, feedings. He realized that he never had enough time to execute all the business he tried because he was always at his desk in the office and this could have attributed to the failure. *Of the many millions Ugandan civil servants I seem to be the only devoted one who always care about duty first but now I see that, the motto of duty first is leading me to nowhere.* Peter thought.

It was one afternoon when the idea of resignation was very strong in him that Andrew put a call to him. He was meditatively reading the commercial page of the *"THE EYE OF THE NATION"* newspaper when the telephone rang. He lifted the receiver and said.

"Hello"

"Hold on for Andrew" he heard his secretary saying.

"Hey boy good afternoon" Andrew said without introducing himself because he had heard what his secretary told him.

"Good afternoon Andrew. How are you there?"

"I am fine and you?"

"No good Andrew."

"What is wrong?"

Nothing is working out right with me. Have you heard of my disaster again with the charcoal business?

"No."

"I am out of the race Andrew."

"Why?"

"These corrupt Railway Corporation has made the condition too stiff especially for those of us who are beginning. You know Andrew it is enormously difficult now to start anything. Nearly every business in Uganda is congested by rich fraudulent competitors with billions stolen bucks and we with mergers money just can't try to complete with them. They do not care the terms or the conditions given. They pay for the items and sell their goods at any price. Meanwhile we the beginners want better terms and conditions to purchase the commodities at a fair cost and sell at big profit in order to recuperate the capital spent, but this is not working presently. This is what has happened with this charcoal business. It was quite lucrative I agree and my nephew was determined to help me. But now you get these big fish in the Railways Corporation because of conflict of interest in the business, are giving us impossible conditions. They are the ones who are selling charcoal in the good sheds in Kampala in different names. I mean they employ people from outside to do the business for them. They transport their bags of charcoal in the carriage luggage bogie free. Meanwhile any other person like me is charged 1000 shillings to transport a bag from Opit to Kampala. What price will I sell it to realize any profit taking into account the labour charges for the boys I hire to assist offloading the bags here, the eating and drinking at the good shed, the storage charge which is now 800 shillings for every night the bogie stay at good shed? Secondly it is very difficult to get the bogie from them. And worst of all you have to buy empty heat resistant gunny bags for packing the charcoal from them before loading them in the bogie. You know the dirty trick behind that? When you are returning your bags to Opit to refill them you are required to book them in the train where you will pay not less than 50shilling per bag. So you can see Andrew I bowed out, and wish them success."

"Sorry Peter, I don't know why I was pessimistic about that charcoal business when you told me that you had taken it up. I had the premonition that something wrong would crop up sooner or later because of the number of big people who were involved in the business. I overheard that the first lady is in it too. And you know any business where those lineages are, there are always lots of inconveniences. I know it was quite lucrative business as you put it but with the many tycoons, plus the senior staff of the Railways Corporation in it, I knew you were not going to resist the stiff competition. One needs a big capital to compete favorably in such a business. The tycoons of Uganda are infiltrating every sector in the country. They own everything. The majority of Ugandans are out. I think the best one could do is probably get export licenses now for this charcoal you are talking about. I hear some guys are exporting them to some Arab world. May be you could get some information about that from John Kiwanuka the owner of Moon Rise bar opposite the Uganda National Theater. I hear he deals in it." Andrew suggested to Peter.

"Andrew, I think I am now through with the charcoal. I want to rest from it. I have even now finished with the bit I got from it."

"What do you intend to do then. I have a friend who came to me yesterday with what I thought I should talk it over with you. May be if anything works out it might bring us some money we might live on for years."

"Is that so Andrew? And what could that be?" Peter grasped the suggestion with excitement

"Well he talked so fabulously about it. May be we should give it yet another trial."

"If you think we should, why not?"

"That is why I am telling you Peter."

"It is alright I will have to hear what hot line we have to chase with you this time I hope it doesn't ice out in our hands as it is always the case with me. I have seen many rough days. Lines as hot as acetylene flame but soon turned block of ice in my hands. It looks I am just naturally unlucky. I ask myself why all these failures one after the other may be if I get mixed up with commercial man like you I could be taught how to go about it."

"There is nothing like that these days in Uganda Peter. All you have to do is trials and errors succeed or fail. Gambling is the word.

That is what it is. You have seen illiterate guys all over the country who are carrying their pot belly stomachs everywhere. They do not know how to write their names not even any letter in the alphabet. Tell him to write one he will draw a line for a name but look at his business, it will be the most successful one employing those PhD holders in commerce. You need to visit markets around Kampala. You don't need a degree in commerce in order to sell *matooke*. Time, money and transport are all that you need and more money will flow in your account."

"Don't you think that is a fantastic advice you are giving, time, capital and transport? All those people you talk about have all these and these are the prime items in business I think." Peter said

"You are right Peter I will see you in the evening and we talk about this one. It's quite a hot line so long as we can take the courage to do it."

"Take the courage. What do you mean?"

Don't worry my honest friend I know you hate to hear about dealing with anything illegal but that is what Uganda is today to succeed you must risk your neck in all kind of trade clean and dirty ones and most of the time you succeed on the dirty ones only if you have a strong gut. You heard what people say "Behind a millionaire there are tons of rots. I am not encouraging you to................."

"I know Andrew you aren't. All what you are saying is the truth of life in our country today. You try to be honest you will eat from the rubbish bin of the aristocrats and walk the street with shoes where your toes are out of them pointing the way. Can you imagine that a pair of shoes, what they call the latest or soonest whatever the case, is costing 250,000/= shilling? Even in Bata the cheapest you can get is 200, 000/= and that is already nearly my salary gone." Peter lamented

"Forget it Peter I will be in your house at eight and we discuss this new turn up with you. Cheerio."

"Cheerio." Peter said and they both cradled their receivers.

Peter was perturbed by the undisclosed information Andrew told him. He didn't know what to think about. *He said there are some risks in the business, what type of business is this and what risks are involved has it got something to do with smuggling the illegal trophy out of the country or is he planning to swindle some money from company and he wants me to be a party in it. He is an administrative chief Accountant may be he is thinking of that. He talked of life in Uganda these days is a gamble you try and succeed or fail what does he mean by this. I am almost sure he is thinking of swindling the money from his company or smuggling some of these illegal trophies. I could risk my neck in the later but the former certainly not. I will advise him against that if he is thinking of doing so. I don't want to be a fugitive. I would rather die poor than steal. It will destroy all the trace of happiness I know now.* As he thought he remembered what Rose one day told him. *If ever you become too poor to live, never steal any money to make you rich to live, as it will kill you instead. You will be an unhappy man throughout your life. Even if someone is not after you, your conscience will not let you free it will keep telling you everywhere that you stole, that is why you are rich. She gave him the example of the army officer who was their neighbor. Do you think with their salary they could be having all they own today? I don't think so. They can't own buses, tractors, cars, radios television buy everyone in their families and relatives, bicycles? Those are nothing but death.*

It was 5 p.m, the time to stop work. The secretary walked into his office with more file, put them in the '*IN*'tray and removed those in the outgoing tray. She greeted him good night and left the office for home. Peter remained in the office for a while clearing the work he had started on. When he was done he got up smoothening on his old blue wrinkled necktie Rose had bought for him for their wedding anniversary. The blue shirt she also bought together for him was already showing tears on the collar. These were the few dresses which survived the plunder they suffered in their house because he had them with him when he went to bury his late father, Robert. Peter read through what he had written in the file closed it and pushed the chair backwards as he stepped out. He took his old jacket he had hooked on the door, the inner lining of which was already tom, he put it on and walked out of the office to the waiting Land Rover to take him home. When the driver saw him walked out in the compound, he came and helped him with his palm leaves basket containing some of his books and the newspaper.

"Hello Mukisa how are you?" Peter greeted the driver as he picked the basket from his hand.

"I am fine thank you." Mukisa replied the greeting and walked to open the door of the Land Rover for Peter. Peter climbed in and Mukisa pulled the door closed.

He walked to the driver door climbed in and ignited the engine and soon they were rolling out of the gate.

"Shall we pass through the market I want buy some vegetable and beans for us." Peter requested the driver.

"Sure why not." They went to the market and Peter bought whatever he wanted to buy and the proceeded home.

"Hello sir welcome home." The house boy of Peter, Daniel said as he came to receive Peter and collected the basket of raw food and drinks Peter had bought on his way home. Peter was expecting Andrew to call on him any time after 5p. m therefore some coffee and a bottle of *Uganda Waragi* won't make the evening too dull and boring. Businesses are normally best discussed with low dose of alcohol in the head.

"Thank you Dan. Daniel was an elderly man about five years older than Peter. He was a tall thin man with plenty of hair on the head but no beard nor muse touch. The temple of his bushy air on the head had started showing grey. Dan worked as a cook from his childhood up to that age. Changing bosses one after the other. Peter was the most recent he was working for. Peter had no idea of employing a cook in the house in the past when Rose was alive although they had a Samba boy whose works were to care for the compound and wash their clothes. Peter and Rose always cooked for themselves.

"I don't enjoy any other woman's cooking." Peter one day told Rose as they cooked together in the kitchen. But when Rose died he saw the necessity of employing Daniel a very experience cook. Daniel had been working for an English Constructor building the estate at Bukoto. Since the departure of the man from Uganda, Daniel lived with his brother at the foot of Kololo hill. His brother worked as an Accountant in the Bank of Uganda. It was Andrew who introduced Daniel to Peter. Peter immediately employed Daniel and the two lived as brothers in the same home. After work Peter always come home and sat chatting with Daniel particularly when Daniel had finished his work.

"Make some coffee ready. Andrew is coming to see us this evening" Peter told Dan. Dan collected the foods and drinks packed in the basket and walked with them in the house. When Dan had removed all that Peter had brought home the driver of the Land Rover ignited the engine and drove away. Peter walked into the house and into his lonely bed room and took off his valuable blue neck tie, kissed it and hooked it on the hanger on the door. He also took off his old jacket he had on and looked at the inner lining which was almost falling to pieces as if some acid was sprinkled on it. *Ah... he sighed, if*

I don't get a new one soon I might have to go, without one. A permanent secretary of all people go out in such a jacket and worse still because he has failed to afford a new one. Isn't it too sad? Peter thought as he hooked the jacket on the hanger. Before their home was plundered Peter and Rose wardrobe was packed tight with all assorted suits, shirts, trousers and neck ties for Peter. He was smart. Peter never put on the same dress twice. He was nick-named among his friends *"Smart Permanent Secretary."* Rose being one of the Matron of the Nursing Sister at that time made sure that her husband looked the husband of a matron of Mulago Hospital and Peter was always after the latest dress for ladies in the market for Rose. A good percent of their salaries every month was starched away for new dresses. The family of two was immaculate. But after all the disasters which befell Peter, at the wrong period of the year when salary of a Permanent Secretary is no better than that of Samba boy's wages Peter had to devise a means of survival first before he thought of a new jacket. It was on that day that he realized that his only jacket was getting too old and smelly for him to go in. Day in and day out, it was on his back there was no time to wash it.

Peter walked out from his bedroom in his navy blue trousers and the light blue shirt he had on and came and sat down in the sitting room scanning through the ***"THE EYE OF THE NATION"*** he got from the office in the morning. It was at that moment when he heard the spectacular sound of Andrew's Citron slowing down at his gate. *Andrew has come* he thought and glanced at his watch an old Oris he bought about ten years back. The nylon strep was torn in many places. Peter had never noticed all those, but that evening for some unknown reason he noticed that in fact he needs to refurbish all his dress. There is nothing he puts on which dignified him. Was it because then there was no one to criticize his dressing. He became a carefree man. Whatever he put on didn't matter. But to others they sympathized with him. Erroneously they believe it was mental break down.

Peter was angered when he realized the occulted facts. His pair of shoes the only pair in which he survived the motor accident had the heels all worn out on the sides so that he almost walked on the leather of the shoes. *What a Permanent Secretary* Peter thought as he got up and walk to the door to open for his friend Andrew.

"You are welcome boy." Peter said as he shook hand with him and led him to a cheap sofa set he had obtained back from the Ministry of Works.

"Thank you Peter. And how is your joint."

"It's fine, and how is madam." Peter enquired into the health of Andrew's family.

"She is quite okay thank you." Andrew said and they both sat down.

Peter tossed "***THE EYE OF THE NATION***" he was reading back on the dining table as Dan walk in with a tray containing two plastic blue mugs turned upside down in the tray, two coffee paper bags, a table spoon lying lonely in the tray, Peter used it for sugar instead of tea spoon, two pieces of fried cassava on two separate saucers, another bigger plastic cup stood up right with sugar in it and a metallic kettle containing hot water for the coffee completed the setup of the tray Daniel put on the coffee table in front of them. Dan was beginning to serve them. But Peter stopped him saying, "Dan, we shall do that, you can go and do other thing."

"Okay Sir." Dan said and walked back to the kitchen.

After their coffee, Peter brought out the bottle of the *Uganda waragi* he had brought with him on his way home with two metallic cups and put them in the try on the coffee table.

"I thought we could talk while playing with this liquid."Peter said and shot a dose in his cup and swallowed.

"It is a brilliant idea. It will make me think fast." Andrew agreed and followed Peter's example. The two friends started talking about the common problems of the people in the country. Whenever Peter was with Andrew he forgot almost about all other things except Rose because he always recalled how the three of them used to sit and talk together. There were very few things which Peter did which did not remind him about Rose.

The time was coming to 7: pm. they had gone through half the bottle of *Uganda waragi* when Andrew decided to introduced the topic which they had briefly talked about on the phone earlier. "I used to trust people but these days I have learnt to trust no one in Uganda." Andrew said and nodded towards the door of the kitchen which stood a jar.

"Peter understood the message and went and closed the door."

"You don't even trust me? Peter asked.

"Not even myself he said and they both laughed. Dan closed in the kitchen shrugged and continued with his work. *May be they are discussing some government secret or maybe they are talking about their social affairs which they won't like me to hear.* Dan thought

"You could be right Andrew but I still trust you." Peter said

"Trust but not too much. I too trust you." Andrew said and they both laughed again.

"Peter." Andrew began.

"Yes" Peter answered and put the metallic cup of Uganda Waragi on the table beside him and relaxed on the chair and began to listen to Andrew attentively.

"I met a Somali friend in my office yesterday morning. He is a driver with our company. He is based in Kenya. He operates between

Mombasa and Nairobi but he comes here whenever he has official job for Uganda especially his."

"What is his job?" Peter asked promptly.

"Hold it. I am going to let you have every detail of it. I told you this morning that you need a bit of courage to do the job. It's an illegal trade but if you handle it carefully you could not be very far away from the queue of Uganda tycoons." Peter heard the stimulating introductory speech of Andrew with a smile. He began to think of his need for money. *I definitely need a big sum of money to rehabilitate myself. I have tried it the honest way but the results were frustrations only. I am now determined to do any lucre job to earn me some money. I hate to see my worn out shoes which are no better than these of the bums you see in a markets. Yet those bums though they dress like that could be having more money than me the Permanent Secretary. Life in Uganda is now upside down. The so call educated are the beggars and they should be beggars are the milliners. You know how they made their millions through illegal practices. So why not try my luck with this offer coming forward.* Peter thought as Andrew talked on.

"Peter, you know, what I told you this morning is quite true. You may believe me or you don't. That is, to be a milliner you must have been a crook at one time especially in our present Uganda. If you try to be honest in all you do I can assure you, you will never afford to pay your electricity bill tomorrow and don't be surprise to use a latten lamp in this house and cook using charcoal stove." Andrew said and drank a mouthful of the *waragi* swallowed it and blew his seeks.

"I agree with you Andrew. I am actually heading to that." Peter acknowledged.

"Yeah man." Andrew said and continued, seeing that Peter was getting interested. "This Somali, a lanky sun burnt guy with thick growth of hair on the head, with the rapacious protuberant eyes that do not seem to miss any site where there is money. When you look at him you will know that he is a smuggler."

"What does he smuggle exactly?" Peter interjected.

"Yes, he himself admits that there is nothing in the world that is worth money he cannot take outside any country. He showed me about a kilogram of emeralds he smuggled recently out of copper belt around Ndola in Zambia and some heroin he got from Japan."

"How does he do these? Most countries in the world are very sensitive to smuggling."

"I have no idea. He told me he is at the moment looking for opium and the elephant tusks so here you are Peter, if you think you can lay your hands on any of these items you let me know I will contact this man and you will spend the whole of one of your evenings these days counting money. He has the money; there is no doubt about that. I am going to take you to him first if you would like to see him. A simple, lanky man. But he has the brain to do his professional work."

"Well Andrew that is very brilliant information you have given me but where do I go for such items?" Peter asked.

"I am sure Peter you must know many of these boys who come to your office from the Northern or Western part of Uganda. There are parks in those places. I don't mean to say you should now go with them running everywhere in the parks depriving the elephants of their tusks. What I am thinking is, some of these boys who come to see you in your office know where the tusks could be lying somewhere in their areas. Why don't you tactically talk to some of these boys? We might be lucky and find a boy who knows where to go and we shall follow him up and get the tusks."

"And how do we get the opium?" Peter asked

"The same procedure. All we have to do is, carefully find out from friends who have and of course who is going to lead us to where those things are found, since, if we go it alone, we might not get anything, even if we may be walking over them. Who would trust a stranger asking for such illegal goods? Even if I am the one I wouldn't stick out my neck that I have tons of them without knowing who you are. How would I know you aren't a government agent sent to trap me? That is why I told you at the beginning that I have stopped to trust Ugandans these days. You eat, walk stay with him together every day and yet he is spying on you. Tomorrow you wake up in a jail then you begin to wonder how you got there. So if we are going to be introduced by someone who knows the person keeping the commodities, we may get it at the first visit." Andrew explained.

"All these are lucks Andrew because we are going to trust none either the guide or the owner of these commodities, for the reason that, they might turn us to the authorities. As you know this government has employed millions of the so called "ears of the government "everywhere on whom they are spending billions of shillings every month throughout the country." Peter remarked.

"It is quite a home work. We have a quiz in our hands already; we start immediately tomorrow to investigate into the possibility of obtaining these commodities. If we get them we shall ask the Somali guy any amount and I think he will pay up. He doesn't know the use of Uganda money. He has a boot full of the dough and he must leave the country in a week's time. He wants to fly straight to New York where he will sell all those tusks, heroin and the opium. It is subtle to imagine how audacious some guys are. To go to New York Airport! And expect to pass the customs with all those illegal goods! One must be mad. They would detect you before you even land on the ground. Those guys are smart in their checking." Andrew said

"This is when I think *juju* exist. A man who is widely travelled like him has all sorts of potions with him so that even if you were as clever as a rabbit, if he spray you with the portion you would be as stupid as a hyena." Peter said

The time was 8p.m when Peter emptied the last bit of the *Uganda waragi* in Andrew cup.

"You take the last dose." Peter said as he shook the last drop of the *waragi* in Andrew cup.

"Thank you. It has been quite an evening." Andrew said.

"With lots of new ideas." Peter commented.

"It's up to us to implement them." Andrew agreed.

"I think we shall. I am on them tomorrow, start." Peter confirmed

"So am I." Andrew remark

Peter got up and walked to the kitchen he opened the door and found that Daniel was seated on the kitchen stool with their supper ready.

"Are you ready Dan?"

"Yes Sir I – I didn't want to disturbed you otherwise supper was ready about thirty minutes ago."

"Sorry Dan we were only talking nonsense really. You could have knock on the door. Anyway lay the table and let's see what you have for us."

After their supper they had yet another cup of coffee each and Peter escorted Andrew to his car. Andrew drove away home leavinghim in his solitude world of meditation about Rose.

"Are you dead Rose? Are you really dead?" Peter whispered as he walked to the house hands folded on his chest.

Chapter Four

After hours of sleeplessness in the night of meditation on the new project Andrew discussed with him, Peter slept at 3 a.m. in the morning. He woke up in the morning at 6 a.m. and looked at the double bed he used to occupy with Rose. Her side was empty without her. It was not because she had gone to the kitchen to prepare breakfast as she always did but because she was no more in this world. Peter looked at their wedding photograph hanging on the wall just at the foot of the bed one of the few items left by the thieves and looked away. He yawned and stretched his arms. The smell of the alcohol in his mouth was bad enough to make another person sick. With a tensed head Peter struggled on his feet and ambled to the bath room. He cleared his throat and spat thick mucous saliva in the sink turned on the water and washed it down the sink. After, he filled the bath with warm water and he entered it slowly as if he feared to drown in it. After the warm bath he walked outside and stood nod toweling himself before a mirror in the bath room he brought back from the Ministry. Peter slowly lowered himself on the stool in front, of the mirror, held his head in his hand and thought of how they used to towel each other after bath with Rose in front of that mirror. He felt strong indignation mounting up his head. How he wished the mirror was stolen but because it was fixed on the wall, the thieves could not easily remove it. He wanted to smash the mirror as if it was the cause of his wife's dead.

Why destroy the innocent thing? It has done nothing wrong. It is merely serving it duty as a faithful servant does. If anything I am responsible for her death of Rose not even the car which burnt her to ashes. Peter thought and clenched his hands into tight fists and bit his lips as he got up from the stool, put on his night dress and with the towel around his neck he walked out of the bath room into the bed room. He went and sat in front of an old dressing table delivered in his house by the Ministry of work after his personal one was looted out by the thieves. Peter sat in front of the mirror looking at his haggard image in it. His fat smooth face he had a year ago has been replaced by a tired thin face exposing the high cheeks bones. The once handsome eyes were sunk in their sockets and making him looks less attractive. The once dark black hair admired by all was as brown as if he had rubbed in a dye. The skeleton of his body could be numerated with ease. He sighed and whispered *I will soon follow you Rose but don't know how to do it myself I won't worry about you again.* He got up and began to dress.

Daniel had entered the house when Peter was in the bathroom. He quickly prepared breakfast, and laid the table for Peter. After that Daniel went to the dirt basket where Peter always left his few dirty linens for washing to check if there were some for washing. As he lifted the lid of the basket, the handle come off and the lid dropped down on some empty bottles which stood near the basket. Peter startled in his room. He opened the door and peeped out.

"Who is it?" He asked

"It's me sir Daniel replied

Oh. It is you Dan?"

"Yes Sir." I was checking for washing in the basket here sir." Daniel put in politely when he found an empty basket.

"I know there isn't much for you to wash these days. Perhaps you can keep yourself busy washing the floor and do general cleaning in the house." Peter said feeling hurt at the question of Daniel. *There is nothing in the basket today?* Peter thought. Peter and Rose used to have two baskets full of dirty linens to wash every day. So that their house boy was kept busy washing from morning until noon and in the evening he was kept busy ironing from 4 p.m. to 8 eight a.m. at night. To evade all these thoughts, he asked Daniel if breakfast was ready, even though he had no appetites to eat.

"Yes Sir. It is on the table waiting for you sir."

"Well I will come up in a minute." Peter said and finished dressing in his same blue shirts, blue tie, navy-blue trouser showing a tear between the legs and he hung on his back the only jacket and walked out in his worn out shoes into the dining room.

He had just finished nibbling on the last piece of cassava in his hand when the Land Rover hooted at the gate. The Ministry driver had come for him. Dan went and opened the gate and let the Land Rover in. Peter collected his palm leave basket he used for carrying his papers instead of a brief case and walked out with it into the parked Land Rover.

Peter got to his office and started work immediately signing documents he left over the previous evening at the same time thinking. *How will I get this information from these boys? When I talked to them about this it will be news all over this tiny little place where rumormongers are with their ears to the ground for any slightest incidence and then you hear the gossip. How will it sound if they exaggerate the news that I have now broken down so much that I find relieve only with opium dealers. Then what about the elephant tusk?* ......

The telephone buzzing on his table interrupted his thought. The time was 10 a.m. He picked up the receiver and said "Hello".

Hello. He heard the voice of his Secretary.

"The District Education officer of Lira is here he wants to see you."

"Oh give me five minutes and let him in." Peter said and cradled down the receiver. After exactly five minutes the Secretary allowed Okullo-Okullo to go in. A tall thick set man wearing a red short sleeves shirt over which he wore a grey half walker safari jacket and carrying a brown leather brief case walked in the office of Peter. When Okullo-Okullo entered Peter got up to welcome him and waved him on a sofa chair near his big office desk. They shook hands and exchanged greetings. The two men first talked about trivial matters about themselves, the country deteriorating political systems the weather, how busy the people upcountry were at that particular time especially Lira where he came from and then Okullo-Okullo introduced the topic which brought him to Kampala. He had come to request for the Government assistant for scholastic materials for his schools and office furniture. After they had exhausted all points Okullo-Okullo excused himself to go, stood up and extended his hand for a final hand shake to wish Peter good-bye. In the process, Peter saw a beautiful bracelet bejeweled with beautiful beads made from the hair obtained from the tail of the elephant. Peter had seen it when they had the first hand shake but did not want to talk about it. Now that Okullo-Okullo was leaving he thought it would not be a bad idea to find from Okullo-Okullo if he might have any idea as to where he could find the elephant tusks and the opium.

"Hi Okullo-Okullo you have a beautiful bracelet." Peter said nonchalantly.

"Thanks. I bought it only yesterday from a police man at the Police station in Nsyambya.

"What? Does he still have more?" Peter asked with amazement how a police officer could deal in such an illegal trade.

"You like one too?"

"Yes. It is quite good looking."

"He had about twenty left. I don't know if they have not all been taken by now. There were many people there after the some especially the people coming from the North."

"They are beautiful aren't they?"

"They are."

"Does he have any other thing beside these bracelets?" Peter asked

"What do you mean?"

"I mean if he is selling any other handicraft other than these bracelets."

"He has some bangles made from ivory also."

"Has he?"

"Yes."

"You won't know how many?"

"No. I wasn't interested in them because they were not fitting my wrist. They were either too small or too big. But they are beautiful bangles."

"I wonder where people get such elephants trophies." Peter asked.

Okullo-Okullo laughed and said "It seems you don't live in Uganda Sir. The most obstinate people in the all world today are Ugandans. You tell them please don't do these. They go ahead and do just what you said they shouldn't do. Tell him to sit down he will not only sit down but lie down. So, you see there is lot of hunting or may I say poaching going on in the parks of Uganda, especially Kidepo National Parks. These animals move in and out from Sudan.

The poachers always monitor the movements of these animals. They mainly intercept them as they return home from their trips in Sudan."

"They must be having plenty of tusks around that place". Peter put in.

"They do. Thousands of them wrapped in polythene bags and buried in the ground. If you are a stranger and you go there with the intention of obtaining some, you won't see any unless you go with someone who knows whoever has them, and then you will buy even two trailers full." Okullo-Okullo remarked.

"Peter laugh and said that's very interesting isn't?"

"Depending on what you mean by interesting."

"Do you personally know of anyone who is having them?"

"You sound interested in them?"

"Not me but a friend is. I don't have money to buy anything of such value. Just take a look at me; do you think I can afford to buy even a kilogram of the Ivory?" Pete asked looking at his worn out shoes. Okullo-Okullo looked at Peter without amusement. He had noticed the deteriorating appearance of Peter. Not the usual attire and look he used to see in Peter each time he came to Ministry to see him before the death of his wife. Okullo-Okullo sighed and changed the trend of thoughts.

"The same police man showed us two small elephant tusks. He said he brought them as samples, to find a market. He asked us to find for him buyers then he would take the police truck with him and exhumed the tusks from their temporary graves in the park. Who will stop the police truck anyway at check points?" Okullo-Okullo said and they both laughed.

"Is he really a policeman or just some lay man visiting a police man?" Peter asked bewildered.

"A Superintendent of Police, with three pips!" Okullo-Okullo answered affirmatively.

"A Superintendent of Police!" Lord Jesus." Peter said shaking his head.

"What did I tell you just now? I told you that Uganda is a difficult world. How we are surviving from day to day defeats me. Because there is no one who is living on his salary. No. You must do something to supplement your salary in order to finish the month. If you stick in your office because you are a faithfully civil servant, then you must be one of those who have underground banks in their homes with free money flowing in their fat bank account or your office feeds you in style otherwise if you are none of those and you have a family you will go home and meet miserable empty-stomached children crying for food. That is when you will reconsider being a faithful civil servant. Fish starts rotting from the gills. When you go to the market and you are buying fresh fish you check the gills don't you. When you opened it and you see bright red gills then you are sure you are buying a good fish but dark! No good. Thisis where we are now my brother."

Peter listen to what Okullo-Okullo was explaining with concern thinking, *Okullo-Okullo, though was the District Education Officer, looked well fed and neatly groomed than me the Permanent Secretary with a higher salary.* Then he recalled when people used to call him' smart' because of his superlative tidiness.

The thought sickened Peter as he looked at how bad his clothes were. *I need something new but how? Where do I get the money? May be if this deal works out this time.* Peter continued to think and suddenly asked Okullo-Okullo. "Do you remember the house number?"

"Nsyambya police barrack Road Plot No. 36."

"I will see him this afternoon."Peter said adamantly.

"Do so if you are in need."Okullo-Okullo said encouragingly

"What about at your place in Lira?"

"There we don't have anything. Those who are interested always travel to Kitgum and Moroto towns near the park areas where they collect them."

"Collect them? You mean they are all that plentiful."

"I have already told you that if you are guided to where they are and you have the money go with the transport that will collect your goods. The guys have the tusks and the giraffe tail-wigs."

Peter sighed sorrowfully and said, "I will find it out from the Police Superintendent first before coming to Kitgum or Moroto."

"Please do. He is not scared of anyone. I am sure he could even sell the ivories to the President office if anyone there should want to buy some. I will be passing that way again today at my brother's home before I go back to Lira. Mind if I mentioned to him that you intend to look him up?"

"No. Leave it to me. I will see what I can do. May be I won't get my friend who wants the tusks and making appointment with him may mean an obligation for me to go.

"Okay then. I must be going." Okullo-Okullo said

"Thank you very much for the useful information you have given me."

"I am glad if it has been useful". Okullo-Okullo said and they shook hands before Peter saw him off at the door through the Secretary office.

Peter returned to his office feeling so much exhilarated that he thought the end of his financial problems was in sight. He was full of hope for success. *If I fail this, this time, then I will know I am naturally unlucky.* Peter thought as he pressed the button on his telephone connecting him to the Secretary's set. The secretarial set buzzed, and she picked the receiver of her phone.

"Hello Beatrice will you give me Andrew please?" Peter said with lot of excitement in his voice.

"Yes Sir hold on the line." Beatrice said complying with his excitement. Beatrice dialed the number of Andrew in the Trans-Ocean. She got the number open. Soon she head Andrew phone ringing Tu---T, Tu---T. The ringing tone of Andrew telephone came clear to her ears. A minute passed before Andrew lifted the receiver and said, "Andrew here?"

"Hold on for Peter."

"Oh Beatrice, that is you? Your sweet voice is of course unmistakable it is unique to you alone."

"Thank you for the compliment." Beatrice said and shrugged. *This married men how they can flirt. They think they are the most powerful. They can't get satisfied with their wives. When they see young nice girls they want to demonstrate their man-hood in them."* Beatrice thought as she connected the two friends.

"You are through to Andrew Sir."

"Thank you."

"Hello Charm." Peter bellowed in the mouth piece

"What is itching you at that end Peter?"

"I have some very exciting information to give you."

"You do?"

"Won't talk on the open line?"

"No. You'd better trot down to my office straight away now." Peter said emphatically.

"Okay boy don't burst your arteries. I am on my way to you now." Andrew said and got up almost immediately from his chair. Andrew was nursing Peter's sentiments. He wanted him to overcome his many problems and begin to lead a decent life. Andrew got out of his office and walked into his Secretary office. The two always teased each other whenever one dressed well or used expensive perfumes. That morning, Sofia was very busy on her typewriter her fingers moving on the keys like some electronic digital counter.

Sofia did not qualify as a Secretary for her talent in secretarial duty only but her charming beauty qualified her more for the job. Sofia knew she was beautiful not only was she told by her dressing mirror but also by the men who always acknowledged her appealing beauty. So whenever she sat at her desk, she sat up with her slender neck high up in the air with her full breasts stuck out from her chest well above the desk.

"Hello Sofia" Andrew called her as he walked in her office.

"Yes Sir" Sofia answered him and stopped touching the buttons of her electrical typing machine. She pivoted her elbows on the desk and looked right in the eyes of her boos. The smell of the perfume she wore that morning seemed to be issuing from the small succulent nostrils.

"You scent is sweeter than the sweetest roses. Where did you buy the perfume from? It must have taken you an awful lot of time to select that heart paralyzing perfumes. It really matches with that face. No ugly woman would dare put that perfume on to turn the faces of men vis-à-vis her ugliness." Andrew commented as he inhaled lungs full of the scent.

"Oh come out of it Andrew, I know the way you always tease me. This is not the first time you are doing it. When you get out of the office now there are queues of them waiting outside to receive the same compliment. Anyway, thank you for my share you have just located me." Sofia said and they both laughed.

"I am going to Peter."

"Say Hello to Beatrice" Sofia said

"I'll. You don't say hello to Peter".

"Please do. How is he these days? Is he pulling out of his troubles?"

"I think he is improving. He's not very much outside minded when you talk to him as he used to be. In the long run he might be alright."

"That is good to hear. All these are because of you Andrew. Thank you for that."

"Peter is a friend. A childhood friendship I cannot leave him to deteriorate to the last. I will be inexcusable like Lucifer. But I have heard of some people who actually killed their childhood friends because of rivaling over girls or even jobs. Can you imagine that?"

"These are heartless people. Have you not heard of people who killed their own wives, husbands and parents and what is a childhood friendship?"Sofia put in while glancing at her work on the typewriter. Andrew saw her logic and did not want a mini debate with her but walked out of the office closing the door to the Secretary office behind. He walked down the step and out of the building to the parking ground where he had parked his car. He entered it and drove off to Peter's office.

Because Peter and Andrew were intimate friends their secretaries got to be close friends too. Occasionally they help each other with stationeries in case one did not have some. Peter and Andrew never missed talking to each other on their phones in any day, so that their voices were monotonous on the line to the two secretaries. Andrew knocked and opened the door to the Secretary office. He opened it and walked in. Beatrice was very busy on the typewriter. She knew who was coming because that method of knocking on the door was attributed to Andrew.

"Hello Beauty how are you?" Beatrice looked at him with her white eyes and later exposed for him her well chiseled set of teeth, which germs seem to fear to infect.

"Who sucks on those delicious succulent lips Beatrice?" Andrew asked.

"Which ones?" Beatrice asked nonchalantly.

"You want me to show them to you with my rough lips. They may bruise if I hang mine on them. I mean your lips of course."

"They are for the owner."

"What a lucky man he is. I wish they were mine I would use them as my chewing gum."

"What about those at home Andrew?" Beatrice asked and eyeballed him.

"Forget about them I am not talking about them. Have I made any reference to them?"

"No you haven't but they are the one you should be dreaming of as you walk along the street. You have read or heard about a book by Armah a Ghanaian I guess the title is "The Beautiful Ones Are Not Yet Born?" Beatrice asked.

"Whatever he meant by that is not my concern but the truth is if I wasn't married to a pretty wife I would have taken you now, now, now." Andrew remarked and bent towards Beatrice.

"Taken me?" Beatrice laughed and said "Andrew you are comic. You want your friend of course? He is free. He has just finished with the last visitor from Lira who has just left." Beatrice said dismissing him from her office.

"Well if I am boring you, I will go and see Peter but please-----." He let his words die away. "If Peter is not thinking of owning you then we shall talk about …."

"Yes he could be". Beatrice said carelessly.

"Oh well, then I am out of the race this joint."

"You must be Andrew."

Andrew eyed her erotically and opened the door to Peter office. Peter was busy at his desk signing many letters which were passed on to him.

"Hey boy will you finish up these heaps of files?" Andrew asked

"More are on their way here." Peter said, put down his pen, and got up to shake hands with Andrew.

"How are you again?" Peter said

"Fine" Thanks

"I have some exciting new for you Andrew." Peter said.

"You do."

"Yes."

"What is this I must hear?"

"I have just received a visitor from Lira, the District Education Officer of Lira, Okullu-Okullu. He is telling me that there is a police superintendent, living on Nsyambya Police barrack road 36. He has what we are looking for."

"Sure about that Peter?"

"That's what he told me."

"I'm not sure Peter. A police officer of such a rank to trade openly is such illegal commodities? I can't bring myself to accept that statement. What if the police officer is mole planted there by the Government with those illegal tusks with the intention of trapping the illegal traders in the ivories? He could be pretending that he is a serious ivory dealer. So when we show our interest, he could offer to lead us to where the ivories are and when we have purchased our commodities, then he lays ambush for us on the way he lands on us red handed when we will be laughing with our successes. He will make us talk to them behind bars. Peter it is not nice to jump on this finding as you have just said especially when a high ranking police officer is involved. We may get ourselves talking to the police against our will. What we could do I think, is to connect this police officer to another person for the first time and see how it works out. Should anything blow up we shall take cover. This person will act as a buffer between the law and us."

"But what will that help and what will be our benefit? Peter asked desperately.

"We shall give him the money to buy for us as he buys his. In this way you will not be directly apprehended. It will give us time to maneuver our cards."

"How?" Peter asked desperately getting irritated that Andrew is not showing interest in the job by diving in it and walking to the police superintendent at Nsambiya and go to the park exhume and empty the tusks from their graves. How he wished he had the money. *May be Andrew would have been more interested if he talked to Okullo-Okullo.* Peter thought.

"Don't tell me that you are a stranger in Uganda Peter. I am sure you have heard several times on radios what happened to some unlucky guys in those areas you are talking about. Only last week the **Eye of the Nation** reported in the front page displayed the photographs of two men caught in Moroto rock hotel with Rhino horns this time. The Rhino horns were heap piled in front of them and the brutal police men stood guarding them. Your guess is as good as any what might have happened to those men now. Peter as we involve ourselves in some of these dirty trades we should be a little careful not to let our names shout out notoriously. I agree there is always big money in them once the deals succeed. You will smile for a long while." Andrew advised Peter and sat back in the chair

Peter sighed and fell back on the tall backrest of his office chair and closed his eyes and almost in a whisper said "Andrew you are right but I don't think there is any fear or risk in this particular one. If we have the money, we could just go and pick the ivories and walk away safe. I repeat and walk away safe." Peters aid emphatically and leaned forwards on the desk resting his fore arms with the fingers clasped together on the desk and stared at Andrew. Andrew saw the desperation in Peter and he knew how much he wants that something must be done to bring him money.

"Yes I see." Andrew slowly began to talk. That could be true. But the second snag is the Somali guy drove back to Kenya last night. Thirdly we do not know the current cost price and the selling price of the ivories in kilograms if we are to find an alternative market. If we make a hasty move without finding out all these we may lose. I am not stepping back on this issue Peter but I want a sure job done.

"How long will he be away in Kenya?" Peter asked

"He could even be back tomorrow or later depending on availability of consignments to be brought to Uganda."

"In that case don't you think we could buy the ivories and stash them in our homes while waiting for the Somali guy or find a new market?"

"Peter, I don't want to disagree with you, but look here, supposing we bought these ivories at ten thousand shillings per kilogram and we begin to search for the market and find that it only sells at eight thousand shilling per kilogram. What will we be doing? It will be too much for us Peter. I would advise that we hold on until this Somali comes back. I am sure he is not going to stay away long. The mistake I made was I didn't ask the price he normally bought them at." Andrew advised

"He would have told you the lowest shelling price even if you think he has excess Uganda money. I am now beginning to see that we have a lot of research work to be done before we embarked on this. It sounded exciting and easy at first but now it doesn't seem palatable as it was." Peter said after reconsidering his earlier hast in the deal.

"Sure let's investigate into that."Andrew agreed.

Peter and Andrew had based their investigations on the cost price for the ivory per kilogram only. They didn't bother about the grades of the Ivories according to the slang used in the trade. Before they could find the source to give them the information they needed the Somali returned to Uganda expecting Peter and Andrew to avail to him the opium or the elephant tusks or both. He contacted Andrew in his office to confirm whether he had found the ivories for him. To avoid disappointment, in the evening of the same day Peter and Andrew went to the police superintendent at Nsyambya Police Barrack Road 36.The police superintendent had only two tusks of a young elephant weighing twenty kilograms each. They bought the two small elephant tusks at the cost five thousand Uganda shillings per kilogram. Meanwhile the police superintendent reassured them that he was a true dealer in those trophies and that was how he was supplementing his meager salary to maintain his family. When Andrew heard what the police superintendent told them, he got convinced that he was not a Government agent. He later asked him when he would get a new supply. He promised them in a week's time. Peter and Andrew were excited to be in possession of the trophies for a start. They drove away home happy.

"I think we are going to have a start in these trades." Peter remark excitedly.

"It's looks so, but I don't know how much they will fetch from him? Andrew answered

"I was told by a friend that these might bring us between ten to fifteen thousand shillings.

"What? Ten to fifteen thousand shillings?"Andrew yield

"Yes."

"You aren't kidding?"

"That's what I was told."

"Okay we shall see." Andrew replied skeptically.

The following day in the morning Peter and Andrew drove to Nakulabye slum where the Somali had rented a small dingy hut of tinned roof, mud walls with cracks on all sides exposing the reeds used for thatching. Peter and Andrew drove through the muddy dirty road passing between the huts of the slum until they reached a local bar where the slum inhabitations of Nakulabye spent their free hours. The Somali had directed them that they would meet him there at 10 a.m. in the morning. Peter and Andrew drove and parked opposite the bar. They looked round and walked out of the car. It had just rained and the mud on the road around the bar was about a foot thick. It was difficult to walk on foot especially in ordinary shoes. High neck gumboots were more preferred, the only ideal shoes for the area. All the same they wadded through the mud and got to the steps leading to verandah of the bar which was once cemented but because of the continuous stamping and dancing on the verandah, the cement was torn in many places exposing the bare bricks and foundation stones in some parts. Peter and Andrew kicked the mud adhering under their shoes on the steps and walked up to the verandah.

There were very few customers at that time about three in all. A short stocky man with bold head, thick fat nose sat at a corner table with a middle aged woman light in complexion fair beauty drinking the local bear from their guards. Next to the door was lanky sun burnt man with plenty of hair on the head that at a glance one would mistake him for a girl. Andrew knew him. He was the smuggler sitting doing nothing but waiting for his catch. It was believed that anyone associated with the Somali was either a smuggler or has something to smuggle out. When Andrew went and shook his hands and sat down beside him, all those who were in the bar knew that the elephant had fallen. The one the vulture was patient waiting for. They all glance at the new arrival with interest hoping to catch a gleam of what was passing between the two parties. But nothing suspicions was at sight. Peter and Andrew had left their trophies in the boot of their car.

"We look strangers here aren't we?" Peter asked Andrew when he saw how the bar maids and the other customers glancing at them suspiciously.

"Of course we do. A Permanent Secretary and Chief Accountant (Administration) Transocean Kampala region in Nakulabye slum where freaks and bums ferret isn't it strange Peter." Andrew remark

"Not strange in Uganda. I can go anywhere for money these days."

"I am behind you Peter. Andrew said and they all laughed.

"We must get started." the Somali said

"Sure it's getting late" Andrew agreed.

"I do not want more people to get us here." Peter said.

"Where do we go? Andrew asked addressing the Somali.

"To my place" The Somali said

"Where is it?" Andrew asked.

"It is just behind this bar. Follow me. The Somali ordered and got up.

"Let's go". Andrew said and they all got up and walked out leaving all who were in the bar staring after them. They got out on the veranda and stood at the door step.

"Shall we take the car with us?" I mean is it possible to drive up to your place?"

It's not possible. You could only push her up to that building then that is that. We shall walk to my place. I hope you will not hate the walk, because there is too much mud there." The Somali warned with a sneer.

They all entered Andrew car and he drove them to the spot where they were going to leave the car. They got out and cleaned their shoes on the dry ground and walked in the Somali hut. It was scantly furnished. Three wooden chairs, a wooden bed on top of which was a thin sponge mattress covered with a blanket, a folded mosquito net was tied on four nails driven in the walls over the bed hang above the bed. The Somali waved them on the wooden chairs and they sat down.

The environment of the hut was appalling. The open sewage draining the entire Nakulabye slum flowed only a yard from his door. The damping pit was full of peelings of potatoes, cassavas and rubbish of all kinds rotting behind his hut. The atmosphere smelled awfully. The Somali choose this horrible place other than the Apollo hotel or one of those De-lux Hotels in the city of Kampala because it was a strategic place for transacting his business. With that sort of environment, no police would have any suspicions that a high degree of smuggling would be going through the hut which looks like a kennel.

"Why have you chosen to live in this slum other than in the city center?" Peter asked. The Somali laughed and said.

"There is too much trouble in the city. I like it here."

Peter shrugged and said. "If it's your choice."

"Is it well wrapped? The Somali asked well knowing that the two understood him.

"Yes they are" Andrew replied.

"How heavy?"

"Forty kilograms."

What? Forty kilograms only? What is it anyway opium or what? The Somali asked.

"We do not have the opium. Andrew said.

"I am sorry I don't buy toys like those. Because of two reasons one; they don't sell well outside in Europe or in U.S.A. There they need big good staff not toys and you will earn all the good dough you want. Secondly; we smugglers are subjected to many risks. If you are netted with any of the illegal commodities in any airport, you will have had it. You talk your head off. At times you are put behind bars for years. So to go behind bars for forty kilograms only, everyone will laugh at you as an idiot. I am sorry gentlemen if these were good materials I would have paid you well for them now."The Somali said and lifted his thin mattress off the bed to expose carpet of notes in Uganda shillings.

"It's okay if you can't take them. We shall try to find another market." Peter said disappointed. *It's yet another flop.* He thought as he walked away toward the packed car.

"You won't find a market for small items like these my dear; these are too small for anyone to buy. I have dealt in these things for years and I can smell good staff which sells for good many. But these ones, not to disappoint you, I am sorry they won't fetch a dime."Peter walked away in silence and opened the co-driver door of the car, climbed in the car and slammed it shut. He rolled in the window glass and rested his elbow on top of the glass. He held his chin and stared outside the car pensively. He thought of the money wasted in buying something that couldn't sell. *Why didn't I buy something else? I don't know what I will succeed in? Everything I try doesn't work right. What is wrong with me? Oh dear I have lost everything in the world and any attempt to earn a new one is always futile."*

Each time Peter's attempt to make money it flopped, the thought of Rose and their stolen properties intensify. He felt warm tears irritating his eyes. It was at that moment that the Somali and Andrew walking slowly after him making another arrangement for better deal got to the car.

"I will try." He heard Andrew said.

"Hay boy this is not the end of the world. Do not fall in complete despondency. I have all hopes that next time we shall succeed. Because these are some of the anomalies we didn't know. We thought anything call ivory is good for the business but we made the mistake. Now we know that small ivories are not marketable. So next time we shall find only the big one. All we have to do is take a risk to Kitgum as Okulu-Okulu has advice we might get those good tusks there." Andrew said

"How do we get to Kitgum? We can't afford to go in your car it's expensive to run a car of your type from here up to Kitgum. I can't take out Land Rover out too, because it is the only one in the station at the moment. So unless you can organize a free transport there it might be useless to try." Peter commented.

"We shall not go there before we get everything right." What I mean Peter I have an uncle working in Kitgum as a Veterinary Officer. I am going to send him a letter explaining all we want and I will ask him to reply as soon as he gets the line straightened out there."

Peter shrugged and said. "You go ahead and do what you think is right. My brain has stopped thinking."

"Okay let's go home and rest. We can't return these miserable tusks to that police officer again in any case he said he was on transfer. He could have left. I will keep them, may be if we get big ones in future we might add them together and sell them together with the big ones." Andrew said and inserted the key in the key hole and ignited the engine. It fire and he eased the car into gear and they drove off.

"To establish a sound business Peter it is very difficult. You may try for years and you will fall in complete despondency and it is bad. I am sure we shall succeed one day." Andrew comforted Peter.

"When will that day be Andrew? We are aging every day. We need to get something now or never. At time I think I must retire and go home so that I see what I can do to earn a better living. But when I look into my bank account I see red. How do I dream to start any business with the meager money like mine? If my properties were looted, but Rose was left with me I would not be worried but now I ......

"Oh come out of that Peter let's forget about it at the moment. Let's think of something better now." Andrew said as he swung the car at the gate to Peter's home.

"I will come and pick you up in the evening we must go to Kololo night club tonight for a change."

"Night club!" Pete exclaimed

"Yes Peter. Andrew said resting his hand on his thigh. Peter shackled and shrugged. *"What dress shall I put on?* He wondered and looked at how badly dressed he was." Andrew glanced at Peter and looked ahead of them as Daniel come to open the gate for them.

Chapter Five

About one month of oblivion crawled passed without any news of hot line to chase. Peter financial position continued deteriorates. Debts especially from Andrew although he was not expected to pay back piled high. He never used his salary which he called his monthly allowance for himself but for reducing the numbers of debtors before he incurred new ones. His bank account was nothing other than the minimum money required by the bank to keep the account open. Peter laid in bed on his back thinking about what to eat that evening. He had already bought some crushed groundnuts and millet flour for lunch, it was a Saturday. He had spent all his time in bed thinking about his past life with Rose. He thought of his present life and strain his mind trying to imagine how he would overcome the financial constrains should he lay his hand on big elephant tusks or opium. *I must get them I must leave no stone unturned for these things.* Peter thought and got out of bed only to meet Daniel at the door way.

"How are you Dan?" Peter asked.

"I am alright sir but we have no salt and washing soap now. Sugar is left for evening tea only." Peter scratched his head and silently walked back into the bedroom and pulled a draw where he kept his money. There was a bundle of one thousand shillings in one hundred shilling notes which was the only money in the house. He picked it silently and walked with it to Daniel. He gave him the whole of it and said first buy salt and soap we might have to do without sugar for sometimes until a Good Samaritan comes my way."

"If there will be some money left enough to buy even a kilogram of sugar I will buy it." Daniel insisted.

"The money is already with you Mzee." Peter said and walked behind Daniel into the living room. He had just sat down on the chair when he saw a man with a red bicycle in a blue dust coat ridding in. He knew the Corporation which owned the bicycle of that colour. He even knew the boy because he had been doing the same job for years. The boy came in whistling happily doing his duty. He stopped near the house jumped off the bicycle and stood it on its stand. He took bundle of envelopes from the bags and sorted out one from the rest and walk straight to Peter's door. He knocked and Peter said "come in." They boy walked in and greeted him.

"Your electricity bill Sir."

"Thank you." Peter said as he received the bill from the boy. The boy turned and walked out of the house.

Peter opened the envelop and pulled out the electricity bill which stood at five thousand shilling (5000) which was about his monthly earning. Below the bill a warning foot note written in red stated that *failure to square the bill within fourteen days would lead the Uganda Electricity Board (U.E.B) to disconnect the power from the home. The U.E.B worked independently they could disconnect electricity even from the state house if the warning was ignored. So who am I?* Peter thought as he tossed the bill on the table. "Five hundred thousand shilling!" He repeated quietly. Peter thought of using charcoal for cooking and the latent lamp for lighting his house as Andrew predicted before but when he thought of the cost he found out that it was cheaper to use electricity. One bag of charcoal at that time was one hundred thousand shilling and he needed at least two to three bags to complete the month. A gill of paraffin cost fifty shilling. And to fill the latent lamp you needed five hundred to one thousand shillings. Yet the five thousand shilling was what he owed the UEB in three months accumulated bill. *From whom can I get help this time? Andrew is already fed up with me although he doesn't seem to show. Is this really me? I don't think so. I look a stranger in my own self. So everything has a beginning and an end. I thought I would never bow down to this kind of life. And I don't think I should really. I will try all the possible means to retrieve my lost financial pride alone without Rose this time and I must make it.* Peter thought. Peter walked back to his bedroom and stood with his arm folded over his chest in front of their wedding photograph and sneered. Tears slopped from his eyes and he walk back to bed. He laid face down and sobbed bitterly at the memory of Rose.

Since the death of his wife the most boring days in Peter's life were weekends and public holidays which people with happy families' background longed for. Peter hated weekends and public holidays because of solitude. As a result, during some of those days, if Andrew didn't come to him, Peter walked back to his office to finish his pending works.

It was during one weekend that Peter bored with his solitary life decided to walk to the office. He had just past the first plot from his home when an old friend he knew during the early school day came driving his Citroen saloon car he had just bought with a lady sitting in the co-driver seat pulled up near him. Peter was puzzled to see the car stopped near him. He did not know who the occupants were. But Walter had noticed Peter as he walked miserably to his office down town. Walter rolled down the smoked widow glass by switching on the automatic buttons roller and walked out.

"Hay Pal Peter, where are you going in the early morning?" Walter asked as he jumped out of the car. He shook his hand affectionately with the excitement of a successful man who has met a frustrated old friend. It's long not see. What have you been doing to yourself Peter? Walter allowed his question to flow. Peter felt shy. He felt like pulling his hand away from the meaty hand of Walter gripping on his bony one. He looked frightened like a rabbit in a net as Walter continued to survey him up and down.

'How are you Peter? Walter continued to pour his question.

"I am fine thank you". Peter answered curtly.

"Where are you going Peter?"

"To office."

"What? To office? Not on a Saturday Peter, come on. Come with us. We are driving off to Lido beach. I need a company of a man like you to talk too. I am getting bored with female talks. Peter giggled shyly and said "I am not prepared to go out now."

"Well I'll take you home and you change."

Peter felt as if the world was turning upside down. *Go home to change?*

In what? Since I am now in my best and this son-of-bitch tells me to go home and change? Peter thought and felt like spiting on the smooth well fed, well shaven face of Walter. Walter was dressed in a grey suits a sky blue shirt and brown neck tie. His shoes were shining black he had an omega wrist watch with a golden metal strep on his wrist made him desirable man to any woman. The fragrant smell of the body lotion he had sprayed on his body made him super sweet to women. Peter looked at the attire of Walter and inwardly denounced the world. He felt that if he rejects the invitation of Walter, it will be a weakness on his part. He needed someone to talk to especially a wealthy man like Walter he might give him a lead to where the life he is searching for is crouching. After all, the main reason why he was going to office was because he was bored with the solitude life at home. Why? Everyone knew of his misfortune he wasn't like that from birth. He was also among the top smartest men in Kampala."How long are we staying there? Peter asked stupidly.

"Well as long as we want to stay there." Walter replied.

"Okay we can go. I didn't work on Friday afternoon so I thought I should go and clear up the files pending."

"Were you chasing money line?" Walter asked.

"Oh no, I don't have any money line to chase at all, I was a bit feverish." Peter lied well knowing that Friday he was with Andrew at the Somali guy's place at Nakulabye.

"On Monday you will do them. Work never get finish my brother." Walter remarked. The girl in the car remained sitting in the car shaping her finger nails with a small nail file avoiding the dark red cutie she had applied on them.

Walter walked in front of the car and opened the door of the car for the girl.

"Hay will you come out and meet Peter my Old Boy in Nyapea College. The girl, a short barrel-chest girl with big frog like eyes walked out of the car and stood in front of Peter. If it were not because of the high heels she had on she would have been shorter than the door of the car. "Hello Peter nice to meet you". The girl said as she put on a smile showing the gap between her upper incisors which made her looked less attractive. Peter wondered why Walter had pick on the girl for a broad day light outing. He knew Walter's weakness for beautiful slim girls but that girl was the direct opposite of Walter choices.

"*May be he wants a change to fat girls*". Peter thought as he shook hands with the girl.

Peter is the Permanent Secretary Ministry of Education. He is an old friend as I have already told you. He has had very many misfortunes in life recently. He lost his Daddy, his properties were all looted from his house when he was at home for the funeral rite of his Daddy. And worst of all he lost his dear wife and their car in a motor accident when he was coming back to Kampala." Walter introduced Peter in detail probably to make the girl understand the station of Peter why he looked the way he looked in spite of his status.

"Sorry Peter very sorry indeed." They girl said wringing her hands and later held them over her breasts

"I am really sorry for you." The girl repeated emotionally.

"Well thanks for your late condolence it is just as comforting as new." Peter said with a sneer.

"And by the way Peter this girl is…… Walters said and paused "What are you by the way?" he asked the girl. Peter would have laughed his head off if he was in the mood instead he looked at them as if he was looking at a clear pool of water. "I am Alice Namubiru I work as a telephone operator in the Ministry of Wild Life and Tourism.

"Yes that is Alice and her profession Peter. She is a telephone operator with Wild Life Ministry I think people who work with that Ministry are wild aren't they?" Walter joked while looking down at Alice.

"No they are not." Alice interjected.

"I don't know why I have that imagination." Walter continued with his joke.

May be someone there gave you a hard time when you visited the Ministry." Alice commented.

"I think so. You could be right."

"I hope it's not me?"

"You look wild enough to give any devil a scare." Walter said and they all laughed.

"Peter come on in let's get going I must drop Alice first to her destination before we continue to Entebbe. I wanted her to come with me but she turned me down. Probably that is why........"

"Oh come on Walter I am tried. I want to go home and sleep. Next time."

"But I am not." Walter interjected.

You are a man moreover a special man would never get tired of women." Alice said as they entered the car. Walter drove Alice to her home at Kymukya before he continued with Peter to Entebbe Lido Beach.

"I thought she was with you I mean she was coming with us to Entebbe."

"Forget. I don't know why I picked on her last night I think I was too drunk. I hate everything about her now."

"But she said she would come out with you next time."

"With whom? Me? I will put a real swine in this car in her place for a girl friend if I am to come out with her again. There is nothing good about her. She is the lousiest girl I have ever shared bed with. She is full of gas. That fat stomach you see is nothing but gas. I didn't sleep last night. I thought there was war outside the house boom blast I had to fumigate the all house this morning to change the smell of the house. I will be an idiot to see her again."

Peter was happy that there was no girl in their company but he didn't trust Walter, he could pick on girls anywhere at any time as they travel to Lido Beach at Entebbe. How he wished he didn't. So that he could introduced to him his financial problem and see how he could support him with some free one hundred thousand shilling if he explained his position well in order to clear his electricity bill.

After all they never disagreed with each other since their early days at school.

Walter a slim tall copper skin young man nearing his forties never was married. He believed in go-go life without any seriousness in possessing a wife. He had girl friends among all the tribes of Uganda and that meant wherever he went he got one. He changes cars as he changes women. Walter was a very close friend of Peter and Andrew before Peter and Andrew got married. They used to go outing together in night clubs, bars hotels and pick girls from different bars and hotels in Uganda. But when the two got married, because of respect for their families and partly because their wives exerted pressures on them to leave the indecent way of life, the friendship between them was flimsy. Walter worked as Principal Accountant in Bank of Uganda, the post which enables him to own anything he wanted in the world.

The time was thirty minutes to twelve mid-day when the Citroen of Walter roared, tearing through the cool breeze of Lake Victoria at Kitubulu loop road heading towards the Katabi check point mended by the military personnel residing at Katabi Barracks. He slowed down the car as he approached the road block and swung the car at the side of the road. He braked as the car nodded and settled on the road. A soldier in a combat uniform carrying a GSU gun attached to an RPG got up from their tent pitched at side of the road and walked to them.

"Good afternoon sirs."

"Good afternoon. How are you?" Walter greeted the soldier.

"I am fine thank you. Identity cards please? The soldier ordered. The two men fished from their pockets their Identity cards and gave them to him one after the other. The soldier checked their car and peeped in the car to check the inside. Finally, he ordered Walter to open the boot of the car.

"What is in the boot?" The soldier asked.

"In the boot, I have, a suit case containing some few dresses, spare tyre for the car, and a jack". Walter numerated the content of the boot.

"Open." The soldier ordered. "May I have a look at them?" The soldier asked as he walked towards the boot.

"Sure why not". Walter said and jumped in front of the soldier inserted the key in the keyhole of the boot and opened it. You want the suit case open too?"

"Yes please."

"Why are you doing all these? Don't you trust senior Government officials like us?" Walter wondered.

"These days the *big fish* we want to trust are the people carrying deadly weapons with them. Last week we arrested a Deputy Minister here with six grenades, two GSU gun and sub-machine gun. He also arrived here the way you come. He looked as innocent as an angel. When he got here without our order he opened the boot of his car the doors of the car so that we had a full view of the car. When we look at his identity we wondered why he behaved like that. We become suspicious because guilty people sometimes make you look a fool when they have all the dangerous weapons in between their legs. So, as we suspected we scrutinize his car, we gave it a thorough search and you know what? My friend observed that the car was tilted backwards in spite of the empty boot. We thought it was strange. He knelt down to see if the car had mechanical problem. It was an embarrassing finding. What did we see? The man, who was as courageous like Jesus facing death, was nothing but a trembling leave. Have you ever seen a man trembling because of malaria infection? I tell you he could not handle the paper in his hand. They were actually vibrating. My colleague saw the bundle well fitted at the bottom of the car. We ordered him to remove the bundle. He did and when we unwrapped the package, we all caught our breath unable to speak. Being a big man we did not roughened him. All we did was to bundle him with all his loots and dumped him at the Nile Mansion. I am sure you all read about this in the *Eye **of the nation.***"The soldier said as he peeped in the boot and checked thoroughly before he asked Walter to close the boot. Walter slammed the door of the boot closed.

"What happened to him then?" Peter asked nervously.

"You big fish in Kampala should know. What do we people know there after when a big fish is netted?"

"Don't you follow up your case?"

"Umm unless you are called to explain the circumstances under which the arrest was made you may end up with a kick on your ass. Some of these fellows have connections."

As they talked another car drove in at the check point.

"Clear your car out of the way please". The soldier order Walter and Peter climbed in the car and they drove off. They got to Lake Victoria hotel at about five minutes past mid-day.

"Why don't we have some lunch here Peter before we go to pass time in Lido beach?"

"I have no objection we could eat. Peter replied shyly. *I used to take friends out in imperial hotel, speak hotel and Apollo hotel and feed them to their satisfaction and now I am unable to take even myself to any of the decent places. Instead I am being taken.* Peter though, as Walter swung his car to a stop into the parking lot near the swimming pool in front of the hotel. There were few people at the side of the swimming pool enjoying their swimming. A fat woman in a tight swimming costumes stood at the diving stand looked like a female elephant squeezed in the swimming costume dived in water in time as Peter and Walter walked pass to the balcony of the hotel. The splash she produced when she fell in water was like a planet which fell from the sky in the swimming pool.

Peter and Walter stopped to see how she was going to emerge. They feared with that fall she could have hit the bottom of the pool and has broken some bones on her body. But they first saw the meaty buttocks squeezed in the swimming costume and her large back and the head with a red ribbon tied around the black long hair. She stood up in the water and wiped the water from her fat face and waved to the people sitting with her at the side of the swimming pool.

"Are you alright?" One man asked

"I am quite perfect." She replied.

"I thought with that fall you had hit the bottom of the pool."

"No I am alright." The fat woman said as she swam to the side of the swimming pool and hauled herself out.

"If she swims here every day she will weaken the foundation of the hotel." One lady joked and they both laughed. Peter and Walter walked to a two seater table in the outdoor bar and sat. A bar attendant dressed in white coat with dark red strips on the sleeves came to attend to them.

"Two cold Nile Special beers please?" Walter addressed the bar attendant while looking at Peter.

"Anything will do". Peter replied. The waiter disappeared and soon came back with two bottles of Nile Special lager and two glass tumblers lying on his tray. He came and stood the tumblers and the two bottles in front of Peter and Walter, and he flipped the tops open. He pulled the receipt for the two beers from his packet and put it on the table and walked away with the tray.

Peter and Walter tossed to their health and began to drink. Walter put his glass of beer down and glanced at Peter, meditatively.

"Do you know what? I am trying to recall where I saw that fat woman. Her face is familiar to me." Walter remarked.

"Your problem is, you know too many female. I don't know how many you pick in a year?" Peter said and they both laughed

"I don't know either. Walter interjected and they both laughed again. "But I think this particular woman has nothing to do with my usual way of knowing women. You know I hate fat women. They are lousy in bed. You turn them like turning an elephant. If you want to change position you need to stand up put her the way you want her to be then you come on her. While doing all these, your desire keeps dying. But the slim one, you can swing while you are on the job man, and you can reach them anytime at any angle."

"You are really a sexologist. Peter said flashing his memory back to Rose. He recalled all he used to do with Rose it was exactly what Walter was describing. If Walter knew what he used to do with Rose he would have suspected that Walter was saying all those to hurt his feeling. Peter shrugged and asked, then where did you meet the woman?"

"I am not sure but I think it must be when she came to me in the bank. She came to the bank to buy some pound sterling to travel to Britain.

"If she is the one then she should be call Helen Namayanja."

"Is she married?" Peter asked

"She is a Miss. No one can manage such a woman. After all she has the money she needs, why marry? She can hire men whenever she needs one. I will find out from this boy who she is. She should be coming from Mengo in Kampala."

"Well here is not far from Mengo she could be spending her weekend just as we are doing."Peter remarked

"I tell you, you don't know Helen if she is the one then she is here on business. She is rapacious for money. She wants all the money on earth. She could kill for as much as one cent. Can you imagine a woman with so much money to sell her sex for money? I don't understand it." Walter said and tapped the bottom of the empty bottle in his hand on the table. The bar attendant who was standing near them sprang forward and came to Walter.

"Two more please", Peter said assuming he understood what he meant

"Pay the first ones please." The bar attendant said.

"Come on I am not going to run with your money." Walter rebuked

"No Sir, I don't mean that but the cashier will ask me for the money."

"Okay, get it and keep balance Walter said and pulled out one-thousand-shilling note and tossed on the table. Peter enviously looks at the note. *How I wished Walter gave the balance to me! I would have used the money for buying some salt, or sugar at the end of the day for my home.* Peter thought and felt like crying. The bar attendant took the money and the receipt lying on the table, walked away and soon was back with fresh cold bottles of Nile Special. He opened them and offered them to Peter and Walter and put fresh receipt on the table as he did before.

Helen and her group had stopped swimming and where sitting under the umbrella near the swimming pool sipping their beer. They were talking and laughing mirthfully. Helen had her back on Peter and Walter, the other man and the girl who joked with her when she was in the pool sat in front of her. The two looked lovers or very closed acquaintance. They sat with their arms flung around the shoulder of each other. The man seemed to be a humorous man he was the main speaker while the two ladies were only laughing.

Walter called the waiter to him. He came and stood near him. "Pull that chair and sit down here I want to talk to you."

"No sir we are not allowed."

"Not allowed to do what?"

"To sit down during working hours."

Okay then you stand and listened what I am going to tell you very carefully. I don't want you to start looking round the bar to arouse suspicion of the people here. I am going to talk to you about that woman who is sitting behind you. Do you know her?"

"You mean Helen?"

What is her other name?"

"Namayanja."

"Oh well I thought she is the one." Walter said.

"Why do you want to know her?"

"Just for fun. She once came to me in the bank. She wanted loan but that was a long time. She was not that fat." Walter explained.

"She is a very rich woman but she has the lust for money. She won't give a tip to anyone in this bar. I have been here for seven years now and I knew her when she was a slim girl as you said. All that meat she built as I look on. She is an international business woman. That man you see sitting in front of her is Kironde Samuel he was the fiancé of Helen. They were to wed but Helen was too smart for Samuel she fell into big money before their wedding. She thought that if she married him Samuel would fall into free money so she kicked him out. Samuel was disappointed, he nearly committed suicide. Thank God he didn't. When Helen heard that she came to console Samuel. She promised to be his friend but not wife. That exposition affected Samuel as a result he decided against marriage. That beer she is drinking and everything she is enjoying here is being paid for by Samuel. Helen does not spend a cent of her money. The best miser there is on earth." The bar attendant explained to Peter and Walter.

"What about that girl sitting with Samuel?"

"Those are some of the floozies we have around Entebbe. What do they want anyway food, drink and a bit of sex that is the lot. Have twenty of them at once so long as you are able to satisfy their need all you will be called a champ or a king of kings or any name that will make a hole in your pocket."

"What does Samuel do for his living?"

"A smuggler."

"Only that? No other job?"

"I think he does that only. He is permanently book in this hotel. He moves throughout Africa, Europe, U.S.A., and Asia. I believe there is no one in the entire world who has seen more of the world than Samuel. Ask him about any town in Europe he will tell you stories after stories about the town. He knows all customs of Africa, Europe et. cetra. He gets along with people very easily. Just a matter of saying 'Hey Samuel', then he will pull his chair near you, and then you should prepare yourself to hear stories and laugh dead."

"Samuel seems to have plenty of money too."

"I think he has an account which can build three hotels of this size and there will be excess money to pay the workers for three years without any constrain. To entertain a woman like Helen, or must I say to buy the love of a woman like Helen cost a lot." The waiter said and paused. "I must attend to other customers. If you want more about this town I will let you have them after duty. Are you staying in for the night?"

"No we are not booked in yet but we might if we find it worthy."

"You are from here. You look strangers here in town."

"Well we aren't quite strangers. We are from Kampala."

"You live there?"

"Yes."

"You intend to go back to Kampala?" Why don't you book with us and enjoying the tranquility of Entebbe and rest from the monotonous gun shots of Kampala?"

"I won't sleep if I don't hear the gun shoot." Walter joke.

"Oh well in that case we have our boys at Katabi and old Airport barracks we shall ask them to blast a few to send you to sleep." The waiter said and smiled.

Another group of customers sitting next to Walter and Peter tapped on the table and the bar attendant excused himself and left to go and attend to their need.

"Isn't it interesting? Peter remark. Why has the boy told us so much?"

"Well that's how it's here give tip to anyone and asked questions he will answer your question plus. He will even tell you what he or she assumes might be useful to you in future."

'If Samuel is such a rich man and Helen is equally rich why don't they get married?" Peter remarked.

"May be Samuel is short of Helen by a fraction." Walter answered and added. "Those types of women are like that they would never use their earning but grasp more and more from men."

"What does Samuel deal in? He is a smuggler what does he smuggle? From Uganda here I think there is very little to smuggle?" Walter remarked.

"I don't think so. Recently I come across a Somali a lanky sun burnt man with plenty of hair on the head he is also a man who seems to know a lot about the trade. He is a driver of Transocean East Africa based in Nairobi. He is interested in things like opium, elephant tusks, Rhino horns, leopards' skins, crocodile skins all these are item he said he smuggles out of here but I haven't known what they smuggle into the country. It's a risky trade but the moment you get out successfully you will breathe the breath of a rich man." Peter said persuasively.

"I can't imagine passing through the customs places in International Airports like in London or New York in the US and elsewhere in the world without being spotted out."

"They know their tricks. Those customs boys and girls there also need additional British pounds or USA dollars free on top of their salaries. So what do they loss if they let them go at the cost of some kilograms of ivory or Rhino horns?" Peter said.

Walter glanced at his Omega wrist watched and said, "Oh we must eat something now you like it here or we go in the dinning."

"Let's go in the dining hall." Peter said and drained the last beer he had in the glass. Walter tapped on the table and the waiter came to them. He paid for the beers and they left for the dining hall

Peter, whenever he went to a hotel to eat always chooses a table in the corner of the dining to enable him have a full view of the customers in the hall. He always enjoyed seeing different ways people behavior at table. On the contrary Walter always liked central table so that he is the central focal person for everyone especially the women. When they entered the dining hall Peter walked straight to a two cheater table in the left hand corner of the dining hall while Walter slightly protested that they should go and sit on a four cheater table in the middle of the room.

"Let's sit where there is enough light." Walter suggested

"It's better in the corner there where you will have better view of the hall." Peter insisted.

"Fine let's go." Walter gave in. He thought Peter was not in his best attire may be the dark corner chosen was a hideout from the eyes of the many men and women dressed in their latest, eating richly. They took their seats and a waiter came to attend to them. They studied the menu for the afternoon meals that was on the table. "There isn't much to choose from." Walter said.

"No." Peter agreed.

"I will start off with mushrooms soup and later chicken with rice. Peter made his order.

"Bring us two of each" Walter said and placed the menu back on the table where it was.

"Let them give us another beer each as we wait." suggested

"There is going to be a long waiting. They will have to serve those who came in first. So we could have a beer each as we wait."Walter said and tapped on the table. Most of the waiters in the dining hall were busy moving up and down delivering food to the customers waiting impatiently. Walter waited, no waiter seems to pay any attention to him. He tapped again. The cashier heard it and came to attend to them. He come and gave them their beers. They had just drunk a mouth full each of the beers from their tumblers when Walter asked Peter.

"Tell me Peter. How did you come in touch with that Somali guy you talked about?" Walter asked

"I was introduced to him by Andrew."

"Andrew did?"

Yes.

"You know why I am getting interested about that Somali guy". Walter said and paused, and asked again."Did he tell you his name?"

"No. Not in my presence. He didn't tell us, but I believe Andrew knows him well because he works for them. Even if he doesn't he could find that out from their Head Office in Nairobi. All I know about him is that he is a smuggler. He smuggles anything worth money out of any country. And he couldn't pay money for worthless good he smuggles"

"You Know what? About a week ago a Somali who suit your description came to our bank and withdrew fifty million shillings from his account in Somalia using VISA card. We were all shocked to see a man of his look carrying the large sum of money out of the bank. Now I am beginning to think that, that money was meant to pay you.

"Could be but we missed it because of the size of our tusks. Peter said lamenting.

"How does he categorize his goods?"

"He bases his assessments on quality and quantity, because, one would be an idiot to be caught with small amount of poor quality goods at any custom port. The idea behind this is that you can't raise money to set you free when you find yourself in such scenario."

"I think he is very correct because first smuggling is an illegal trade and to add on valueless goods not worth the risks are not a very good combination is it? Further I think valueless goods jeopardize the trade." Walter remarked and went on, "Don't you remember hearing and probably reading in the *Eye of the Nation* that some people in these days of scarcity of sugar bought brown sands mixed with equal amount of brown sugar for real sugar? And some bought bars of plywood coated with thin layer of washing soap nicely labeled and properly packed in the usual papers cartoon for the soap? And these commodities are being smuggled into Uganda through Kenya boarders at Busia and Malaba. You must be careful with anybody dealing with you in such dangerous business, because sometimes you end up losing your money for worthless commodities.

I have heard so much of miscellaneous transaction going on in Uganda these days. There are boys who come from Rwanda with fake gold, I understand they are fillings from pressure stoves, you know they look like gold, some people bought them for gold and when they were tested the so call gold dissolved in the testing acid. The poor victims paid all their capital on such worthless commodities. You see Peter, you are young in this illegal trade, what I am advising you is thoroughly know whoever you are dealing with, ascertain that what you are exchanging is a commodity worth the money you are giving or receiving, otherwise my dear brother don't try it. I appreciate your effort in all you've been doing to revive your standards of living but don't be over ambitious to achieve it within a short time. It is easy to destroy but difficult to rebuild. You had all you needed in the world but everything was destroyed within few months only. I am terribly sorry that your dear wife didn't survive to struggle with you to revive your standard of living. Meanwhile you should learn by now what the world is. There are lots of ups and downs in our lives. When we are down, only true friends and relatives come to our aid and try to lift us up, but many friends and relative, would not turn their eyes to look at our directions not withstanding our shouts out for assistance. They block their ears and walk away. On the contrary, should you stand up on your own or otherwise, you see them routing in for help."Walter lectured Peter and drank beer from the tumbler. Peter sat in front of Walter listening to him like a child taking advice from a father. He was aware of Walter's character whenever he was tipsy he became too talkative. Peter reacted when Walter reminded him about his wife Rose. He felt like walking away from the hotel. After their lunch they walked out of the hotel and regained their table in the outdoor bar.

Chapter Six

They had just sat down when Samuel with his girlfriend walked out of the hotel, immediately after them and continued towards their table under the umbrella near the swimming pool.

"Ha she eats a lot." Walter and Peter heard Samuel commenting as they came near them. They would have doubted for whom the remark was meant if they did see Helen in the hotel demonstrating her appetites on the full chicken with a full tray of *matoke* she had ordered. Put in the talking mood by the Nile Special Walter called Samuel to him.

"Hey Sam."

'Yes Pal". Samuel replied. He always suffixed pal to answer anyone call.

"Welcome home." Walter said following what the waiter told him about Samuel.

"Thank you but this was a week ago when I flew in." Samuel replied

"Yeah but I haven't met you since you came back." Walter lied as Sam stopped to shake hands with them.

"I meet very many people pal and I tend to forget their names. But they remember Samuel. Where did we meet pal?"

"'I am Walter and he is Peter." Walter proceeded with introduction ignoring Samuel question knowing well that they hadn't met before. You should know him well. He is the Permanent

Secretary to the Ministry of Education. In case your child will need a scholarship to go for study abroad this is the man to talk to."

"It is nice to meet you Peter". Samuels aid, shook hands with him and glanced at Peter from head to foot apparently noting how poorly dressed he was. After, he shook hands with Walter as well. The girlfriend of Samuel stood in silence next to them with her hands folded over her breasts she also shot a glance at Peter after Walter introduction. Peter noticed the way the two glanced at him he knew they were wondering that if he was the Permanent Secretary then he was either one of those careless punks who won't care a damn about their outlook or he was one of the civil servants who were hard hit by the inflation or at worst a drunk. He fidgeted on his chair blinked twice and cleared his throat as if to say something but he sipped his beer instead.

"And what about you............"Walter said and paused looking at the girlfriend of Samuel. Shapely build girls about five feet nine, copper colour in complexion, flat inviting stomach hang on long slender limbs with narrow waist. The white frock she had on with a blue butter fly on the nipple of her breasts had V. shape opening on her chest which ran along the line of her breasts exposing just a bit of the smooth firmed base of well-oiled breasts. She had a white hat with a black feather stuck in the white ribbon round the hat on the head which she wore romantically slanting slightly covering her left eye matched well with the frock and the white pair of shoes she had on. She was the type of girls that would send Walter secreting saliva like a hyena on seeing meat. Walter wanted to know her. The beer he had taken with that beauty near him left Walter with no other world but a world she belonged.

"Joyce meet Walter and Peter will you?" Samuel said and Joyce walked forwards stretching out her long smooth arm for handshake.

She shook hands with Peter first and then with Walter. It seems she intended it that way may be she was expecting it to happened so. Walter shook hand with Joyce and clang on it for a while. The soft tender feels of Joyce slender fingers with a quiet sent of perfume crawling up Walter nose dazed him to madness and sent his heart thudding wildly in his chest.

"Nice to meet you Joyce." Walter said with a shaky desirous voice.

"Same to me." Joyce said shyly and gave him an expensive romantic smile. Walter got the stung of the smile right in his heart like a fish which has swallowed bait down the throat ready to be pulled out of water. He adjusted himself confused in the chair and returned her smile.

"Why don't you sit down and have a beer?' Walter broke in inviting Samuel and his girlfriend.

"There are not enough chairs at your table Joyce replied."

"Oh well we can organize that if that is the only problem?" Walter said and got up and pulled two chairs from the other tables and brought them to their table. He squeezed one on his side and another between him and Peter.

"Perhaps I should leave you my chair and Samuel takes that one Walter gabbled to Joyce and sat on one of the new chairs he put next to Peter which put him between Joyce and Peter. Peter knew what was going on. Walter will never leave any beautiful girl on her feet. Accompanied or alone Walter always made a pass at them. He on a number of occasions got into trouble with some hot head guys because of their chicks. Walter tried married life twice but they never held on because of his desire for outside life. The number of illegitimate children he had outside were enough to start a nursery school.

Peter show what Walter was starting as something very risky. Samuel was a tall athletic powerfully built man with long fat arms, fat finger which when made into fists would scare any devil. His protuberant brown eyes with fat nose on a bold head gave him a belligerent look. Peter thought that should Walter provoke Samuel he might pick him with his chair and toss him outside the fence like a piece of stone. He didn't like to see that happening. He felt like cautioning Walter about the risk he might face should Samuel be provoked. *May be the best he could do is to exchange address with the girl and learn more about her later. This could be follow up case and avoid physical confrontation with a man like Sam who looked strong enough to stop one's breath with a blow.* Peter thought and changed the trend of discussion to emphasize his thought.

"Itis apparent I am the only one here introduced in detail. The rest of you are known as Joyce, Samuel, and Walter. But I was introduced as Peter the Permanent Secretary to Ministry of Education. I hope it's not bad to know who we are in that detail so that in future in case I need Samuel's help I will know where to go just as much as he now knows mine." Peter said and sipped his beer from the glass. Well when that is being done my I do one thing. What do you take by the way Joyce? Walter came in boastfully.

"Get me Sweet Martini or Chinzano."

"Any other sweet wine you will take?" Walter asked. Joyce only smile at his remark.

"And you Samuel?"

"Walker-on-the-rock."

"Walter called the waiter and placed in the order of the two guests.

"Well now we can go ahead with Peter's request it's important. We apologized for that omission." And thank you for reminding us." Walter said apologetically.

"Shall we start with you Joyce tell us who you." Samuel said and they laugh

"'I thought it will be formal for you to introduce her to us Sam". Walter said.

"I think she can talk for herself but if I must introduce her myself then Joyce is the Personal Secretary to the Minister of Health in Entebbe here." Sam said.

"Oh I see. Peter said shyly knowing that Joyce must have notice the contrast between his tidiness and her boss who is also a minister.

"Where does she lives?" Walter asked.

"That detail you can find out from her". Sam replied.

"'I live on 16 Gower Road opposite shell petrol station." Joyce said.

"Satisfied?" Sam asked Walter.

"Very".

"So when you want her for any assistance you could ring the minister's office she will be the first to receive the call but if you want her outside working hours then try 16 Gower road second flat on the left." Sam remark suspiciously.

"And who you?" Walter intercepted Sam.

"Me? Sam said pointing at his chest. At the moment I have no profession." He said and kept quiet

"I mean you must be doing something to earn you that good living you are enjoying now." Walter insisted as the waiters placed the orders to Joyce and Sam in front of them. Peter and Walter pretended be ignorant about Sam activities revealed to them by the waiter who was serving them.

"If you must know I always tell people openly that I am a smuggler because I need people to bring things to me and I carry them out. I do not fear anyone. Even to the police I ask if there is anything I could smuggle out. I have the money to shut up devils who try a fuss against me. The police of these days will allow you to smuggle all the money from the Bank of Uganda so long as you can blind fold him with some bundles of the five thousand shillings note. He knows his salary per month. Give him anything like fifty thousand shillings he will defecate in his uniform and clear you with all you loots.

"So you are a registered smuggler?" Walter asked jokingly.

"If you like it that way, then I am, because there is no one who can stand in my way."

"Before we forget you, who are you." Joyce said addressing herself to Walter.

"I thought I was going to escape that." Walter said and they all laughed. Walter smoothened on his neck tie and sat back on the chair and belched out some gas of the beer and said "excused me". Umm-I am a very simple man really. I am just an accountant with the Bank of Uganda."

"Chief Accountant." Peter corrected.

"I thought that was not important."

"Quite a juicy post, that's why you look money," Sam commented.

There was a moment of silence among them. Each one of them was meditating what topic to open as they sipped their drinks. Peter put down his glass and thought it would probably be a good idea to talk to Sam about his activities. He might be the answer to his financial handicap. As he broods over the way to put it to Sam, Walter who wanted to know a little more about Helen broke in.

"Hey Sam, you were three, where is the other lady."

"'Are you missing her?"Sam asked jokingly.

"I am not but I thought she should be with you."

"'I wish she doesn't come here. You don't have enough money to entertain that swine." At least me you can knock me dead with a bottle of walker but that swine, the fat in her seem to absorb all the alcohol and nothing is left to ascend her brain to make her tipsy. The more she drinks the more she sobers. Well if you are interested to know where she is, go back in the hotel and you will find her with the heap of foods in front of her. And by the way she will be eating in the true sense. Always she orders double plates for every meal she eats. She takes minimum of one hour to eat. I normally, whenever I meet her, I don't wait for her at table. I always spend about five hundred thousand Uganda shillings to feed that punk here in every meal we eat here. So you can see. If she comes here you will hate yourself for having come out to Entebbe. She does not spend a single sent of her own. She comes here every day and hooks on men and siphons their money from their pockets dry.

"Who is she by the way?" Peter asked.

"She is Helen Namayanja, a very wealthy idiot."I am calling her so because she is real idiot. A miser is and an idiot isn't that true? Why make money just for storage for you to see. Then the money losses it meaning and you the miser is an idiot because you don't know the meaning of money. Helen is a rich miser. She has businesses in every town and trading Centre in Buganda. Shops, restaurants, bakeries grinding mills, taxis, buses and you see all the money she gets from these entire business she does not spent a shilling. She wants men to buy for her, her dresses, soap, foods, each and everything. Can you imagine that to happen? I can't. To tell you just how much she loves money, Helen and I were engaged for marriage. I was by then a lecturer in the Faculty of Veterinary Medicine."

"So you are a veterinary doctor?" Walter interjected.

"I was, but I am not now. Now I am a smuggler as you prefer to call me." Sam. said and went on. "I was then with Makerere and this Helen was a school girl in Makerere High school. I met her in the baptismal party of the child of one of our staff. I was boozed up to the last hair on my head and so was Helen. I spent most of my hours during the party wooing the bitch. She was by then a plumb fleshy girl the type of girls I love their feel; you know they give you the sensation of a woman, smooth, thick and nice hu… that was Helen. After party I took Helen home. I was a bachelor of course so there was no emergency technique in the bush or dark corner. I took her home properly lay her on the bed and the day broke when we were together. We started knowing each other better. I don't know whether it was because of me or she was just not going to make it, Helen failed her higher examination. I wanted her to repeat but she refused. She wanted nothing but to marry me. I was a bit reluctant not because I didn't love her but because I was not quite ready to marry. You know the sudden shock we Ugandans had during the privatization, 40% cut of our banking. But it taught us many things. Without that privatization I would not be what I am. I don't know whether to thank the despotic. Anyway as I was saying I wasn't ready to marry. I asked Helen to give me one more year to prepare I explain to her every problem I was facing and the obstacle I wanted to overcome. I thought she saw my points and understood. As I told you there were lots of good and bad the regime change brought. Some hopeless people like me for instance gain quite a lot but some unfortunate people lost their properties and lives as well. The later was the case with the unfortunate parents of Helen which gave her fortune of today. You have heard of the wealthy business man of Mengo who owned trailers, buses and fleet of cars. He had restaurants shops and bars all over the town in Buganda in fact the Business Helen is now running. This man the late Kizito and his wife were killed in cold blood in their home in Mengo because they were strong supporters of the previous regime. Kizito was a very popular business man. Everyone in Kampala knew him."

"I heard of the man." Peter said.

"Yes that was him." Sam said and went on.

Helen escaped the butchery because she was in Makerere with me. We were shock to hear about the deaths of, to be my in laws, Helens parents, brothers and sisters. We mourned them much. Then Helen went to her uncle to find out what was going on. She found out that all the properties and business of her father were intact no one had temper with them. She went to her father's lawyer to claim all those wealth. There was no obstacle or question. She was the only child of Kizito left and had all the right to inherit the business and properties of her father. So that was it. She dives into the money. The lawyer, I think helped her to get the letter of administration transferring all the properties of the family and the account of her father into her own. It was then that Helen stopped calling on me. I try to get intact with her but she would not respond I did everything to make her realized that I was then ready for our marriage but she turned ears with stones in to me. I didn't know that she had fallen in all those fortunes, and then one day I met her suddenly in town in Drapers. She was shopping. I greeted her with the excitement of lovers who have been away for a long time but the bitch looked at me with icy eyes. Contemptuously she said hello to me and turned away to discuss the price of the dress she wanted to buy. I stood behind her ashamed and humiliated.

Well let me wait and see. I thought and stood waiting."Sam said and swallowed the last drop of whisky in his glass. He pushed his glass to Walter and said "My glass is empty pal I need more." Sam said and stretches his legs under the tables. "I like people who make me talk especially when they provide the energy to make me talk like this I will chatter until next year." Sam said and they all laughed. Walter called the waiter and ordered another round for all of them.

"This is it." Sam said as the waiter laid their orders in front of them. "I was telling you Sam said and went on. "I stood behind the bitch expecting her to see me and come and talk to me. When she finished buying the dress she gave it to another lady who had stood beside her. I learnt later that she was a shopping servant. Her work was just to go out with Madam Helen whenever she went shopping. Yes, Madam Helen walked out and met me at the door. The ice in her eyes had not thawed even a bit. If anything she was harder and vicious when she heard me said, "Helen, honey". The usual way we used to call each other you know. I didn't know what was up. *Am I talking to a stranger in this town who resemble Helen or am I talking to Helen herself.* I' thought and I asked her, "I am sorry madam if it is a mistaken identity, are you Helen Namayanja I asked her. You know what she said.

"I am and so what?"

"So do you know the Samuel Kironde the Lecturer in Veterinary Medicine Makerere? The one you were betrothed to in marriage?"

"I know but I am too busy to discuss anything like that with you now perhaps later." She said and walk to a 280-black Mercedes Benzes park in front of the shop. A man who had stood near the car dress in a black suit sprang into motion and snapped the door open and Madam Helen I used to know as higher school girl dropout entered the car and the man slammed the door behind her. The woman the shopping servant lugging the basket packed tight with all sorts of items walked and stood behind the boot of the car. I stood at the door perplexed I did know what to do but stared at Helen with livid eyes. I thought it was a night mare but it was reality. Things were happening.

The suffer walked to the back of the car and opened the boot and put the basket in and both of them walked to the front seat. Helen in the car did not turn her eyes towards me standing like a dead body near the car. She pretended to be reading a copy of ***The eye of the nation*** she bought that morning. I didn't know what to do to fall dead was impossible to pull the bitch out of the car and strangle her was impossible because I had no strength. I had that hollow feeling you get when you are expecting sad news. I wanted to cry but I couldn't. I wanted in fact to do everything but I could do nothing. The Benzes280 started and was soon lost among the traffic. I knew, at the distant the disappearing car was Helen who turned me into calf love and now because of some wealth, she has deserted me. For some unknown reason I had built up my love for her and her sudden change of idea affected me. Well with the privatization which was bullying me left, right and center plus the loss of a lover, I thought it was not a good combination I decided to go on leave. I went." Sam said and drank the whisky in his glass, put it down and licked his lips. Yeah, Walter the man of dough, you aren't bore with my story?" I always talk until my listeners have no strength or are bore with me then I end my story abruptly and walked out of them. You know what my fuel is? The Jeri cane is always labeled Jonnie walker with the picture of a man striding in a real tail coat, black sailor hat white trousers with a black stick in the hand. Pour that fuel in me and you hear any story in the world. Don't mistake me for a miser. I want people to spend for me when they want something from me and I spend for anyone anytime." Sam said drunkenly and drank some more whisky from his glass again and put the glass down. "Yes gentlemen I went home for leave. This is where I ended. I was bore stiff I didn't know what to do to myself. Each day I thought of the Helen still eating. Have you seen how long she is staying away? Do not be deceive she is gone somewhere or sitting in the hotel there doing nothing. She is munching and crunching the bones. How glad I didn't have money then, I don't know how we were going to get along. In bed she is not the same as she was. With that weight she is the lousiest woman you can love. Maneuvering her in bed is just like turning a mountain on its base. Anyway that is not important now. The most important thing was, I was in financially fixed. Then a friend come to my rescue I complained to him about my financial position and social life. You know what he told me. "He said the days of Moses for manna's from heaven are gone when people use to complain to God and they got whatever they wanted. These days' of Adam and Eve are days of sweat a toil. You have your coffee pouring down from the trees like rain from heaven why don't you pluck the bloody things and ferry then across to Kenya and remove that boredom and poverty." He said

"How do I go about that? I have no canoe or a boat to do that. And I don't know anyone who could help me both in Kenya as well as in Uganda to take the coffee there." My friends said "I never knew you were so much behind news. You mean to tell me that you have no idea about coffee smuggling going on between Uganda and Kenya?" I told him I didn't know and honestly I didn't know. Beside, even if I knew I needed courage from a person like that of my friend to make me sit in a boat or canoe which could just be shank by the army marine boys at sight. With courage from my friends I prepared ten bags of coffee and we set off to Kisumu in Kenya. I tell you, you can now go and accuse me, even to the president, my case will never go in court. Because I have the keys to make men talk or keep quiet in Uganda today. And all this by the way I owed it to my friend who gave me that encouragement and the advice. We went to Kisumu I sold the coffee. I got Kenya money and that money, as you know, is as precious as gold in Uganda. You know about it. What I was further told by my friend to do was to buy sugar and salt to come and sell home here. Those were, I don't know their value. In one trip only I found that I was nearly a millionaire. I came back home I pluck each and every coffee beans which I was leaving to get wasted on the trees. I went to the extent of collecting those which fell on the ground. I went back with fifteen bags this time and come back with more salt, sugar and soap. I opened my account in Kenya Commercial Bank in Kisumu. At home here my banker the Uganda Commercial was recording 2.5 million and in Kenya I had two hundred thousand Kenya shillings and that was a hell of money if converted in Uganda shillings. So with that money, I began to recover from my mental stress about Helen and my financial position improved. I thought it was not worth going back to Makerere to waste time. Working for thirty days and get just three thousand shillings the equivalent of what earn in one hour now on my own. I decided to tender in my resignation. I did and that was it. I came out here now. I am dealing with all commodities that may want to find their way outside Uganda and I also bring anything I see people are interested in". Sam said and emptied his glass.

"You want to give me more, Walter?" Otherwise I have finished detailing to you what you wanted to know about Helen and me. Joyce is at the moment my only girlfriend. I love her and her loves me too don't you Joyce?"

"Of course you know that Sam." Joyce said resting her head on the massive muscular shoulder of Sam. Sam smoothened her head under the hat as Walter looked on enviously like chain starved hyena being teased with a red meat. The scene reminded Peter about Rose, he recalled hours they used to romance with her in the drinking places like that whenever they were tipsy he felt sick at the scenes. To dispel of the worries Peter started thinking of what Sam has been narrating to them. *He was disappointed by Helen at first. That disappointment helped him to work hard for transformation in his life. He had his coffee which started him off. I tried farming. I planted coffee but the weather let me done. I would have done exactly what Joe has done. How the world has changed in Uganda! The so called adverted are the worst hit by privatization, as a result they are all running out into business like smuggling, running bars, shops, canteens and even becoming taxi drivers in order that they earn their livelihood. Those who would have been bums and freaks are the guys living like kings and lords. They even owned fleets of cars and Lorries. They have herd of cattle, flock of sheep and goats.* Peter thought. He must talk to Walter about his problem but how is he going to go about it since Walter was getting drunk increasing his sexual appetite. Peter was sure Walter was not going to go back home alone. He must pick a woman and how will he talk to him his problem. *May be I shall invite him and talk to him about that at home. I need some money to go and square the electricity bill. My sugar and soap are gone. What if I get a visitor tonight what shall I use for breakfast? There must be an end to this financial suffering. My salary does not last me a week yet I use it with maximum care. If there was a way out, I would have resigned from the Government service. There is no emolument I am getting from my present post. The post meant something in the past but now it is just like being a sweeper in other countries. But if I resign now how will I start life outside without foundation. I have no capital the least I had I lost it with Andrew to that police officer. We bought something not worth showing to anyone. May be we could let Sam have a look at them and see whether he would like them. I'll mentions to him and see his feelings.* Peter thought.

"Okay gentlemen it has been quite a nice afternoon with you we must be going." Sam said and got up holdings Joyce by the waist. As they got up to go Helen ambled down the hotel entrance steps her hand bag swinging on the meaty arm back and forwards. "Haa the swine has at last finished eating, see."Sam said pointing at her. She is now coming out of the hotel she must have eaten a barrel of food." Sam said as he saw Helen tumble out of the hotel steps and lumbered towards them. The butterfly colour *gomaci* she had on gave her the appearance of a moving hut. She had tied a red headscarf on her head and was wiping her fat oily face with another white handkerchief she had in her hand. She humbled on and come and stood akimbo near Sam. Later she put her left hand on his shoulder and said, "Thank you very much for the delicious lunch you gave me honey!"

Joyce laughed and she was beginning to say something to Helen when Sam interrupted her by squeezing her left hand he was holding and addressing Helen he said, "I thought that words disappeared from our mouths many years back?"

"Did it?" Helen asked.

"You want me to remind you?" I know you wanted lunch I gave it to you and that is the lot."

"I want to give you supper in my home tonight."

"Both of us?"

"No you alone."

"That won't happen. If we are to eat in your house Joyce and I will be there. Without her I will eat with her in the hotel or at her place. In any case she has already asked me to be with her for supper. Helen I must be frank with you, I did not start this. You started. We can remain talking friends but no more of the relationships we had before. I now have Joyce and her alone." I am proud of her and she is of me. Sam said as Joyce nodded her head approvingly.

As the two were arguing where to eat their supper Peter took the advantage of this and ask Walter if they could be alone for a period as long as one hour.

"Certainly there will be time even longer. Now we are going to Lido beach I expect we shall be on our own". Walter said and went on, "I in fact want to talk to you. Even if I don't talk to you now, on our way back home I will. The coincidental meeting of today was very good."

"Hopping that you will not pick up a chick." Peter warned and they giggled.

"Well give it time and we watch the development. But I think I won't for tonight that swine of last night drained me dry."

"Joyce had stood near Walter as they talked to Helen."

"How did you like the afternoon Walter mumble to Joyce."

"Sorry I didn't get you". Joyce said and leant forward to Walter

"I'll give you a ring on Monday." Walter gabbled. Joyce smile and turned to her group. Sam caught them in the act as he turned round in time to see the smile on Joyce lips dying out. Scare at the look on Sam face Walter in fear said "I was telling her that Helen eats like chicken from morning to dusk without rest."

"Ha yeah that is what she is. A normal human being can't sit at table for one hour eating, eating and eating like termite."Sam repeated his joke and they all laughed including Helen herself. Peter and Walter shot glances at Helen who stood in front of them like an ant-hill and looked away. Sam is right such a woman is impossible in bed. *You just can't reach her. Look at the buttock two big hills behind her. One could safely sit on them without falling off.* Walter thought as his sex appetite drained away.

"Hay Sam where could we locate you if need you."Peter asked

"Ha that you can contact Joyce. When I am in the country I live with her."

"I want to sit down". Helen began to complain. We haven't a chair good enough for you here may be we should go back on our forms under the umbrella." Sam interjected.

"Okay we go". Helen agreed. Holding Joyce by the waist Sam. and Joyce walked away to where they had sat before.

"We are leaving you gentlemen." Joyce said and eyed Walter and Peter waving good bye to them her slender fingers flickering in the air.

"Thank you very much for your short company. I hope we will continue to meet and talk like this sometimes. Sam said as he walked away romantically with Joyce.

"Thank you Sam and Joyce it's been quite nice meeting you and the nice story from Sam. It's very informative and we have learnt quite a lot." Peter said as he shook hand with Sam. "I will prepare his fuel and he should prepare story for me also." Walter said and shook hands with both of them. They waved to them good bye, and they were left alone at their table.

Walter sighed and shrugged. "He is quite a character."

"He is a very adamant man." Peter replied and added, "that is what it is with successful people. He is quite right. In Uganda of today what matter is money? If you have it, you can do anything in this country. If anyone tries to talk against you, all you have to do is slap his mouth with a bundle of money and he will keep quiet forever. If you want him to talk dangle the bundle in front of his face and he will yell all there is in him. Even if you are a professor or a doctor of divinity or any highly placed professional but if your pocket is hollow as mine, you are dead. Any slight mistake will throw you behind bar for years.......”

"Let us leave that for a moment."Walter interrupted Peter and looked round for the waiter. "Shall we have one each before we go to Lido Beach or we could go and have it there?”

"We have been here too long let's transfer." Peter said.

"Well let's get going then. The two got up and walked to where they had parked their car and drove off to Lido beech.

Ten minutes' drive brought them to Lido Beach, a love nest for milliners of Kampala and Entebbe. Lido beach, a small bay about a kilometer to Entebbe International airport lay on left hand side of the Road. The sandy beach extends up to the road. Opposite the beach is the old Entebbe international Airport. Walter spent most of his time on Lido beach during weekends so that he was well known by the beach attendant as a "beach lover". They knew what he drinks and what he ate whenever he went to the beach. All he has to do was to pop in and show his face to the waiters at the Hotel beach and they would flutter after him with all he cares to eat and drink. If he is accompanied as that day all he did was to put two fingers up, and his usual order would be double or only one finger in such case the waiter had to come and take the order of the accompanied.

That afternoon the beach was sparingly populated when they drove in. Walter park on the parking lot and walked out to the Hotel bar. He showed his two fingers to the man at the counter. They exchanged smile and he walked out and took a table which was under the umbrella near the lake. They sat down and immediately a waitress, a short plumb girl came in with a tray containing two Nile Special right from the heart of the deep freezer. She came greeted them and placed the bottles on the table gave them the glasses and flicked the tops of the bottles open with her opener.

"Thanks you". Walter said and pure the whole beer into the glass, a long neck glass about a liter in capacity. Peter follow suit and they push the bottles back to the waitress who was still standing near them waiting for cash. Walter took the dough tossed it in her tray and she walked away.

She has over bleached her face. "Look at her. A polychromatic lady the arms and the legs dark, the face brick red the lips dark red the eyes brawn blue and I don't know how the down stair is like bet its painted white." Walter said.

"You have x-ray eyes you can see ladies through their frocks. Peter put it mildly.

"The usual set up of such artificial girls they paint all the sensitive parts on their body so that went you open up you find it the way she looks, made up thing there is nothing natural about them" Walter remarked.

"You could write a book about women of Uganda today couldn't you?"

"I could but I have no time for that. I don't even have time for writing a letter home and you talk of writing a book. Anyone can find about women of today by himself. Undress many and you will know their demand how they dress and polish themselves from head to foot." "Anyway Peter now that we are alone, I want to change the subject of our discussion before I start introducing you to my acquaintances in this place." He said and drank from his glass. "I had a talk with Andrew Yesterday. I met him in the International hotel." Walter said and sat back on his chair and smoothen his neck ties and looked sympathetically at Peter. In fact, as I have already said, that meeting you this morning was a very good coincidence. I was coming to your home this evening all the same. "I – I do not know how you will take it but I mean nothing other than what I am going to tell you. True, since your down fall Peter", Walter said and put his hand on the thigh of Peter. Peter stooped forward on the table supporting his head with his left palm and the right arm folded on the table, listened to Walter attentively. You have been struggling to sit up and walk financially but each time you tried you flopped down. There was no one to hold your hand and make you walk out of it other than our good friend and brother like Andrew. Together with him you tried many but you were partially successful. We need to find resources which can make you buy basic commodities like soap, sugars and pay water and electricity bills." Walter said. When Walter mentioned the lack of money for sugar Peter felt the 'thud' in his heart he blinked and the mouth turn salty with exasperation. Small beads of sweat beaded on his nose in spite of the cool breeze of wind from the Lake pounding on his face. "Anyway, to make long matter short, Andrew and I have agreed to help you if possible out of this mess you are in. We have been good childhood friends and I believe we are now more or less brothers. Your problems are ours, and Andrew's should be yours and mine, mine should be yours and Andrews. Because of that Andrew and myself have decided to assist you with a few not much that is we have bought for you some dress which I have in the boot of the car I will let you have them when we get home. I don't know if they will fit but we try to guess your size as much as we could, we got for you also a pair of shoes. May I say the content of that suit case in the boot are all yours. And as far as this trade you have started is concerned, I will try to help you if you still need to try. I tell you it's quite a healthy trade but the risks overwhelm the beauty of the trade. It's only when you are like Sam that you could carry the bloody thing on your head and walk the street of Kampala from the Bats Valley to Jinja Road. No one will talk, if anyone does you throw a red bundle on his mouth and you see him flinching away. But a beginner is always dragged behind bars to eat cassava and beans with donkey work during the day. And by the time you walk out of it you will be a dead man. My uncle in Gulu has friends who have plenty of those ivories. They get them from Sudan as I said if you are still interested we could go home together in the train and bring that stuff here and we shall let Sam or the Somali have a look. It's not safe to go by road. There are too many road-blockcheck points on our road these days we could easily get netted up and it will be a fine story among the highly placed people." Walter concluded.

"I – I' don't know what words to use to you two to express my gratitude. I can only say that I am very grateful to both of you for all the assistance you have been rendering me. *A friend in need is a friend in deed.* The English say and we believe anyone who comes to you and sit with you when you are aggrieved is truly no one other than a brother. I don't need to go all over what you have just stated. I entirely agreed with every word. But my only worry at the moment which you two will know is that I have no financial strength at the moment to assist any of you when you will need my help. Moral supports you will get it in plenty. As far as the trade is concerned, I am determined to go ahead and pursue it. I don't see anyway, where I could raise money sooner than through this dirty way. I know it's risky but if I should get my hand at it, Sam might be my immediate buyer." Peter said holding his head with both hands elbows resting on the table.

Chapter Seven

A week after Walter and Peter spent their weekend at Lido beach, their investigations revealed that Walter's uncle could have ideas where to find the elephant tusks in Gulu. Friday came, Peter and Walter booked the upper class in a train bound from Kampala to Gulu to go and explore the possibility of obtaining the elephant tusk sin Gulu. At exactly 6 p.m. the train rolled out of Kampala railways station heading for Jinja. The first major town in Eastern Uganda. Because of jolting and swaying in the train they didn't have good sleep on their way from Jinja to Tororo where they changed the train to the Northern bound line. The time was 5.30 am when they left Tororo for Gulu. At noon, they a day after they left Kampala, they reached Aloi Railway Station, one of the most popular stations along the Tororo-Gulu line. All local foods of all kinds were available in this station. They were hungry and they needed some lunch. After their lunch of chicken and millet bread at Aloi, they embarked on their last segment of the Journey to Gulu. Peter and Walter mounted their beds and laid on their backs as they talked about how to move when in Gulu. The jolting and the swaying of the train lulled them to a deep sleep. They travelled through all other stations without knowing. It was not until the train came to a stop in Gulu station, their destination that they both woke up. It was wet and raining when they got to Gulu. It had just stop raining and switched on to a drizzle. Pools of rain water stood everywhere between the railway lines in the station. Gutters draining the rain water made noise like waterfalls.

"Where are we now?" Peter who was sleeping on the toped bed asked Walter who was sleeping on the middle bed directly opposite the window of the coach.

"We have arrived in Gulu". Walter replied as he rolled up the window glass of the coach and peeped outside.

"Oh dear we have slept so much within this short distance. From twelve mid-day up to now. And its six p.m. by my watch is that right?" Peter asked

"Yeah mine is one minute behind though." Walter said glancing at his wrist watch.

"That is good enough." Peter remarked and yawned.

Peter and Walter picked up their brief cases and walked out of their compartment and into the corridor of the coach. The rain had made the window glass frosty so that it was difficult to see outside through the glass. Peter rolled the glass window up and they peeped outside the train to see how bad the weather was. As they did, another train from Pakwach, the terminal station on the Northern line, pulled into the station alongside the Kampala train, and parked. Passengers from both trains started coming out from the coaches carrying their luggage on their heads, children on their backs, and rushed away with them to the waiting rooms. Peter and Walter with only their brief cases to carry climbed down from the train and skipped over the puddles of rain water to get into the veranda of the station office. They got to the veranda and kicked the mud from their shoes and flick away the rain water from their jacket. Peter had put on his new grey suit Walter and Andrew had bought for him. It fitted him well as Walter had said they had made guesses about the measurement as near as possible. The blue neck tie with diagonal, red and blue strips match well with the light blue shirt all of which were gifts from Walter and Andrew. The new shoes made of crocodile skin with leather soles made him as new as in the days of Rose. Beside the wears, Walter and Andrew gave Peter, they also gave him fifty thousand shilling each as his working capital to start on the elephant tusks business he was interested in. Elephant tusks, Leopards skins Rhino horns, and mineral like diamond and gold, were all being illegally sold in Gulu. Walter was willing to help Peter to purchase any of the items. They went for the items which were most paying at that time, the elephant tusks and Rhino horns. These were their target when they left for Gulu. But, failure to get those items they could collect whatever were available.

The drizzling rain increased again into a heavy down pour for a short while and reverted into drizzles again.

"We are going to stay with my uncle in the village most of our time here." Walter said.

"Is your uncle's home far away from here?" Peter asked

"Yes about eight miles on Gulu-Kampala road and about two miles inland from the main road.

It sounds far away from town why don't we go to town and book in Wilobo inn or the Pacholi Inn?"

"There will not be much to hear and see as far as we are concern if we stay in town. My uncle is well informed about what we want." Walter said. As he talked an open boot taxi Peugeot 504 pick-up pulled and stopped near them and immediately two bare chests young boys, about eleven and fifteen years old, wearing torn pair of shorts jumped down from the boot of the pick-up where they were couching from the drizzles and started calling for passenger who wanted a ride to town. With shaky voices they shouted, town-town-town, informing the waiting passengers that the pick-up was going to town. The driver turned off the light of the pick-up and cut off the engine but remained inside because of the drizzling rain.

"Let's climb in the front seat." Walter said and without waiting for Peter's reply picked his brief case and jumped into the rain and opened the front door of the pick-up and climbed in. The driver, who was rolling down the window glass on his side, turned for a brief moment to see who were coming into the front seat. When he saw them he turned back and continued with his job without saying any word to them. Peter got in and sat next to Walter. He was closing the door of the car when a tall fat old man held on door from outside. Walter duck in front to see who the intruder was. A fat, old man with wrinkle face, carrying a bifocal spectacle on a thick nose stared back at Walter. "May I come in?" The old man asked. The old rain coat he had on, and the torn old brief case in his left hand, gave him the look of an old professor. The fluent English he spoke, the courage he had, differentiated him from the old scrap of the village.

"May I come in?" The old man repeated seeing that Peter was not making any move to accommodate him in the front seat.

"It's full." Peter put in curtly.

"Where will you sit my dear old man I am also in plus the drive and him I......? Walter said.

"The back is over flowing, otherwise I would not be bothering you gentleman." The old man polity interrupted Walter. "I must go when it's still bright enough my sights are very poor and worse still I have to walk the most dangerous road in Gulu these days." The old man added.

"Where are you going sir?" Peter asked not yet decided whether to let the old man in.

"I am going across Layibi stream. My home is directly opposite the road to St. Joseph College Layibi."

"But the pick-up, is going to town my dear old man." Peter corrected.

"I know but I want to avoid tripping on these metals in the station here. I am going to be left just at junction across the main road. I told you I will be walking home. And that road at night is as dangerous as walking between the queues of hungry lions. You get all sort of railroad bums on the road with all type of weapons ranging from pocket knives, clubs, bows and arrows, spears, and guns along the road." The old man said and added "it's a short distance but if you walk along that road after eight and you don't bleed then you could be a ghost or one of the bums."

"I really do not know how four giants like us can fit in this small space but as you have explained let us see how we can fit you in." Peter said and left the handle of the door.

"Please remove off your rain coat its wet?" Peter reminded the old man who was already squeezing himself in with the rain coat on.

"Oh dear sorry excuse me". The old man said as he took off his old rain coat and put it in his old bag and squeezed himself in the narrow space Peter had provided for him. Peter sat forwards his knees touching the dust board of the pick-up as the old man squeezed in slowly and slammed the door of the car hard behind him before he sat down with half of his back against the door. The old man picked up his hand bag held it on his thigh and said, "Thank you gentlemen. You will excuse me for being a burden. It is only a few yards to the main road and you will be alright."

"It's okay old man we appreciated your difficulties", Peter said and adjusted himself further. The passenger at the back of the pick-up, as the old man put it, were parked with their luggage like bags of beans. When he was satisfied he had parked enough the driver tipped the two young boys fifty shilling each and he ignited the engine. The pick-up spat smoke, heaved and began to roll away in the dark. The boys immediately ran to the dark veranda looking happy, stood side by side shivering in the cold weather.

"Oh dear poor kids, they are dying of the cold weather because of money" the old man remark as he leered at them through the window. Peter chuckled and said, "that is Uganda of today my dear old man. You either go it the hard way like that or you perish. They are lucky they have got some money. They may eat some pan cakes with it, but there are some who are worse than they are, sleeping hungry." Peter said and continued, "I tell you what we saw yesterday when we were at Mukono Railway Station a place about fifteen miles from Kampala...."

"I know Mukono very well. I lived in Mukono for about seven years as a district Veterinary Officer." That was from 1955-1962. The old man interjected.

"You are retired Veterinary Officer?"

"Yes. I am. We used to call ourselves "bull fighters" not Veterinary Officers you know. That was because we used to wrestle with those long horns Ankole cattle when treating them we held them by their long horns. It was quite a fun." The old man remarked.

"Wasn't that very dangerous?"

'It was but we had to do it that way....."

"Anyway I was telling you old man, when we got in Mukono Peter interrupted the old man, "a boy about twelve, not mad, was walking naked with the body was full of sores. He was wading in the puddles of rain water along the railway lines collecting bones which people had eaten and thrown down. He was picking the bones and gnawing at ligaments which remained on the bones like a dog. These types of kids are very unfortunate. They are either without parents, or have irresponsible parents; as a result they are forced to do that because there is no other way to survive."

"That is what we say the survival of the fittest." Walter said.

"'Uganda is badly mismanaged since we got our so call independence an independence lead by greedy selfish leaders with very poor primitive family backgrounds which have resulted into destruction of lives and properties of individuals and Government infrastructure." The old man said and went on, "for instance, there are lots of embezzlement of Government funds, mismanagement of factories industries, roads and rails. The education systems are destroyed. Makerere University which used to be one of the best Universities in Africa is no longer better than an institute. All the lectures have left for better pastures in other countries. The semi-literate rulers have erroneously convinced most of the Ugandan that education has no value by giving big business and job to their illiterate friends and next of kin who actually do not know a bloody thing about whatever they are doing. As a result, we are adapting one of the most primitive trading systems, the batter trade. Where will that take us? Illiterate people, one getting big job and drive fantastic cars which are convincing most parents that there is no need to waste their money on education." The old man said and asked the driver to stop at the main road to Gulu Town. "I am getting out here." The old man told the drive.

"I know you are." The drive replied without looking at him. The drizzling rain had stopped. The old man got out of the car and thanked Peter and Walter.

"Nice meeting you gentlemen I must be going before it's very dark. Although my days are numbered I still want the few more days God is giving me. I don't want to snap it up. I wish we could meet and talk more. Are you here long, and where are you going to stay for the night?" The old man said.

"I don't know how long we are here and we are trying to find room in Wiloboor or Paacholi inn"

"You will certainly get one. I advise you check with Wilobo Inn first. I don't like Paacholi inn much these days because there are too many armed men there. It looks more of an Army officers' Mess other than a public inn. And you know, they could be chaotic sometime when they are drunk. If there are no rooms in Wilobo, then you may risk Paacholi Inn." The Old man advised.

"Thank you very much Bull Fighter" Peter said using the name the old man fancy. It has been quite a pleasure for this accidental meeting tonight. As you said, we are looking forward to having another chat with you one day presumable with glasses in our hands. Do you play with the stuff by way?" Peter asked.

"Much. I started it during my Veterinary train in Kabete. It was helping me to fight those real bulls in Kenya you known. And now I drink it to wait for my last days, the "D" day. Eat your death son hope to see you again." The old man remarked and started to walk away.

"Okay bull fighter have a safe journey home don't hit your toe against any rock."

"I will be alright. It's still early enough to see clearly."

"Cheerio" Peter replied as the drive eased the gear lever of the pick-up and accelerated to town.

A few minutes' drive brought them to Wilobo Inn which stood only one hundred yards from the town Centre along Gulu-Kampala road. Wilobo Inn catered for boarding and lodging. And behind it, there was a night club.

"We are checking for rooms here" Walter said to the driver.

"Shall I wait for you?"

"No, take those people in the boot of the pick up to town. We can find our way to other places if we should fail to get rooms here". Walter said.

"May be before we depart, where can we get taxi if we want one?" Walter asked the drive.

"There are no taxis here at the moment. I am the only one."

"Where do we get you if we should need your help?"

"Obote Avenue plot 30."

"Okay we will call on you should we need your help as we are likely to. We might be going to Abilli tomorrow in the morning and we definitely need transport."

"You could take Kampala buses and drop down at Abilli. It is cheaper that way." The driver advised.

""That could have been okay if we were stopping at Abilli trading center, but when we come out of the bus at the trading center at Abilli we need to move some distance inland." Walter said

"I will be at your service up to mid-day. After that I will go out for other business." the driver acknowledged

"Okay we shall try to be in time. In case we you don't see us by mid day, you are free to go. Cheerio."

"Okay". The driver said and drove off.

"Do you believe him that he is the only one who owns a taxi here?" Peter asked Walter.

"We shall find that out. Don't worry."

Peter and Walter walked to the entrance of Wilobo inn. A girl, brown in complexion with a smooth baby like face, wearing ivory necklace and ear rings, with the hair on her head straightened standing on end which gave her the look of a girl wearing a black hat, sat at the Inn reception counter. She was reading a novel as Peter and Walter walked in. She lifted her head in time as the two stepped on the cemented floor in front of the reception counter.

"Hello you are welcome." She said as she close her book and gave them a persuasive smile which reminded Peter about Rose. Peter thought he had seen the ghost of his wife Rose. The smile, the hair, the dimple on her cheeks when she smiled the setup of the teeth, the immature canine tooth on the left jaw, matched well with those of Rose. Walter also noticed the resemblance between Rose the late wife of Peter and the Receptionist of the Inn. *She is well chosen for the place. Her position as a receptionist was an asset to the Inn. It must have taken the owner of the inn a bit of time to find her."* Peter thought as he stared at the girl at the counter.

Don't you think she is the twin sister of Rose Walter? Don't you believe me?" Peter asked emphatically.

"Yeah I – I agree with you." Walter answered.

Walter and Andrew the only two close friends of Peter knew all his problems. He was a devout to his wife Rose and since she died Peter was never tempted to have an affair with any girl. He always talked of Rose that Walter and Andrew were afraid to suggest to him not to cry over spilt milk but to remarry. That night, when Peter exclaimed his surprised in the resemblance between his late wife and the receptionist in Wilobo inn, Walter thought it was wise to encourage Peter to have a start.

"I am Peter Lapyem the Permanent Secretary Ministry of Education do you know Rose Idaganono from Palabek? She was my late wife."Peter asked stupidly and extended his hand for a hand shake with her. The girl was shock dumb. No customer has ever approached her like that since she was employed in the inn.

"I don't get you sir. You want rooms or something?" The girl replied

"We want rooms alright but my question is, do you know Rose from Palabek the daughter of Idaganono?"

"Oh dear, me! I have never been to Palabek and I have never known of anybody call Rose Idaganono. I am from Anaka the daughter of Amen." The girl replied with a smile and added. "I doubt very much if we have any relative in Palabek. I am sorry sir I don't know Rose. I could be her relative but I... I ...."

"People resemble don't they". Walter put in carefully.

"No-no-no you must be a relative to Rose. Peter insisted with his eyes rolling on the receptionist. What is your name anyway?" Peter asked.

"Now look here gentleman let us finish with business first. What is your business here?" The girl asked looking serious.

"We have come to find where to sleep tonight." Walter interrupted.

"I have three single rooms and two double rooms still free."

"I think we shall take two single rooms what do you think Peter?"

Peter did not answer he only stared at the girl at the counter, and said

"Why the resemblance if you are not related to Rose?"

"Okay book us in two single rooms." Walter added.

"The girls took down their particulars and book them in the rooms near each other in rooms 12 and 13.

"Supper time starts at 7.30p.m. and ends at 9p.m. so please try to be in the dining hall within this time. And breakfast tomorrow morning is from 7.30 a.m. to 9a.m. The bar and the dancing hall with the band playing live music will be open throughout the night so you can go enjoy yourself. But do not go out of the Inn. These army men in Gulu here are ruthless at night." The girl explained to Peter and Walter and got up from her stool she was sitting and walked to the cupboard with a glass shutter where various keys for different rooms where hung. She pulled the knob of the shutter and picked the keys for Rooms 12 and 13. She gave the keys number 12 to Peter and 13 to Walter and returned to sit on her stool and began to read her book. Peter and Walter thanked her and walked up to the second floor and checked in their rooms. They went in Peter's room first .The room was self-contained. A carpeted lounge with two heavy Western types of sofa sets with a coffee set in each lounge.

The single bed covered with smooth beautiful blanket was large enough to accommodate three people yet it was used for a single person. The telephone and a bed side lamp stood on a stool near the head of executive bed. The inbuilt in wardrobe was directly opposite the bed.

"What a luxury! I did expect the place to be luxurious like this. Walter said.

'It's superlative". Peter agreed.

"I am not going to sleep alone on this bed tonight." Walter vowed.

"I hope you are not thinking of the girl at the reception desk?" Peter said.

"If you won't talk to her then it could be her or any other I will bump on in the bar in the dance hall."

"Okay I think I must talk to her." Peter said vehemently.

"That will be great Peter. It will be a new leaf in your life I was longing to hear and see." Walter said.

"That won't mean I will forget Rose and begin to mess about with all the floozies I meet on the street." Peter warned sternly.

"I don't mean that Peter but don't you think it is no used to ……. I believe we are all going to go the same path Rose has gone though under different circumstances. You are still young and you are not going to finish up your life like this Peter. If you don't begin to occupy your mind with something new you might find yourself taken to the bottles and that will be more disastrous than taking on another faithful woman. It's not against the law. You know as much as I do that if Rose were alive you would not be thinking about another wife." When Walter finished talking Peter sat pensively on his bed and suddenly stirred and got up from the bed scratch his head and said, "I won't be taken to the bottles dear brother but I am going to talk to that girl and find out more about her."

"That will be great Peter and we shall see if we could invite her for supper."

"We shall find it out from her." Walter said and walked out with his key on his left hand while the right hand held his briefcase. He walked and stopped at the door to his room inserted the key in the lock, opened it and walked in. The setup of the room was identical to that of Peter. He tossed his case on the bed and walked out locked the door and walked back to Peter's room.

"Let's go down." Walter ordered Peter. Meekly Peter got out of the chair he was sitting on in the lounge of his room meditating over what Walter has just told him. He walked out after Walter and locked his room before they both walked down.

"Here are our keys". Peter said and the girl lifted up her head from her book she was reading. She closed the book with her finger keeping the page and received the keys from them with a smile and hung them on their numbers.

"That book must be very interesting. Peter asked the girl affirmatively.

"Indeed it is."

"Who is the author?"

The girl without a word turned the title of the book to them so that they read it. It was by James Hardly Chaste and the title was *"You are safe dead."*

"Umm. I like James Hardly Chaste writing. I have plenty of his writings." Peter remarked.

"Do you? The girl asked as she sat up on the stool.

"Yes I have a number of copies. My late wife, whom you resemble, used to love James writing. Peter remarked insinuatingly.

"You are a widower?" The girl explored

"Yes I am."

"Sorry." the girl said and added "But you look strangers in Gulu town where do you come from? Nevertheless, you said your late wife is from Palabek and I haven't seen you in Wilobo inn night club. Very many gentlemen of your class don't miss our place here every night."

"We are not strangers in the true sense of the words. This is our home town and our homes are not very far from town either except our jobs does not enable us to show up often as to know most people especially beautiful girl like you." Peter said lowering his voice down and stooped over the desk so that he was looking right in the eyes of the girl.

"Thank you for your compliment. But I am not that beautiful". The girl said.

"What are you expected to say anyway. I knew you would say just that. If I were you I would have said the same. Any woman who resembles my late wife is beautiful." Peter said and paused. "You've had your supper yet. There are not many customers coming in at the moment why don't we go and eat and you come back?"

"We are not allowed to eat at this time. In any case if I am going to eat I will go in the staff room and not in the dining hall." The girl corrected

"At what time are you allowed to eat?"

"8 o'clock".

'Ten more minutes."

"Yes, if the girl who is coming to replace me comes in time."

"And where will you go."

"Eat and Go home."

"Now listened." Peter began to talk and moved nearer to the receptionist. "As you correctly said that we look stranger in Gulu but I corrected and said we are not very strange because Gulu is our home town. It is a long time I came home that was to bury my father and later my wife." Peter said and looked at the girl in the face probably to attract her sympathy. The girl reacted with a nod of the head and said "sorry for the loss of your dear ones."

"Thanks." Peter said and went on. You said you are not allowed to eat in the dining hall. Could we go and eat elsewhere in town? Am sure you know of good eating places in town." Peter said well aware that he may not be able to afford to pay for the meals. But there is something in this girl if it means borrowing money from Walter he was ready to do so.

"I don't go out with ….." The girl had started to talk when Peter interjected. "You need to make a start at it." Peter said. The girl smile at Peter and almost turned to her book. Determined to win the heart of the girl, Peter forgot about his main aim to Gulu. *If I could go back with this girl, the ivories could wait.* Peter thought.

"Your friend is waiting for you to go and eat." The girl said as she saw that Walter was pacing the lobby of the inn reading the posters display on the wall advertising the few items to customers.

"He is not too hungry nor am I. But please after your supper will you come back here. I very much like to have a word with you. I will be disappointed if you slip away home. I would like to talk to you about my wife you resemble so that you do not be surprise why I am interested in you like this.

"I will try". The girl said and turned to her book as Peter walked out to join Walter.

"Let's go and eat Peter said to Walter."

"How is it? Any luck?"

"You know our bloody girls. It's difficult to deal with them and you cannot predict whether you've started well or not. Anyway after her supper she is going home and another girl is coming at her place."

"She said that?"

"Yes and I have asked her to come back at the counter with the friend."

"That is good. I call it a good start and you will be through Peter don't worry. The friend although I haven't seen her, is already a victim, Walter utter.

"She might not be of your taste."

"A hungry man has no taste." Walter said. In any case I don't believe any sane hotel proprietor would stock ugly girls in his hotel to scare visitors off. Especially if she is to work at the reception desk, she must be succulent.

"I know you need one tonight. This long boring journey must have heightened your appetite."

"It has done quite a lot." Walter said as they took their seats at two seats table in the corner of the dining hall. The hall was pack tight nearly every table was occupied. Few people were leaving while their seats were being occupied immediately. When they sat down, a waiter came and stood over them as Peter and Walter browsed through the menu placed upright on the table like the Bishop's Miters.

"Get us chicken with rice and……

"Chicken has just got finished."

"But your menu still says chicken is there."

"It was, but it's now finished. There is duck and turkey if you feel you must eat something like chicken meal tonight. Otherwise there are various traditional dishes on the menu you could still choose from.

"Okay bring us the turkey." Walter proudly said.

"With rice and half *millet bread* for me Peter said."

"And for you sir?" The waiter said addressing himself to Walter. Double his order and you get mine."

The waiter turned and bristly walked away towards the kitchen shouting "Two turkeys and two half rice and half *millet bread*" to the man dishing out the foods ordered. The man dished the orders in four plates. With the four plates artistically balanced on his arms, the waiter walked back with the food to Walter and Peter.

"I don't want to go out of the hall with my suit smelling the soup." Walter warned the waiter when he saw him nearly tipping the plate on him.

I have handled these plates for the last ten years and they know me well that's why they always adhere on my skin like ticks on cows. Don't worry about them I could carry ten plates at once and these are only four, six less. I have been trained for the job." The waiter assured Walter.

The band in the night club playing the disco music, thundered with all the melodies in crescendos world which kept everyone eating in the dining hall rocking with their spoons and forks in their hands at the rhythm of the music. The girls were flirting with their boyfriends reassuring them that they were there for them. Everyone looked gay that evening. Even Peter who, since the death of his wife had never thought of owing any other female that night turned on a new leaf. He brooded over the question which Walter raised to him whether it was wise to cry over spilt milk. *Well I loved her if she was still alive I wouldn't be thinking of any other woman. Time to remarry after the death of a wife like this is allowed so why am I here living like a Catholic Bishop. I must capture this girl tonight if she accepts to marry me I will do it because of her resemblance with Rose.* Peter heard a soft law voice whispering at the back of his head. The whisper become louder and louder as the sentential music caressed his ears salaciously accentuating him into carnal desire.

"You don't like the food do you". Walter asked Peter when he saw that he was absent mindedly chewing his food.

"I do but......."

"The music is bothering you? It is quite a good band. It reminds me of the dance I had in Apollo Hotel last weekend with the Ultra Sonic Jazz Band. They are the best band I have ever danced to." Walter interrupted Peter.

"I never expected to find some fantastic musicians like this up country town like Gulu."

"I understand that the proprietor of this Inn is hiring some boys from Zaire. Mainly the vocalists and the drummers, in fact most of the band members, and they are only coaching the local boys here in the arts."

"The authenticity of the music is indubitable."

"Eat and we go dancing man." Walter said as he bit on the turkey meat. He chewed it swallowed and pulled another chunk and chewed it like a lion assaulting the carcasses of an animal it has victimized. He finished the meat on the thigh of the turkey and tried the bone but it was too hard for him to crunch. He tossed the bone back in his plate, and pushed the plate gently away from him. He sat back resting his back on the chair and stretched his legs under the table as he looked at Peter struggling with his food.

I am left with one tusk of wooing that girl for the night. If I go through, then the night will be a gorgeous one. Peter kept thinking and eventually finished eating. The two walked out of the dining hall to the lobby of the hotel. The reception counter was manned by any person.

"Where have they all gone?" Walter asked as he saw a look of depression on Peter's face and walked behind the counter and took the keys to their rooms.

"I think they could still be eating." Peter put in not sure of what to say and added." Let's hope she has not furtively left for home."

"No I don't think so. Let's go and bath and change into something lighter for the dance. We shall come back when they are already in."

"My wife once told me that it is unhealthy to bath immediately after a heavy meal like this". Peter advised

"I don't think that one time in twenty years would be dangerous."Walter said and walked up the steps and Peter followed him there. They bathed and Walter changed into a red short selves shirt with blue jean trousers while Peter with not much to change remove his neck tie and the jacket only and remain in the blue long sleeved shirt with dark blue trousers. They walked out looking fresh and cleaned. When they got down the reception desk, there was no one still at the desk. *Peter could be right.* Walter thought as he hooked the keys on the nails. *It's about an hour since we went up. If they don't show up within the next five to ten minutes then she is gone. Well we know where she works we shall trace her out.* Walter thought as he walked out in the lobby of the hotel. He dragged Peter by the hand and they began to look at the posters on the walls of the hotel. They had gone past one poster only when a door next to the counter swung opened and two girls came out laughing gaily. Peter and Walter turned to see who they were. The receptionist, Peter was desperately waiting for, was in front with her book in her hand. She walked out of the room first and her friend followed her from behind. She allowed her to pass before she closed the door and they both walk to the counter. Peter and Walter immediately started to walk to them.

"I am sorry if I kept you waiting for your keys but you could have taken them if you wanted to go into your rooms." The girl apologized

"We did just that. We are in fact waiting for you." Walter said emphatically.

"Waiting for me? What for?"

"Take it easy Miss." Walter said giving the girl his erotic smile. As he predicted the new girl was a tall dark girl with white eyes. The smooth thin lips, the smooth proportionally placed small nose. The sticking out ears gave her the look of an angel. She wore a white rose on the side of her straightened dark long hair. She looked rosier than the rose she wore. The flat stomach and the narrow waist were real love nest. Walter surveyed the girls with his eyes rolling on her up and down as if she was a suspect he wanted to describe to the police. The girl saw how he was studying her and turned her back on him and began to walk to the boards where the keys were hooked.

"Most of the people are still out." She said. The dark red open back frock she had on revealed a smooth clean back carrying long slender neck which no man like Walter would miss to caress. The resilience buttocks look warm enough to excite a frigid man. Walter adjusted on the ground where he stood and said.

"You want to put them to sleep now?" His voice sounded like sand papers rubbing on the mahogany wood. He hated it because it has shown that he was worked up already.

"The sooner they come, the better."

"Why?"

"We want to go home."

"You don't go dancing."

"We have no money and there is no one to take us for the dance."

Peter looked at the girl seated reading her book. He didn't know what to do with a girl who is too bookish like her.

"Are you a student?" Walter asked the girl reading

"No I am not. Why?" She asked.

"It is because you are all the time reading. I guess you read even when you are sleeping." Walter joked.

"How do I do that?"

"I mean you are all the time reading."

"Try the book you will not let it go .That is why I must go through it tonight."

"How many pages left?" Peter asked worried.

"Five."

"Well not a bad speed. I guess that is about five minutes or so."

"I have a very poor reading speed." the girl said and smile. The dimples on her cheeks made Peter swallowed thick salty saliva.

"Are you both on duty now? Walter asked addressing himself to none of them.

"I am the one on duty". The new girl replied.

"She is here to finish her book?" Walter asked the new girl.

"No she is waiting for me. We always walk home together."

"Yes". The old girl confirmed.

"Where is that?"

"You wouldn't know the place even if I tell you. You look strangers in this town."

"Why do you think so? Gulu is our home town so why on earth do you call us strangers in our own town?" Walter interjected

"Because I have not seen you two since I came to work in this town."

"When did you come here?"

"Ten years back." And I mean it." The girls said and turned to look at Walter.

"By the way I think we need to know each other now by names so that we are no longer strangers. Peter suggested.

Let's begin with the ladies. Who are you? Walter asked the girls reading book next to him.

Who? Me? She said as she sat up.

"Yes."

"I am Rose Marry Akol.

"You are who? Peter asked surprised nearly shouting."

"Rose Mary Akol is there anything wrong with the name?"

"You will know Peter said and paced the floor with his hand in the pocket while Rose Mary turned to read her book.

"And you?" Walter asked the new girl.

"I am Lilly Aber."

"The name suits you infinitively."

"Thank you for the complainant" Lilly said and turned with a snigger which caused Walter heart to wobble in his chest.

"You've known our names what about yours?" Lilly said as she took the register for the clients and went through it to check the numbers of rooms still empty. There were only two rooms left. Lilly closed the register and stared at Walter expectantly.

"Yes you are right Lilly." Walter said

"This is Peter Lapyem the Permanent Secretary Ministry of education and I am Walter Lamon the Chief Accountant in Bank of Uganda."

"Nice to know you." The girls said and they shook hands with each other.

"When did you come to Gulu?" Rose Mary asked them addressing her question to none of them.

"This evening by train from Kampala."

"By train? "I thought you…………."

"The domestic flight is rather expensive for us to afford Walter interrupted Rosemary."

"The Government should pay for you. You are big Government officials." Lilly added with sniggers.

"We are not on official duty here." Peter interjected.

"I see," Lilly said and sat down on her stool behind the reception desk.

"Now that you've finish reading the book Rose Mary shall we go in the bar and you tell me the story you have been through in the book." Peter asked inviting Rose for a drink.

"Not in this dress and shoes."

"You want to go and put on your latest dresses and dancing shoes?" Walter asked.

"I have none."

"Then just walk in with those. In fact I want to discuss something very secret with Lilly so the two of you could blow off somewhere in the bar."

"What secret do you have with me since you knew…."

"Do not worry about when I know you. Things have beginning and end that is what is important."

"Come on Rose Mary walk out and we go. Don't you see that these two have something to discuss between them. We are interrupting their discussion?"

The two girls looked at each other and Rose Mary reluctantly got up and walked out of the counter. With her book in her armpit the two walked side by side towards the bar. Peter chose a table for four right at the corner of the bar expecting eventually they could be joined by Walter and Lilly.

"What do you drink?" Peter asked Rosemary.

"Nile Special Lager." Rosemary replied and Peter walked to the self-service refrigerator and brought two bottles of Nile Special. As they drank Peter made a pass at Rosemary and she yielded and they spend the evening dancing, eating each other tongue and lips. Walter and Lilly joined them at 10 p.m. when the Hotel had closed for customers. Lilly handed the register to the night watchman who also did the booking at night should any guest arrives after 10 p.m. With their relationship settled Walter and Lilly walked to the bar hand in hand like lovers who had known each other for years. The band was a good one it played on until 6 a.m. in the morning.

Chapter Eight

Walter had forgotten to draw the curtain when they returned from the night club with Lilly and the sun rays at dawn, beaming through the bed room window, fell on Walter's face, and aroused him from the short sleep. Lilly coiled on him and breathed out breath of satisfaction and woke up also.

"It was good charm". She whispered in his ear.

"I loved it". Walter said and squeezed her on his chest."

"Oh it is dawn already". Lilly remarked as she woke up with a full bladder and she swung her legs out of the bed, got up from the bed, and stretched naked in front of Walter who was also having full bladder. He squeezed her on his chest. She pressed on him and said, "My bladder, let me go and empty it." Walter released her and they both went and came back. After cleaning up, they dressed and walked out of the room.

It was when Peter had finished making final agreement with Rosemary that they would marry, that Walter and Lilly walking hand in hand knocked on the door of Peter.

"Who is it?" Peter asked

"Walter." Walter introduced himself. Peter got up and opened door for them. They were already dressed and were seated side by side on the bed.

"Come right in." He invited them.

"How was the night Walter asked Peter?"

"The most beautiful one I have had in years." Peter replied.

"And yours?"

"Fantastic."

"By the way, we are marrying." Peter interjected.

"You are what?" Walter asked.

"Marrying."

"Congratulation." Walter said and shook hand with both of them and Lilly did the same. "Well - well that is fine Peter. I am sure our trip to Gulu this time has yield the most succulent fruit in the World.

"I have found Rosemary the duplicate of my late wife Rose and no matter who Rosemary is I am marrying her not later than next month from now." Peter asserted.

"I wish all come true." Lilly, said and smiled looking at Walter who seem to hate standing there talking of marriage.

"We must be going home. We are not allowed to sleep in the hotel with customers. And in fact last night has been the first. I don't know why we did it." Rosemary said and got up from the bed dressed. Peter caught her by the waist squeezed her on his chest and kissed her passionately.

"I know why you did it because God wants you to meet me." Peter said and kissed her again. Lilly and Walter were already out on the corridor descending down the steps to the ground floor, when Peter and Rosemary walked out of their room. As the sun hauled itself behind the horizon, men who had picked ladies during the night club dance had started dismissing them from their rooms. Peter and Walter took Rosemary and Lilly up to their flat in Acholi Ber.

"Where can we get taxi to Abilli? Walter asked Lilly as they were leaving the girls' flat.

"I thought you said you aren't strangers in Gulu town." Lilly joked.

"Well we aren't but you don't expect us to know every sand in Gulu town do you?" Walter said with a sneer.

'It is just opposite the Rainbow Inn. I hope that, you know." Lilly said and walked forward and kissed Walter. Walter was not in the mood any more. Lilly was now any other girl on the street of Gulu. He felt the kiss as if he was rubbing his lips on back of his hand.

Lilly knew that she had touched the wrong button not like that of Rosemary. She was dealing with a man who would never stick but only interested in go-go life.

After their breakfast Peter and Walter were back to their struggle to get money and this, is essential, and dire need for Peter. He needed this trip to succeed because, beside the fact that he wanted to rehabilitate himself financially he has now got himself mixed up with Rosemary in a proposed marriage. No marriage has ever succeeded without money. As Peter walked with Walter he thought of what would happened if he will fail to raise money to marry Rosemary. He has now a big debt which some of his good friends were writing off. He swore if it meant staying out of office forever he would do it so long as he got money for marrying Rosemary. *Sam did it and he is now a very successful man.* Peter thought recalling what Sam told them at Entebbe.

They soon reach Taxi Park at the Rainbow inn. The New Toyota sedan for special hire to Abilli was in the slot. When the driver saw them, looking richly dressed, with executive briefcases, he called out at them.

"Abilli special hire?"

"How much?" Walter asked

"Five thousand shillings only."

"We can go in it." Walter said looking at Peter who had his hair on end when he heard that they were to part off with five thousand shillings, while they would pay only three hundred shillings in the ordinary Public Service vehicle (PSV) to the same destination.

"Why don't we take the PSV?" Peter asked Walter.

I know it's a lot cheaper but we shall take long on the way they will be stopping collecting any traveler on the way and by the way they will make sure every inch of the seat is utilized with human beings. I can't stand the smell the heat and above all the delay in the (PSV). It means a lot if you lose what we are chasing because of PSV man holding us for hours on the way because of his interest." Walter insisted. "It's alright let's go in this." Walter emphasized and walk toward the waiting immaculate Toyota sedan. The driver got out and opened the door for them. When they were in, he slammed the door shut and walked to his door. He entered the car and ignited the engine before he push a cassette of the latest disco music hit on.

He eased the brakes and the sedan rolled out of the parking slot down the main road to Abilli. The driver squeezed the paddle of the accelerator on the floor of the car and the sedan groaned and bellowed down the slop and soon they were out of town heading towards the Railway station on the tarred road to Abilli, the speedometer flicking between 180 and 200 kilometers per hour.

"This is a bad speed". Peter remarked as he recalled the speed at which he was driving the day he crushed his car and his wife Rose was burnt to death.

"They are expert they know the roads and their cars" Walter said and adjusted himself approvingly in his seat.

"Accident is accident, if it is to come, you will not be an expert of anything. You could have driven the same vehicle along the same road for years but if accident is to befall you, you could meet it in the safest place." Peter argued.

"I know but don't worry he will take us alright." They crossed the Railways lines and descended down the slope of Layibi River before the ascended the slope which brought them to the Road to St. Joseph College Layibi.

"That could be the home of that old man of last night. He said it is opposite St. Joseph College Layibi" Peter remarked.

"Must be." Walter agreed and in twenty minutes only they were branching along the path to the farm of Walter's uncle at Abilli. The path was not good there were pot holes with puddle of rain water in them. The driver slowed down driving at 20 kilometers per hour bunching and swaying like a canoe on a wavy lake.

"If I drive this car on such a path every day I will have no car. That is why we take a little more for special hire. The PSV always leave their passengers on the road. You would by now be legging this distance." The taxi driver said.

The farm of Obina, the uncle of Walter, was a ten square mile piece of land stretching from the road inland. It was a mixed farm. They had just finished going through the grazing ground for the cattle when they met Obina in his Toyota Land cruiser driving out.

"You see if we came in the PSV, we would have missed him". Walter said when he saw the Land Cruiser bunching coming to meet them. The taxi driver pulled up at the side of the narrow path to left space for the Land Cruiser. Obina came and squeezed at the side of the Toyota sedan and cut off his engine. He popped out is head to greet them as Walter walked out of the car.

"Oh it is you, nephew. I expected you yesterday but......."

"You know what? The train takes two days to travel from Kampala up to Gulu."

"Why did you have to take such a slow tiresome means?"

"We wanted to have the experience."

"So you have it now. Slow means are not good for business." Obina advised.

Peter had also walked out of the car to join Walter talking to his uncle.

"I know Peter well. We were together in Makerere. I was doing my Bachelor Degree in Agriculture when he was doing his Bachelor Degree Education." Obina said and shook hand with Peter. I'll get you home I am delivering this milk in town and I will be back in soon." Obina said and ignited the engine of his Land cruiser. But Walter moved nearer and said, "We are not intending to stay long. We came for these things I told you about on the phone last time."

"You mean…………

"Yeah" Walter interrupted when he noticed that Obina was going to blast out the secret in the presence of the taxi driver.

"Well you are rather unfortunate with the one I said was here. Obina said and looked at the taxi driver who sat impatiently in the car waiting for his money to be paid and he goes back for more. "Why don't you let him go back I could solve your problem in this matter?" Obina suggested.

"It's okay." Walter said and paid the taxi driver.

"There was a "T-junction along the path a little ahead of taxi driver. He drove and turned there. He returned and parked ahead of Obina Land Cruiser. Peter and Walter took out their brief cases from the car and stepped aside as the taxi driver drove forwards.

"They take a little too much money these days." Obina remarked as the taxi man drove away back to town.

"They complain about the escalating cost of fuel, spare parts and bad roads." Walter remarked

"Yeah as I was telling you, that man who had the Rhino horns and the Leopards skins sold them away to the Minister of Finance yesterday."

"You mean he was here for the same?" Pete said.

"There is not very much difference between you and him and you are here for the same." Obina commented and the three of them laughed.

"What next? Peter asked. Anywhere we could try?"

"Yeah there is a man just opposite Layibi College he had some 200 kilograms of elephant tusk with him.

"Two hundred kilograms!" Peter exclaimed with excitement glowing in his eyes. *If we got that we would certainly be rich. I imagine one kilogram in Kampala should sell not less than ten thousand* Peter thought.

"Climb in, let's go and see if he still has them" Obina suggested. Peter and Walter climbed in the Land Cruiser and drove back to town. The idea that the old man Obina was talking about was the old Veterinary Doctor, the 'Bull Fighter' was the man with the elephant tusks, didn't occur to them. Obina drove them back and when he got to the road avenue leading to St. Joseph College, he slowed down and branched along the path to the Bull Fighter's home.

"Is this not the home of the "Bull fighter?"Walter asked.

"Yeah it is, how did you know him?" Obina asked.

"We met at the Railway Station last evening. A pick-up taxi transporting passengers from the station to town brought us back to together. The three of us, plus the driver squeezed in the front seat. He could not sit at the back because it was full. As we moved, he told us stories how he used to work as Veterinary Officer in Mukono, etc. He is quite a humorous man."

"He is, he gets along well with people very easily." Obina agreed as they stopped the vehicle in the compound of the Bull Fighter.

The Bull fighter had just finished spraying his cows and he was returning the spraying kits into the store when Obina swung the Land Cruiser round in the compound and parked it and cut off the engine immediately. He walked out first and Peter and Walter walked out after him and stood near the motor car.

"There you are Mr. Milk man". The Bull fighter said and walked towards Obina and his men. Obina was popularly known by his nickname 'Milk man' because of his dominancy in milk supplied in the area. "You're early today". He added.

"Yeah I am. I met my nephew and my college mate at Makerere University Peter Lapyem the Permanent Secretary to Ministry of Education on the way to my home."Obina said and waved his hand towards Peter, and added" They were coming to see me about the Rhino horns and the leopards' skins which the Minister bought yesterday. I told them about the 200kilograms. I wonder whether they are still there." Obina asked.

'Yeah I think they are still there. The man who has them, live near the stream. I am sure they haven't gone because whoever buys anything from him must pass through me."

"You are an international broker?" Obina said and they both laughed.

"That's how we survive these days. And that is where I get my quid for Wilobo bar. Retirement Pension is no use to the Bull Fighter. The Bull Fighter told Obina as they walked to meet Peter and Walter where they stood near the Land Cruiser of Obina."Hello gentlemen. We meet again didn't I tell you that we would do so."The Bull fighter said extending his hand for handshake with them. They exchanged greetings. And Obina introduced the topic officially.

"Yeah I saw in them. It was written all over their faces that they were hear for a deal. No high ranking Government officers like these ones come out in a train for the sake of it. It is the most boring means of transport in the country and yet a very safe camouflage for this type of deal. You sit for two days to travel form Kampala to Gulu in a train and yet in a bus, through the great north road, although it is very risky because of the bandit activities and the check points, you could get through it in four hours only. And by air ten minutes. You can see the difference. Any way they are welcome, I smelt them yesterday. I could have asked them if they needed my help for the deal but I feared it would scare them. The two hundred kilograms is still there. If you want to see them we can go to his house and talk to him right now." The Bull Fighter said.

"If he will be there, why not?" Peter said anxiously.

"Okay Mr. Milk Man, the Bull Fighter said addressing Obina, "will you drop us at the path to the man's home before you go your way? We will walk home." We will be there waiting for you. I know he prefers to transact his business at night. Now we are merely going to confirm the availability of the commodities and possibly negotiate the cost. The payment and the transportation will be in the evening or........

"Why is that?" Peter asked.

"Illegal trade. You do not have that immunity from above do you?" the Bull Fighter asked. Peter kept quiet. He knew they were for the unusual happenings. They got to the home and confirmed that the tusks were there but as the Bull fighter had said the business was to be done at night.

"Is there anyone who is going to check on us?" Peter asked anxiously.

"No. But suppose you run into police man with them, do you have extra money to spend to shut their mouths?" The Bull Fighter asked

"We don't have any money for that, but I believe that if we bought a mattress and roll the tusks in it and bundle it up properly do you think anyone will suspect it's not just a mattress? Peter asked. Walter was tempted to advise Peter that they should follow the instruction from the people on the ground but when he saw the insistence in him, he let him have his way.

"Well the weight may betray you. I don't think an empty mattress would weigh the same with that you are going to carry. You might need a few hands to carry the bundle which could look so small and this is where the suspicion comes in." The Bull Fighter warned

"We might have to risk that than wait till evening. We should be on the evening train to Kampala. Peter said anxiously.

"Well if you prefer it that way I have no object. But I am not in the game should anything blows up." Olyec warned. Olyec was the man with the tusks.

"Don't worry we shall be alright." Walter spoke for the first time since they got to the home of Olyec skeptical of his own statement. He did so, to give some encouragement to Peter, who has all along been trying to make sense of purchasing the tusks at night. After the remark of Walter, Olyec gave in and the four men walked in the hut where the two tusks of an elephant were being kept wrapped in polyether bags. Walter, who was keeping the money, paid for the tusks and gave some money to Olyec to buy the Mattress at Abilli shopping Centre. The mattress was brought and the two tusks were bundled up in it with strong nylon ropes. Although the tusks could not be seen the shape of the Mattress spoke by itself that it was not blankets wrapped in it. Come what may, the mattress was transferred to the Bull Fighter's home.

Obina return from town sooner than expected. He checked at the home of the Bull Fighter and found that the four men were waiting for him in the living room with the Bundle of the tusks properly wrapped up in the mattress lying on the floor like a coffin waiting for the burial hour.

"Hey how are you guys?"Obina asked with a smile. Look's everything is okay?" Obina continued to ask affirmatively.

"So far so good, everything went on well as you can see from their faces and the bundle lying there."The Bull Fighter said nodding his head towards the mattress.

"Oh dear, you have the whole world bundled up in this mattress?" I wonder how you are going to walk with it to the train without being suspected. It looks quite a small luggage to be lifted with one hand but it is the elephant itself squeezed up into this small bundle." Obina remarked and added. "You know these days there are plenty of these intelligent boys on board in the train checking."

"That is why Olyec warned them, that should anything blows up we are out of the game." The Bull Fighter repeated the warning of Olyec. Peter and Walter kept quiet.

"According to our return ticket the train leaves Gulu station at 5 p.m is this always the case." Walter asked changing the topic.

"It is always between five and six, depending on the arrival of the train from Kampala." The Bull fighter answered.

"Well, it leaves us with four more hours to look around before we leave because it's only 2 p.m." Peter said and glanced at his old wrist watch.

At exactly five Obina drove Peter and Walter to the Railway Station with their mattress. On their way to Gulu, Peter and Walter had paid for returned ticket to Kampala. So, when Obina brought them to the railways station, they went to the booking office first to confirm the coach they were going to travel in. After that, they got their mattress out of the land cruisers. Although they pretended to carry it with ease, the plain clothed crime officer *CO* watching them boarding the train was not fooled by their pretexts. He knew something heavy was bundled up in the mattress which looked small enough to be carried with ease by one person. The shape of the mattress distorted by the two elephant tusks spoke by itself and made him more suspicious. *A sponge mattress of that size can't be that heavy and have a bow shape like that. There must be something strange in the bundle. I must get it checked. It might give me a rank ahead if they refuse to comply should I get anything of interest bundle up there.* The *CO* thought and started walking after the three men. They had just entered their compartment and slot the bundle under the lower bed in the compartment, when the *CO* knocked on their door. Walter opened the door and saw a young boy about twenty in black leather jacket with blue jean, smoked sun glasses standing at the door. The high neck white boots he had on made him looked a mortuary attendant.

"Good evening sirs." He greeted them.

"Good evening." They replied his greetings.

"Travelling?" Walter asked the boy who was already surveying the compartment with kin interest as if he was trying to find out something he has left behind.

"No." The boy said with no interest in them.

"Then what are you doing here in our apartment and what are you looking for?" Obina asked exasperated.

"Take it easy sir I am on duty. The boy said and produced to them his identity card.

Obina ducked his head and glanced at it without touching. The identity card was headed railways police *CO* Branch. That was all he saw. He was not interested in the name, nor the picture, nor the rank of the boy who stood there as calm as a rock, and with no remorse of what he was up to.

"You want us also to show you our identity cards also?" Peter asked thinking that if they showed the boy their cards, by the virtue of their posts in the government he would exonerate them.

"I didn't ask for them and it's not my duty to check on identity cards of travelers." The boy explained.

"Then what duty are you doing here. There seem to be no work for you here then." Obina stressed.

"I want to look at the mattress you have just brought in here." Peter hearts skipped a beat. He felt his fingers making fists. He looked down on the floor and looked up at Walter and Obina who were sitting side by side on the opposite lower bed looking like their portraits. *Will the boy be tough with them? He looked a boy who could easily excite a mutiny in a military barracks.* He stood leaning on the door with his arms folded on his chest, his left leg crossing over the right he starred at the three men expecting to hear from them about his request. He knew he had them at the right place right time for talk. He was not attracting the crowd to the show. They were only four of them. So either they cooperate and give him supper, or else he turns them to the law and he earns his promotion. He had been doing very well at the station by arresting smugglers and prosecuting them and the Chief of the *CO* had promised him an earlier promotion if he should stir up a crime of that nature in the near future. And this could be the one. With no money for the evening the boy thought he was still young, the promotion could wait, nevertheless they should provide his evening. *This Gulu District is awash with smugglers. Tomorrow I may get some of those other guy and I will take them for my promotion but these I must milk them if they have the milk.* The boy thought as he watched the three men.

"What do you say about my request?" the boy repeated his question looking from Peter to Walter and finally Obina who sat nearest to him.

"Come and sit down there?" Walter said pointing to the seat where Peter sat alone.

Peter moved away to the extreme end of the bed as if the boy had plague. The boy knew then that the big fish were beginning to swallow his bait. He needed to poke it further for them to swallow deeper.

"I want to open that mattress you have just brought in. It looks it has not been weighed in. Do you have the receipt from the weigh bridge? Because heavy luggage like that should be booked and put in the wagon for goods not in the passengers compartment like this one, moreover the first class coach not the economic coach for the low class poor people." The boy emphasized.

"But we are also poor." Walter joked.

The boy only eyed him and began to look round the compartment and said "If you do not want embarrassment and more crowds in this compartment, please let me know the content of that mattress. It is my duty to check anyone who boards the train without weighing in the luggage. Beside, you look respectable men who I expected to know this regulation well, the dangers of doing so, to bring in a luggage in your compartment without booking it through the weigh bridge, surprised me. I do not know how many kilograms you have brought on board the train without booking? And I repeat my un answered question, do you have receipt for the luggage?" The boy toughened.

"You are talking like that because you don't know these two gentlemen." Obina said trying to throw a scare in the young boy.

"I don't need to know them I am employed to serve Uganda with all the people in it regardless of tribe or what. They could be minister or higher but if they fail to fulfill what this simple railways cooperation law stipulates, that all bulky luggage must be weighed and loaded in their proper places for the convenience of the passengers, I will not even excuses the president himself if he should behave stealthily with any luggage in this station as they are doing. You are wasting my time. I have many others slyly people outside doing exactly the something as you have done passing unnoticed. I am taking action now." The boy said seriously and got up put this hand in his leather jacket pocket and drew a 0. 28 police pistol and ordered them to stand up. "If you make any fuss you are going to regret it." He warned.

"Don't blow your top for nothing young man. This is a simple case put that chicken leg (pistol) back in your pocket and let's talk." Walter said calmly and set back leaning his back on the wall of the coach

"What are we going to talk about?" The audacious boy said.

"About the mattress." Walter said with a snigger seeing that the statement he made was all the boy was waiting for.

"Okay sit down he ordered Obina and Peter to sit down and he un clashed his pistol and slot it back in his pocket. "Bring it out he demanded."

"There is no need brother to do that. I said we were going to talk about the mattress and see where we end but I didn't say that we were going to examine it."

"Now this forces me to know in detail who you are because you are getting stubborn. I told you I am on duty. And in Gulu especially at night like this you find the unlawful guys very busy doing all sort of unlawful things therefore I must be out from hear quickly."

"I am glad you have accepted to know us." Peter said boastfully I am the Permanent Secretary to Ministry of Education............."

"So what?" And you break such a simple law Permanent Secretary of all people. I am ashamed of you and that one is the Permanent Secretary to the Ministry Smuggling I suppose?" The boy said with a sneer. The three men sat quietly without any smile. They felt like strangling the boy who was rightly executing his duty. Peter sighed, looked at the boy and looked at Walter.

"You are a rude boy very rude indeed." Peter said.

"In fact that is what my job demands from me." The boy said and by the way you haven't got me rude. I have been very gentle and peaceful because my Instinct was telling me that I was talking to the so call Permanent Secretary and who is that one?" The boy said pointing at Walter.

"I am Walter a cook in Lake Victoria hotel." Walter said because he saw that the boy was not bothered about their identities. "Well anything more you want to know form us?" Walter asked.

I want to know if you are exporting some smoked elephant or buffalo meat in that mattress for your customers in Lake Victoria hotel. Now please get serious."

I must do other things. I don't want to start it again or you won't go on this train. Do you want to steal time so that I let you go off without looking at that meat you have bundled up in that mattress?

"Well boy let me tell you we are all Ugandans. We all know what it takes to survive in Uganda these days. No one has a salary which is enough to sustain oneself for a month. We all do odd unlawful and lawful things to add up. We work for each other. Is that right? Obina advised. The boy kept quiet and stared at Obina as he talked knowing that the scare he threw at them was beginning to yield fruits. He nodded his head but said nothing

"Well you very well know the difficulty that we the civil servants are facing at the moment. There is no civil servant who is living within his salary. You hear for instance that the Permanent Secretary get so much per month. It sounds quite a lot of money to people who live outside Kampala and especially to people at home. But to those who actually earn that money are in a real hell of financial problem. They can't buy enough food for themselves to last them the month. They can't do what they should enjoy according to their titles as their positions in the Government stipulate. So there are always many dirty unlawful trades going on among the Uganda which I am sure you very will know as the *CO* in this station. Ugandans have learned to help each other. He gets you with some of the illegal commodities being a man of the people he says brother you also help so that you can go and help yourself on the same. This is what we were expecting from you. That sort of cooperation But now if you pretend that you are not a Ugandan, you never know tomorrow you will be in hotel where I cook these elephant meat I am exporting I will overcharge for a plate. If you treat us nicely I will also treat you nicely in my hotel but if your treat me roughly I will also give you bones to gnaw in my hotel. So let's behave like Ugandans." Walter weighed in.

"You start it and I will follow you". The boy said

"Walter pulled out a bundle of five thousand shilling notes from his purse and gave it to the boy.

"How much is that?" The boy asked.

"Five thousand shilling." Walter said

"For me to behave like a normal Uganda of today, I would like to know from you the content of that mattress then I will value it against the five thousand shilling you have willingly offered me." The boy said.

"We have two elephant tusks weighing about 200 kilograms. They are not very long as you saw for yourself." Peter said.

"Well if that is the case I estimate you are going to sell them at about ten thousand shilling per kilogram."

"No they cost about five only in Kampala." Obina interjected.

"Well say five thousand times 200 kilograms. That is about a million shilling you are going to get because I let you go clean from these end, meanwhile if I prove tough, you will end behind bars with loss of your jobs you see the difference on the other end I may lose mine if I don't handle my end properly. So please add more five to be fair. You help them if they are broke the boy said pointing at Obina."

"You are right we are broke badly actually. We might just travel up to Kampala without food on the way now that we have given you our money for food on the way." Peter said

"The money is still yours. You are buying your freedom and job." The boy said and looked at Walter."

He had just pocketed the ten thousand shilling he received from Walter and Obina and stood up when a knock sounded on the door of the compartment.

"Hello who is it?" Walter asked.

"Open." The voice from outside ordered.

The boy, who was already standing up, turned to the door and tried to open it. It jammed. He jerked it but it could not open.

"What is wrong?" Peter asked.

"It can't open, something must be wrong with it." The boy said as he examined the clutch knob. He jerked again but it could not open. The man outside remained quiet and was waiting to see whether they could open the door from inside.

"We can't open it." The boy shouted. The man outside was the ticket examiner. He had earlier on checked and found that the compartment has a faulty lock, which could only be opened from outside. His intention was to confirm and to relocate them in another apartment. After confirming that the door could not open from inside, he opened it from outside and walked in.

"That is why I have come to you."He said grinning. This door does not open from inside. There is something wrong with the lock. It need checking so please if you do not mind the embarrassment, will you transfer to the next compartment No.2 There are very few passengers tonight and most of these compartments will be empty. If you like this one it's all up to you. The ticket examiner said and walked out, followed the boy.

"What do we do? Transfer?" Peter asked.

"Well I think we should if the door is such a nuisance." Walter said.

"Let us check the room how it looks like." Obina said.

Compartment No 2 was next door. When Obina had gone to check the compartment No2 the train guard on duty wasn't in but came in that compartment No2 almost immediately Obina came back to Peter and Walter.

"It is okay?" Walter asked affirmatively.

"Fine."

"No one in?"

"No."

"Okay let's go." Peter said and opened the lower bed in which they had put the mattress. They pulled it out and put it on the bed. Together they carried the mattress to the compartment No. 2. They were surprised to find the guard seated on one of the bed comfortably combing his beards.

Good evening gentlemen.

Good evening Obina answered cynically. And open up the boot of the lower bed. The boot was containing a bed sheet strip green and white.

"Whose bed sheet is this?"Obina asked the man

"It's mine". The man putting on the uniform for the railways guard answered not even looking at them but in the mirror he held in his hand and continued plucking some fibers from his beards.

"We want the boot for our mattress". Peter said.

"Go ahead and put it in. There is no problem. There is plenty of space there I guess."The guard said still looking in the mirror. The three men pushed the bed sheet in one heap in the corner and put their mattress in and closed it. Peter put their brief cases on their respective bed and sat down.

"It's getting late I must be going." Obina said as he glanced at his wrist watch

"Yeah I think you must. In any case the train is about to leave. Don't you think so?" Walter asked the train guard who was then paying attention to them, his green and red small flags he use for directing parking train lying on the bed near him..

"Yeah we are leaving in five minutes time."

"But you should be working." Peter complained to the guard who seems not to be bother that the train was leaving soon.

"Don't worry; I don't work at Gulu station. I am going to my work station. When I get there I will start to work."The guard replied.

"And that is?" Walter asked

"Aloi."The guard replied curtly and climbed up the second bed opposite Peter

"Okay gentlemen, when do I hear from you again?" Obina asked.

"As soon as we get to Kampala and dispose......."

"Well I understand Obina interrupted Walter. Meanwhile I will make sure this end is taken care of too. The moment I stir up anything of interest I will telephone you immediately.

"That will be very kind of you. Peter said and the train hooted, warning all travelers that it was time to start rocking and swaying on the long journey to Kampala. In a few seconds the train rolled out heading to Aloi.

The train got to Aloi the crossing station by trains from Kampala and that from Pakwach in which Peter and Walter were travelling at eight O'clock in the morning. The braking of the train with sudden bumping of the coaches coupled with the noises which the people selling all kind of cooked foods including live chicken and goats, sugar canes, awoke Walter and Peter from their sleep.

Peter was sleeping in the second bed above Walter and directly opposite the window of the compartment. He yawned and flipped the blanket from his head and sat up. He rolled the window glass to see where they were. Walter had also set up on his bed under which there was the mattress.

"Where are we now"? Walter asked Peter who was poking his head outside below the glass window.

"We are at Aloi now?"

"Oh Aloi. I've slept quite a lot? Walter said and got up from the bed, stood side by side with Peter at the window as they watched people selling food stuff moving from window to window.

"We must eat something here. After this station there is hardly anything to eat." Walter suggested

"Let's wash our faces and brush our teeth before we get anything to eat."Peter said.

"There is no hurry anyway as we have to wait until the train from Kampala clears the line for us."

The train guard laid on the second bed adjunct to that of Peter still covered up in his heavy duty coat. He was asleep or pretended to be asleep. Peter and Walter didn't pay much attention to him they cleaned themselves and walked out where the crowd was very busy shouting selling eating looking as busy as bees.

"What should we eat?"Walter asked Peter

"I prefer the chicken if they are not very expensive."

"I will have chicken with some stick of roasted cassava."Walter added and bought whatever they wanted and walked in the train. When he got to their compartment he found that the train guard who was lying on the bed was not there. His dark green hairy heavy coat lay on the bed. The green and the red flags were not there. Walter immediately checked in the boot for their mattress. It was not there. Peter had remained behind arguing the price of a cock he wanted to buy. He bought it and came in with the cock chuckling in his hand.

Hey Peter our mattress is gone? Walter told Peter who was walking in the compartment with the cock in his hand while chewing the roasted pork he had bought.

"What? Peter yelled hysterically. Who took it? He added his heart thudding in his chest nearly splitting it open.

"I don't know. When I was coming back in the train I saw in the compartment No. 12 on the last bed on top a mattress which resembles ours. I wasn't sure that it was our so I came in here when I checked down I could not see ours I am sure that one is ours."Walter said gnawing on the leg of the chicken he had bought from outside.

Peter threw the cock down and walked straight to compartment No 12 and found their mattress lying peacefully on top of the bed. The compartment was marked *railways stuff only*. A man with a spectacle sat on the lowest bed near the sink. He was reading through a file when Peter entered in, and without greeting him Peter asked him, who brought this mattress here?"

"I don't know I have just come in. Is it yours? The man asked

"Yes I have been looking for it. Someone stole if from my compartment.

"You had gone out?" The man said without looking up at him.

"Yes to buy something to eat."

"If it is your, you can take it. People here in this station are terrible you'd better watch your luggage." The man said glanced at him and turned his attention to the papers he was reading. As he they talked, Walter joined them licking on the chicken bone in his hand. He met Peter single handedly carrying the bundle back to their compartment No2 panting for air.

"Who took it there?" Walter asked. Peter was furious. He was unable to speak. After a brief silence he said. "I don't know who took it there. The man I got there told me he didn't see anyone with the mattress there."

"I think it was stolen by this train guard because even the bed sheet which was there is no longer there."

"Could be him because he was behaving slyly to me. I wonder where he is now."

"Look he has came back and collected his coat and left." Walter exclaimed when he saw that the green coat which was on the bed was no longer there.

"We are going to keep quiet now that we have recovered the mattress. If this mattress was officially taken for checking, in compartment No12through the conspiracy of the *CO* at Gulu station, whoever took it will certainly come back to look for it. But if it was stolen, as I strongly believed it was, no one is going to come back."Walter advised.

"But you know what? Finding that his aim is now frustrated he could easily instigate problem for us. I wouldn't be surprised to see this compartment swarmed by the police on duty demanding thorough search of this compartment for all illegal commodity."Peter said nervously

"I agree with you Peter these people work hand in hand with each other. How can we be sure that all these happening have not been passed on by the CO in Gulu? They are terrible black mailers. If they know they can eat on you, the pass words ahead of you so that everyone of them time you at a spot, shucks you and let you go on and by the time you reach the end of your journey you will have lost all you have through these buying your freedom . I hate it. Uganda the Pearl of Africa is now spoiled and I doubt if it will be corrected. So we better be on the lookout for any suspicious character from here up to Kampala. We are not going to leave the coach together. If you are out I will remain in and when I am out you will remain in." Peter said.

As they talked, they did not know that there was a young man sleeping on the top most bed. Apparently when Peter and Walter were sifting to apartment No2 he was already quietly sleeping there. He was also one of the railways *CO* on duty. He lay flat on the bed and on the wall of the train listening to Walter and Peter talk. He smiled and stirred after he thought he had heard enough of their talk. He had slept in his shirt, trousers, and pair of shoes. He got up and set on the bed with his legs dangling in the air. Peter and Walter thought that they were seeing a ghost. Their hearts skipped beats and they looked at each other with dried eyes. Peter shrugged and lay on the bed. The boy claimed down, greeted them and walked out of the train. Peter leered after him through the window but soon the crowd swallowed him up.

"He looks one of those characters we met in Gulu." Peter said.

"I think so from the way he is dressed". Walter agreed.

"I hope there are no more on top. We might as well pull down the beds to make sure no bed bugs remain up listening to our talks?" Walter remarked

"If we leave this place without any incidence then we could expect a surprise in Tororo. Because most of these stuff on board now will leave this train and go back to Gulu with the train coming from Kampala. The group coming from Kampala will go back with us. They could tip those crews going with us from Tororo to Kampala you know, and they could give us hard time. I pray that nothing of the sort happens." Peter said despondently

The train from Kampala arrived at about 10.a.m. Two hours since Gulu train arrived at Aloi. After a while their train to Kampala hooted and started to roll out. Most passengers were already in the train. A few who were still outside and the crew exchanging trains all rushed to climb the train. It was at that moment that Peter and Walter saw the guard who was on the train from Gulu to Aloi who had disappeared sometimes back came running tearing through the crowds scrambling into compartment No12. This time he had his green Jacket on. He went and check where he had left the mattress he had taken from Peter and Walter. He didn't see it. He took his bed sheet and without asking the man with the pair of spectacles he disappointedly walked out the compartment to check if Peter and Walter were out. He glances back at Peter who was watching him through the window with hatred as if say you won't get away with it.

Peter remain standing at the window wondering what will happen to them if that train Guard should release to the police escorting the train from Tororo to Kampala that they have ivory on board, then they are for a big trouble. There was no doubt the guard was the one who had transferred the mattress. *How did he know that the mattress was containing something valuable? Was he told by the CO boy at Gulu railways station or did he discover it when he was taking his bed sheet. Now he has lost, he is not going to let us have an easy end. He will complicate things for us. So how are we going to avoid this? I know he has seen us quite well. He is going to give a detail description of us to the police whoever is going to watch us. So what, we must do now is to camouflage ourselves. We are going to change dresses and if possible shave our beards. That may fool the police who will base his finding on the mere description he is going to get from the guard.* Peter thought. Peter came back in their apartments and revealed his idea to Walter. Walter fell for it and they started the ceremony immediately.

The journey to Tororo was without any incidence. Peter and Walter were already beginning to think, by any luck they could get away with their ivories. But, it was until they were entering Kampala railways station at six p.m. that Peter and Walter had the night mare. The indicator light at the station was showing red meaning that the line was not clear. The train stopped and hooted. At that time, Walter was standing at the window along the corridor to their compartment watching the rain pouring outside. Peter walked out to join Walter. He had only stood there for a minute when he saw a uniformed police man being followed by a plain cloth man walking side by side along the corridor coming towards them. His heart bang in his chest and wobbled as if all the veins and arteries holding it in position had snapped off. He felt small beads of sweat trickling down his shirt from his armpits. He decided not to look at them as they reach near them and greeted them. Peter and Walter gave them way to pass. The Policeman and the plain cloth man walked passed them two compartments ahead and stopped.

"Which compartment is it?" Peter heard the policeman in a low voice asking the plain cloth man.

"He said it was…. I don't remember very well. Should be two but he told me that the gentle men had beards and they were all putting on red long sleeved shirts."

"Find out from those rooms if there are people who match that description." The policeman ordered the plain cloth man. Peter nearly laughed at them but turned to Walter and smile as the two men entered compartment two. It was empty.

"There is no one here. I am sure they must have been here." The plain cloth man said.

"Where do you think they have gone jumped off the train with the bundle when the train stopped at the signed post or what? May be they have moved out to the third class mixing up with the common people." The police office suggested.

"Could be, but Ocan is at the door to the third class and he is watching them. Ocan was the young man who listened to the conversation between Peter and Walter and later left the compartment without a trace.

Peter and Walter turned wearily towards the third class door and saw Ocan standing with his back against the wall of the coach, with another uniform police officer. He saw Peter and Walter at the window but could not swear that it was Peter and Walter whom he saw in the coach a while ago full of beards and in red shirts. To confuse them further Peter had put on his face his sun goggle he use to wear when Rose was still alive. Since the death of his wife, he hid the sun goggle and never used it again. He looked a stranger in his own right. They walked in and sat on the bed as people began to disembark from the train.

"What are we going to do, that Ocan is in the game now?" Peter asked Walter. He was actually watching us through out from Aloi up to here. He is now with one policeman at the entrance to the third class. They feared we have moved there. All these times, he has been setting traps for us at our last exit."

"That would have been a wise idea if we had move to the third class but it didn't occur to us."

"Nevertheless some intelligent people in the third class would have noticed the uniqueness of our mattress.

"That is true, but now as we have disguised ourselves I don't think even if we go and stand in front of Ocan he will reorganize easily. He believes we have disappeared in thin air. Even the other man who is leading the Policeman; firstly doesn't know in which compartment we are in, secondly he is stuck with the information that we are bearded men with Red long sleeved shirts. I think the only thing which will let us down is the luggage. How do we get it out?" Peter asked.

"I was of the opinion that I get out go and call one of those wheelbarrow boys and bring him to stand outside the window, there we shall lower this mattress through the window into his wheelbarrow and he will roll it back to the meat parker then from there we shall get a taxi to Uganda House were my friend lives. He will take care of the mattress until we dispose them off." Walter suggested.

"What about the rain. How are we going to walk in the rain?"

"We shall do it after the rain."

"No we aren't going to be the last to leave the train after everyone else has left. That alone will make them suspicious and with close on us. Ocan might identify us.

"Then what do we do?" Walter asked desperately.

"I think all you do is you get down, walk up to the main gate see if there is any police activities taking place there. If there is none, then come back carry this cock and the brief cases. I know quite a number of boys at the gate I used to joke with them a lot when I was dealing in charcoal. I am sure if they see me coming they will clear everyone on my way. Therefore, I should be able to walk out easily with this bundle alone. I know it's heavy. But if there is no one blocking my way I should be able to walk faster and drop it outside the gate. Get a taxi ready too when you go out. That will be quicker and safer than the long walk to the meat parker in the rain." Peter explained.

"Okay here I go", Walter said and walked out. As he went Ocan and the policeman walked into compartment twelve. Peter had his sun goggle on and he had put on a real air of superiority and do not disturb attitude. Ocan came and greeted him. Peter replied without looking up at him. Will you excuse us sir we are sorry for interrupting you. From where did you board the train?" The police officer asked.

"Why?" Peter asked still scribbling something in his note book

"We would like to know if you saw two bearded men dressed in long sleeved red shirts in this compartment."

"Peter first chuckled and said I didn't see any. Were they prisoners?"

"No we wanted to ask them few questions." The policeman said

"Were they security risk?"

"No sir."

"Well I didn't see anyone."

"Where are you going Sir?"

"Come on, none of your business. I am here for an important meeting in the Nile Manson I am organizing myself, and you come to disturb me asking me question I don't need to hear? Do I look like your red long sleeves shits boy?" Peter asked furious.

"No sir".

"Please leave me alone then."

"I am sorry sir." The policeman said and walked away with Ocan following him. Peter turned his attention to the book and began to write something. He would have told them that, you idiots I am the man you are looking for. It was until Peter and Walter were seated in Omony's flat in Uganda House, and his wife was making them tea, the bundle of ivories safe under the bed, that they began to realize their existence.

Chapter Nine

O n Monday when Peter reported to office after seven days absence, he found Beatrice very busy at her machine typing the work he had assigned to her before he left with Walter for Gulu.

"Hello Beatrice good morning he greeted her as he walked into the office dressed in his navy blue suit, a white shirt and a new black pair of shoes Walter and Andrew had bought for him. Since he got the gift from his friends he hadn't come with them to the office. The first time he put them on was when they were in Gulu and when he disguised himself against the police in the train.

"Hello sir good morning. You are welcome back. You are very smart today." Beatrice commented with excitement of a wife receiving her husband home. She stopped typing and surveyed Peter up and down and noticed that everything he had on was new.

"Is it only today that I am smart?"Peter asked Beatrice with a smile.

"Oh no, you have always been smart except that you are exceptionally smart today."Indeed, it was not Beatrice alone who commented about his smartness that way. Everyone he knew whom he met commented the same. *You are very smart today*. Peter knew he was smart too. When he looked at himself in dressing mirror that morning he acknowledged his smartness the smartness which reminded him when his late wife Rose was alive. He saw the original Peter people used to call *Mr. Smart* the one his delicious wife used to kiss in front of that mirror and say you are smart. Peter felt the prickle right in his heart when he thought about it. The thought which later merged with the memory of Rosemary he left in Gulu.

"Thank you very much Beatrice how was it here? Have you been very busy?" Peter asked.

"I have been fine thank you. I am finishing the work you left shortly. I have finished putting together the files for the scholarship of these candidates to go the UK next month. They are waiting for your verification. Otherwise it was quiet."

"That is fine." Peter said and walked into his office. He put his basked down inclining it against the office chair and sat down at his desk. He smoothened his neck tie meditatively and sat back on the chair resting on the back rest. He paired his hands together as if he was praying his elbows pivoted on the arms of the chair. *So I was junk of human being. Everyone is commenting the same. It means I must have been badly off. Anyway it looks I have made a start we must get those ivory sold off as soon as possible and the money realized must be propagated. I am sure Obina will let us know about any of those tusks the moment he sees them in Gulu.* Peter thought as he sat at his desk.

Meanwhile Beatrice back to her type-writer thought, *he must have hit a jack pot in Gulu where he went. It is nice, he seems to be recovering from his financial setback. It was making him afraid of ladies. You know a man is social to ladies when he has money. Without money no man talks to any lady. How.........*

The Secretarial set on her desk buzzed interrupting her thought. She scooped the receiver and glued it on her ear holding it with her cheeks pressing on it. Beatrice had grown so used to this way of holding the receiver because she was able to type and talk at the same time.

"Hello P/S office" she said

"Hay Beatrice good morning" Sofia said

"Ho Sofia how are you this morning?"

"I am fine my boss is talking of going to Nairobi this afternoon. He wants to talk to Peter. Has he come in yet?"

"Yes he is in. He is very smart. Will you come and see him." Beatrice said whispering in the mouth piece."

"I think I am coming that way with Andrew."

"Okay let me give him the line. I am expecting you for coffee at ten O'clock."

"I will be with you." Sofia said and left the line to Andrew. Beatrice pressed the button on the Secretary set and connected it to Peter's Office the "TuT" on his telephone interrupted his thought as he scooped the receiver.

"Hello".

Hello. Hold on for Andrew. Beatrice said and cradled her receiver. Peter started smiling, itching for a chat with one of his intimate friends.

"Hello boy" he heard the voice of Andrew at the end of the line.

"Hello boy," how are you the family and everything?" Peter asked generally.

"I am fine and so is my wife and everything. How was your trip?"

"It was fine, with lots of exciting experiences not worth talking on the line here. I came to your house last night at about ten p.m. But you weren't in. I was told by Daniel that you were picked up by Walter so I didn't bother to trace you up." Andrew said

"Yeah you were right. You know Walter well. He misses Kampala so much when he is out of the city. The moment we got home yesterday we first went to his friend in Uganda House where we spent most of the day. We took long there and late afternoon we rushed home to put more fuel in the car and drove straight to the petrol station. Most of them were either closed or they didn't have supper fuel. We were lucky to get it at Wandegeya Shell. After that we went to my home just to let Daniel know that we had come back before we left for Apollo hotel. We remained there until mid-night when he drove us home."

"Ah Walter is very entertaining." Andrew remarked.

"Ah I think there is time to mourn and time to remember and do other things." Peter said referring to his new relationship with Rosemary in Wilobo Inn in Gulu.

"I get you right Peter. I am coming there now to see you because I am flying to Nairobi this afternoon at about 15.00hrs and I should come back tomorrow.

"Going on duty or............"

"The usual auditing of books in our stations."

"I see."

"And of course I want to know how you travelled so that I could go and see what I can do there. I may let our Somali know that you are back."

"Yeah that is a brilliant idea you come here and we drink coffee together and talk over it.

"Sofia is coming with me."

"She will be most welcome. How is she?"

"She is fine and getting more and more beautiful." Andrew said and they both laughed well knowing that she was hearing.

"What are you doing to her? Polishing her?"

Some other guys are doing it. For me I only enjoy the sweet scent of the beautiful perfume in my office." Andrew said and they laughed again.

"You are interesting Andrew."Peter said, while laughing,

"We will be with you for coffee at 10.a.m. Okay? Andrew said and hung up.

At 10 a.m. Andrew and Sofia arrived in his Peugeot 504. They found that the office messenger assigned to the P/S office had just finished setting the coffee in Peters office ready for them.

"Hello Beatrice, how are you?" Andrew said as he entered the Secretary's office pushing Sofia in gently holding her by the waist.

"Hello, I am fine." You are welcome. Sit down let me tell him you have arrived Beatrice said and buzzed the telephone on Peter desk. He scooped it and heard Beatrice saying, "Andrew and Sofia are here now." Peter got up cradling the telephone receiver on the set and walked to the coffee room annexed to his office.

"Hey you look brand new today." Sofia said when he saw Peter standing full length on the floor.

"Thanks you for your complement. But you look more gorgeous. Come in and sit down." Peter welcomed Andrew, Sofia and Beatrice in.

"I was impatiently waiting for you all. The appetizing smell of this delicious coffee is making me very hungry you had better come and let us empty the Kettle." Peter said shaking hands with them affectionately and waving them on the seats in the coffee room. Andrew sat next to Beatrice while Peter sat with Sofia. After their coffee Andrew and Peter excused themselves for a talk.

"Well, well, well, it looks everything is finish in the coffee pot now and … I think the ladies should excuse us for a while." Andrew said

"No *notes. No report* to be taken in the meeting?" Beatrice asked jokingly.

"No report or minute is necessary so Secretaries are not allowed at the moment." Andrew said.

"Okay we leave you to gossip."Sofia said and the two of them walked to Beatrice office closing the door behind them. When the office messenger had cleared the coffee table, Peter and Andrew got down talking.

"Yes, Andrew here I am again. Thank you very much for all you and Walter did for me. I now look different because of you two. I owe you quite a lot."

"You owe me nothing Peter. Let's forget that and talk about your trip to Gulu. How was it? Andrew asked changing the subject of discussion.

"It was beautiful." Peter said and began to narrate to Andrew how they travelled in the train from Kampala to Gulu Railway Station and from the station to Gulu Town. He told him how they met the Bull fighter and later their wonderful time in Wilobo Inn with Rosemary and Lilly. He finally told him their dramatic escape from the police arrest with the ivories. Finally he told him that he was considering going back to Gulu to bring Rosemary to Kampala with him as a house wife.

"Huu-Huu-Huu. That sounds brilliant Peter that you have found a woman of your heart and decided to live with her. Thank God for that and I further thank God that the police didn't get at you. And you said you have left the Ivories in Uganda House flats?"

"Yes. They are now in Uganda House flats with a friend of Walter. But you know what? I didn't seem to like the boy at sight." Peter said.

"Why?" Andrew asked

"Because he looked un trusted boy." Peter said and they both laughed.

"How do their faces look like?" Andrew asked mid-laughter.

It's easy Andrew to detect those types of people. They always look frightened you know. They always look away when you talked to them. They avoid looking in your eyes. Whenever I met such a person I never trusted the person with anything worthy. I am not sure whether the friendship between him and Walter is a genuine. He looked smart. I am sure if these two people are true friends then, the friendship has something to do with girls. Of course when we got to his flat we got him with a girl he introduced to us as his wife but to me a house wife does not look like that girl. When we were there he told Walter that, Walter's girl was at the flat looking for him some days back. You see what I mean about the base of their friendships? The type you could trust with ivories? I am a bit worried. Nevertheless we left them with him all the same because there was no alternative, and above all it was the nearest stopover from the Railway Station where we were escaping from the police. But Walter assured me that it would be alright with that boy Omony, so we left them there."

"Do you think he will sell it and create fake robbery in his flat?"Andrew asked.

"That could be possible also. Since they are not related and yet I believe beyond any reasonable doubt that this man has a dubious character. He knows this trade is quite illegal. He could do anything to the ivories and you won't make a noise if you are to save yourself from going behind bar. You just cannot Andrew. We could go there tomorrow and find his flat locked. You get him on the street he doesn't know you. What do you do in such case?" Peter asked worried.

"I do not think you should worry to that extend Peter. Walter has some hopeless friends, I admit. For instance, one day sometimes in December last year. He introduced me to a young man who actually fitted your description of the dishonest boys. I gave him some money to bring home to my house-boy for buying food for lunch. After about two hours I was surprised to receive a telephone call from my house-boy that it was getting late to go to the market to buy food for lunch. I asked him whether the boy had not yet delivered the money. He said no one had called home since we left home. I then call Walter to confirm to me who the boy was. He told me that they met one night in Kololo night club and they drank together. And that was that. I had to drive to Nakasero market and buy some other food stuff which I took home. So while not dismissing your observation and fear completely. I …. I think give it time with some luck all will be alright. Meanwhile if I get to Nairobi this afternoon I will get in touch with our Somali guy and let him know that you have 200 kilograms of ivory waiting for him. I will want him to come immediately."

"That is if you get him in Nairobi."

"Yes that is the fear. He moves quite a lot."

"Anyway there is nothing much we can do now. I will talk to Walter now and let him confirm to me that, to some extend he trusts this boy Omony, otherwise I would love to get the mattress out of his place today. It's very painful to think of losing it not only because of its value and it significance to me but look at the risk we took to ferry the ivories to where they are now. It was just sheer luck otherwise you have seen the head line of the *Eye of the Nation Permanent Secretary Ministry of Education Peter netted with 200kilograms of ivory.* I am sure you would have fainted. Now after an escape from such humiliating episode and someone walks away with it smartly, I will go to the best witchdoctor in Buganda to make the man mad." Peter said and they both laughed and Andrew got up and glanced at his wrist watch. The time was half past eleven.

"I must get to the office and wind up what I have to do here. And go home to prepare for the trip." Andrew said and started walking towards the door. Peter got up and opened for him the door. They walked to the Secretary's office. Sofia and Beatrice were there talking.

"You have had quite a meeting" Sofia said looking at Peter.

"Sorry for having kept you waiting for so long." Peter said and walked to Sofia touch her chin lovingly.

"It's alright sir. It also gave us time to talk about our problems."Sofia replied.

"Oh my goodness what are your problems you were talking about?"Peter asked.

"We are ladies with a store of problems." Sofia replied.

"One of them is looking for the best cosmetics in the markets". Andrew interrupted her and they all laughed.

"You are always after me for cosmetics. I have many other domestic problems which, if I could give them away to you, you would not like them for a day."Sofia said as she got up from the chair she was sitting and opened door and said. "We must be going." She said as she slung her hand bag with a long strep over her shoulder and walked out in front of Peter. She walked out through the door which was held opened for them by Peter. Beatrice walked behind Sofia. Andrew followed them and Peter walked out behind Andrew closing the door behind them. Peter and Beatrice saw their visitors' right down to the car and came back to their offices.

Peter came back to his office and sat at his table meditating about what Sofia has just revealed to them. *Surely all these pretty girls you see on the street elegantly dressed most of them are harboring problems. Some are unable to feed themselves and all the sophistications are nothing but money siphons for men's pockets. Look at this girl florid as*

she looks she is the girl to cater for all the family welfare. Marrying such
a girl would really be, as Andrew put it, a sift of responsibility from one
head to another. I . . . . . .

The telephone on his desk buzzed bringing him in attention. He scooped the receiver and glued it on his ears and talked in the mouth piece.

"Hello."

Hold on for Walter. Beatrice said and connected them.

"Hello boy good morning." Walter greeted him.

"Good morning Walter I was in fact thinking of ringing you up."

"'I thought you would. I have just been talking to Andrew".

'You have."

"Yes. He says he goes to Nairobi this afternoon and he would be back tomorrow."

"Yes he said so."

"He is questioning me about Omony."

"He did?"

"Yes."

"What was he asking?"

He was actually trying to find out how I knew Omony and how long I knew him to trust him with such a valuable goods which could easily be stolen and you wouldn't make a noise to trace it." Peter summarized his discussion with Andrew

"True I have known this man for quite some time now but what I don't know about him is how much we can trust him with valuable goods like the one in his custody now. All our meeting with him was in drinking places and night club. I never bothered to study him with money. That has always been my weakness. I do not give myself time to study people. I give money to them just like that. Whether they bring it to me the way I want it or not I do not check on that. So I must admit that I do not know much about Omony. Anyway he was here in the office this morning telling me that he has started to find the market for them. He said three different gentlemen have already called into his flat to see them. But he told me that these people said that the ivories were not well preserved."

"How? What does he mean not well preserved?" Peter asked.

"He said that the men said there is only one of them which is good."

"And the others?"

"He said, they said, the other has crack and holes on it which disqualify it."

"I don't know whether to believe him yet. As Andrew might have told you. I wasn't happy with Omony. He appears slyly to me. You know boys who talk too much about themselves and always avoiding face contacts are most of the time dangerous and this I observed in Omony. A bragger who seems to impersonate a milliner so that you are wheeled into thinking that you won't lose a dim if you left a million with him. And yet the reverse could be true."

"'So what do we do now Peter?"

I really do not know what to do. But you see losing these things in the hand of a crook is very painful to me when you recall the suffering we underwent. The risks we bore and the operating cost we incurred. I would rather we sell it at a lost, to refund our money spent to enable us to purchase other better ones if his statement is true than lose them altogether. You have already heard him saying that one of them is not good. Well I strongly believe that Obina and the team will not sell us defective ivories. And by the way did you tell him to find the market?"

"No I didn't tell him anything."

"So you see. I could be bias but you can now see what is coming up, firstly only one of the ivories is good and the other is cracked and has holes on it. Secondly in a matter of a day he has gone through out Kampala looking for the buyer without your instructions or mine. I wouldn't mind if he got the instruction from us. For me, I seem to think that this idea of finding the market is either to make him also get a double commissions these are from the buyers and from us or sell everything for himself. I am sorry Walter if….

"I am even beginning to see something fishy. Because, why is he taking everything on to himself. What if as he puts it, those who came found all of them good? Would they not have bought everything? We would have been surprised with some money or not at all. I think we must get them out from him now or we miss everything."

"I think that is the way forwards Walter, if it will not jeopardize your relationship."

"There is no serious friendship between us. As I told you we met in some of these places and if anything our link is not of any importance socially or economically. I thought of him when we were coming back simply because of the proximity of his home to the railways station and secondly it would have been fairly difficult for us to beat the security personnel in the game."

"Meanwhile what we could do now is to make sure you call Omony and make him understood that there will not be any sale of these ivories without you or both of us at the sport. Even if the buyers come in the mid of the night he has to let one of us know. Give him our house numbers for contact at night and office numbers for office hours. I assume that the telephone I saw in his house is working. Moreover, Andrew leaves for Nairobi this afternoon. He promised he is going to see our Somali friends. If he gets him in the city then I think the man who will buy these ivories should be him." Peter said anxious.

"I think the telephone is working. He gave it to me as his house number and yesterday he rang me from his house."

"Fine if he is on then what we should do is to instruct him that he should not sell anything belonging to us, which we left in his flat, without us. **Full stop**. In any case we are not going to forget him when the deal is done well.

"I will do that Peter and I do not expect him to be offended if he is a reasonable man." Walter said and hung up.

Andrew returned from Nairobi the following day at 3 p.m. He drove straight to his office in their company Mercedes Benz 280. When he got to the office he immediately rang Peter. At that time Peter was clearing files on his table. *I don't like this job any more. You work and work but the money you get from it does not pay the labour. If I could only get a sizeable amount of capital, this time to start, I would quit this paper work and start real business.* Peter was thinking when the telephone of Andrew buzzed. Beatrice picked the receiver and said.

"P/S office can I help you?"

"Hi Beatrice how are you this afternoon?"

"Oh Andrew you are back? You are welcome. When did you arrive?" Beatrice asked. The two Secretaries were used to their bosses so much that they always addressed them with their first name.

"I arrived in Kampala from Entebbe only now."

"And why are you in the office. Don't you think you must go home and let her know you are back home? You need a rest don't you?"

"You are right Beatrice but I should deliver some of the files in the office before I go home. As for her she could wait. In any case I have already told her when I arrived at Entebbe that I am back.

Beside I have many other duties to attend to around town before I get home. Seeing people like you." Andrew said and they both laughed in the phone

"Aren't you damn lucky Andrew to have them fluttering their wings after you like butterflies after roses? By the way, you haven't forgotten my skin lotion have you?"Beatrice put in.

"I did not forget. It is right here in my brief case I am bring it to you right away. Guess what else I have brought for you?"

"My guesses are very poor. A dress?"

"More than a dress."

"Shoes?"

"More than a pair of shoes."

"What then I don't know how to guess". Beatrice said and adjusted the receiver she had held on her ear by her check.

"Myself." Andrew said and held his breath waiting to hear the reaction at the end of the other line.

Beatrice hooted laughter which startled Peter from his office.

"Oh well Andrew you are quite a joker. That is why I like you. You know how to tease me. May I hand you owner to Peter you want to talk to him don't you?" Beatrice said brushing Andrew aside.

Andrew crossed his legs and waited for the line to Peter to be cleared. He heard it. He heard the clicking sound and the voice of Peter came through after a spell of seconds.

Hello Andrew good afternoon."

"Hello Peter good afternoon."

'You are welcome back home."

"Thank you very much."

How was Nairobi?

Nairobi was quiet, peaceful but raining. You know what that place is like. It's very cold especially in the morning I did not like it this morning when we were taking-off. Our flight was delayed because of the bad weather and yesterday evening when I was going to Kabete to see a friend, the flood nearly wash away our car especially area around Kagemi. The flood was great enough to drown an elephant. But otherwise the few hours I spent there was quite enjoyable"

"That was fine if you did enjoy yourself. Here we were also fine with our usual problems poverty, no power since you left and not much change from where you left us."

"Yeah that is why I want to talk to you before I go home."

I did not get the Somali in. He had gone to Voi and he was expected to continue to Mombasa. He is going to stay out for may be a week or so. I left a message for him that he should ring me immediately he gets back. I don't know if that will be alright with you. I am suggesting to you that if there is anyone who can take them away now at a fair price, why don't you let him take them. The Somali is not the only buyer I am sure of that."

"Do you know of anyone who could buy them?" Peter asked.

"That needs to be investigated. What does Walter say about them now?"

"We were in fact waiting to hear from you. Because this Omony the friend of Walter......

"Yes what happened now?"

"There is nothing useful at the moment. But according to Walter the boy gave him reports which almost confirm my doubt about him. I wonder whether he told you anything about the boy calling to see him in his office.

"No he didn't."

"Well it's funny. Immediately we left yesterday he started looking for the buyer for the things and yet we had told him just to keep them and we would bring the buyer ourselves. Now this boy went everywhere searching for the buyers. And you know what stories he came up with? He is saying that he had got three different buyers who come up to his flat and saw the ivories but they all were unwilling to buy them because only one of the two was worth buying and the other has cracks and holes on it so they couldn't buy them."

"Oh no that is bad. How could he unwrap the bundle without any of you around and yet he was warned not to."

"That is it, I do not understand him."

"Why the buyers couldn't buy the one which is good?"

"He said he refused for it to be taken separately. He wanted them to be bought all together."

'It sounds good only if he was given the price and the permission to do so."

"That is why when he told Walter that, I had a feeling that this guy wanted to sell those ivories exorbitantly and later fix his own price for them and later he would bring to us what he thinks is reasonable for us to congratulate him for job well done. From this he is going to claim commission for finding the buyer and selling them."

"That is if he is going to be kind to do that Peter, at worst he may disappear with everything as you have rightly said. I think you made a mistake you shouldn't have trusted that man with such tricky items."

"By all means this Omony boy is a crook."

"What have you two decided to do about it now?"

"As I said we were waiting for your information. We are going there today and get the mattress out of that place and bring it at my place or Walter or even yours where I am sure of the safety but not with a canny boy like this Omony.

"It's okay Peter good luck."

"Thanks." Peter said cradled the receiver and sat back on the chair his finger clasped together rested on his thighs. He sighed and stared fixedly at the door in front of him as if he was expecting someone in. After a brief moment of thoughtlessness, he got up push the chair backward and with his hands in the pockets of his trouser he walked slowly meditatively towards the window. He stood there watching the cars parked below. *How are we going to sell these tusks?* He thought as he looked down at the cars parked.

The door behind him swung open and Beatrice walked into the office with a letter Peter was waiting to sign replying to one the Principal of Comboni College wrote requesting the Ministry to aid them with funds to enable them to purchase physics apparatus for their laboratory.

'Oh it is you Beatrice."

"Have I startled you?" I am sorry

"It's alright Peter said and walked back to his chair and sat down. He read through the letter signed the original plus the copy and gave the file back with the letter attached to the Secretary for posting. Beatrice took the file and walked back to her office. Peter was sliding his jacket on when a telephone on his desk buzzed. He picked up the receiver and talk in it.

"Hello."

"Walter would like to talk to you."

"Okay." Peter said and heard the click on the line and the voice of Walter cameon the line.

Hello Peter. Good afternoon and how are you?"

"I am fine. You almost miss me. I was on the door going out." Peter said. Walter looked at his wrist watch and said thirty more minutes to time, is my watch wrong?"

"Your watch is very correct even mine which is going to celebrate its 22th years of service next week on Sunday is saying the same. I was in fact coming to get you in your office." Peter said

"Do not come I will get you there. Have you met Andrew? He is back from Nairobi. He came to me on his way home.

"I have not met him yet but he telephoned me from his office."Peter emphasized.

"Well, so? What is going to happen now that the Somali is not coming very soon, and we need the money to go back to Gulu." Walter changed the subject and went on, "Sell them to anyone with the money. But what I want to emphasized is that we are going to Omony now to remove the ivories from him."Walter emphasized

"You will get me in the Waiting Room."Peter agreed and hung up.

He walked to the Secretary's office and found Beatrice winding up her work. It was five minutes to five.

""Oh well it's time you can go home. The Driver will take you home. I am waiting for Walter; we are going places to Uganda House." Peter said.

"How do you enter Uganda House after working hours like this? Through the main gate?" Beatrice wondered. This was because after five, no one was allowed to enter Uganda House because of security reasons only the soldiers guarding the place remain at the main gate.

"We are going to see a friend who leaves in the flat."

"I didn't know there are some residential flat there."

"There are but they are not very decent. They are meant for the watchmen and….

"How do you get mix up with watchmen?" Beatrice asked surveying Peter up and down." Peter realized that he had betrayed himself therefore he must check his next statement.

"This particular one is from Walter's home and he wants to send a message home to his elder brother through him. He is going home tomorrow." Peter lied. As they talked a knock sounded on the door and the handle swung down the door opened and Walter walked in.

"Oh have I interrupted your discussion?" Walter apologized as he lumbered in the office where Beatrice and Peter were talking.

"No there is nothing wrong. You come in." Beatrice said inviting Walter in. He had stopped a few steps from the door and was looking at them searchingly.

It's alright Peter confirmed. Walter walked in and shook hands with them.

"Are you ready to go?" Walter asked.

"We were impatiently waiting for you. The Driver will take Beatrice to her home while we go our way." Peter said and he got up as Beatrice took her keys out from her hand bag and also got up followed the two men and locked the door behind them. Walter and Peter drove to Uganda House flats to meet Omony.

"Peter, it's now a week since we brought these ivories to Kampala," Walter began to talk as they drove and went on," and we have not yet found proper buyer for the ivories nor did the Somali showed up. Obina telephoned me this morning twice telling me that he has got more others tusks to be bought including the Leopards skins and Rhinos horns. So this information is challenging to us. If we get these ivories from Omony tonight we must make every effort to find buyers." Walter informed Peter. The information from Obina made the two restless.

"What are we going to do?" Peter asked desperately.

"As I said, we have to sell of these ones and go to buy those in Gulu. We want to generate money from the capital we have already invested in these ones. I am sure those in Gulu will not wait for us if we don't go back soon. No one is interested......."

"What are you talking about?" Peter interrupted and added, "I mean if Obina is going to instruct those people that we are buying them, then I am sure they will be kept." Peter said.

"You think somebody can keep any dangerous goods like that in his house for years waiting for a buyer who, he is not sure of? Look here we are now trying to sell off these ones to anyone willing to buy them despite the fact that our sole buyer was that Somali man whom we aren't sure of his coming. No one can accept to starve because he has been promised a deal with a man who is not showing up. Money is the same. "Walter said.

Walter parked the car at the underground parking and as they walked out of the car they met Mindra at the gate of Uganda house. Mindra was a workmate of Omony the man Walter and Peter were going to check on. Mindra knew Walter through Omony and knew him as a friend of Omony. So when Omony told Mindra that the ivories in his flat belonged to Walter, and that Walter had instructed him to find buyers and sell off the ivories he believed. Consequently, after Mindra and Omony sold off the ivories belonging to Peter and Walter, Mindra was made to believe that the tusks were in fact belonging Walter. Omony did not mention Peter at all in the deal.

When Walter and Peter met Mindra at the gate they greeted each other and stood talking for a brief moment. Walter and Peter were excusing themselves to go and meet Omony when Mindra impatiently introduced the topic complaining that in-spite the fact that it was him who got the buyers for the tusks his commission

Omony gave him was small. Walter and Peter were astonished to hear the information.

"What are you talking about?" Walter asked.

"I mean I found for you the buyer of your tusks and you gave me only five hundred shilling." Mindra insisted. Walter and Peter were struck speechless.

"Tell us more Mindra, you mean Omony has sold the tusks? Is that what you are saying? Walter asked trembling.

"Yes of course and my share as the man who found for you the market is only five hundred shillings!"

"Walter sighed and rubbed his nose. How much did he sell them?"Walter asked.

"You mean you don't know anything about the sale?"Mindra asked

"No. We are hearing from you now."Walter answered.

"Well according to what Omony told the buyer when they first came was that the total weight of the ivories was 500 kilograms. The buyers had their own balance and they wanted to ascertain what Omony told them. In the end either the balance used in Gulu was faulty or that of the buyers we used here, your ivories weighed six hundred and fifty five kilograms."

"Six hundred and fifty-five kilograms!" Walter exclaimed softly shaking his head. *Can this be true* Walter Thought? Peter stood next to Walter as his portrait.

"Yes."Mindra answered emphatically.

"How much did he sell a kilogram?"

"Twenty-five thousand Uganda shillings Sir."

"That mean we should expect about seventeen million Ugandan shilling from him."

"You should expect that if you see him again."

"What do you mean?"

Omony left here immediately he sold the tusks yesterday about mid-day and he is not seen since."

"Don't tell us."

"Well that's what I am telling you." You know when I saw you together in his flat where I first met you and because you speak the same language, I thought you knew each other well."

"Yes I knew him but not so well."

"You didn't know that he was dismissed from the job last month and he was here only waiting for the boss to come before he packed up?"

"I didn't know that."

"You didn't?"

"No".

Well that is what it is. You will be dam lucky to see this man again he is one of the most insincere corrupt character we had in this joint no one gave him money and he got it back all went the same way. He has served many sentences because of stealing and cheating like this." At this Peter locked his fingers and put his palm on top of his head and began to pace the floor tears gusting from his eyes. He whispered to himself, *it has happened again. I thought the end would be like this.*

"You know where he comes from?" Walter continued to ask Mindra.

"Well I have been hearing that he comes from Pader but such a boy could give the name of any place to be his home. His record shows that he is an orphan adapted by the Mission and raised and schooled by the Cathoilc Mission. He does not know the names of his parents. It was rumored that his mother came with him from Sudan and she remarried to an Acholi man who was working as a house boy of the Missionary in Gulu and that is where he got his education. Later his mother got other children with different men, mainly those trailer drivers. How can anyone be sure since it was him who gave these particulars?"

"Was the fact checked with the Mission?"

"Is there any time these days, for doing such thin in Uganda? Who has the time?"

Walter stood with his hands folded over his chest staring at Mindra who stood in front of him as if he had turned into a monster. He couldn't believe he was hearing alright. He thought he was day dreaming. He walked a few steps to the gate and stopped and turned to look at Mindra who was looking after him lips tight. *Is this man hoaxing me or is it's a plan set up by the two. We must go up and see for ourselves if this Omony has skipped.* Walter thought and turned to Peter who had sat on the step with no more interest in the talk.

Walter came and put his hand on his shoulder and said "Iam sorry Peter it' my faults. Peter in return pressed on the back of his hand and "say it's over." Walter slowly removed his hand from Peter and started climbing up the step to the residential flats leaving Peter sitting on the step unable to stand up but holding his stooped head in his palms. Walter went to flat No. 7 which used to be Omony's flat. The pad lock wasn't on as it used to be. Still not believing that, he opened the door and walked in. Papers littering everywhere on the lobby of the flat told him that Omony must have left. He stood akimbo looking at the open door of the flat the window all stood open. He shrugged and turned to go back when he saw a man at the next flat door.

"Looking for him?" The man asked.

"Yes sir" do you know where he has moved too."

No idea he left here mysteriously yesterday and everyone is cursing him to hell because he has disappeared with one thing or another from each one of us in the flat here. He is the most rotten boy I have ever met in my life. I guess he has hit you too.

"Muuu, yeah." He did.

Well he is gone we don't know where to find the same. His record here is very scratchy that not even the CIA will trace him and find him." The man said sadly.

Walter shook his head and walk out of the deserted flat of Omony which seemed to smile happily that the crook has at last walked out of her. Walter descended the steps and found that Peter has walked out and was waiting for him in the car. Walter not sure of how to start telling Peter what he saw in deserted Omony's flat, for the first time remember God's help, and whispered to himself a short prayer saying, *God help me to make Peter understand this and make him accept the tragedy.* He walked out of the gate and climbed in the car where Peter was sitting resting his head on the back seat of the car with closed eyes. He sat in the car beside Peter and looked blankly in front of him not sure of what to do and how to start talking to Peter. He was exasperated he felt like walking on foot rather than drive in the car to avoid accident. He knew Peter was greatly touched by the sad news. Inconsequentially with all the thoughts in the head, he ignited the engine of the Citroen with the gear on. The car leapt forward but he managed to control it before he ramped into the rear bumper of a car parked in front of him. Peter rolled his head on the cheat of the car and looked at Walter and said, "Be careful, I know we are not ourselves now, but it has happened, all we have to do is to take courage. I know I have failed in many attempts but this one has hit me very hard."

After he controlled the car, Walter rested his fore head on the steering wheel of the car, he lifted himself up, shook his head and put his left palm on Peter's thigh and said, "I am sorry Peter I should have let you know that Omony was not a friend I knew well to be entrusted with such valuable commodities. I am sorry Peter. He has disappeared without a word to anyone in this world

Peter sat up on the seat of the car and held both arms of Walter and looked into his eyes and said "Do not tell me more Walter, because you know it will not solve my problems. I am not holding you responsible for the misfortune, even if those where all I was banking on to start a living. They are gone I do not have any hope to do anything better in this world. I am not going to succeed again in life. My entire attempts to raise money are being frustrated why is this so? I do not understand it. It is either I buy the wrong commodities and the money is wasted or someone must hoax me by running away with the dough like this. Peter complained bitterly with tears standing in the eyes. Walter looked at Peter and looked away speechless thinking; *there is no way of tracing him back home to his village? It is dangerous to start this. As we said before it is not possible to bring this case to law. On top of that, his records in the department are very vague indeed. All that is known about him is that he is called Omony Sarafino and he is from Pader, an orphan who does not know the names of his parents and with these information what can one do? It's very unfortunate. We can't recover anything. I am sorry for having introduced Peter to the crook.* As if Peter was reading his mind, as they drove away home, Peter sighed and said, "well, that marks the end of the comic episode. I do not know why I had the feeling that this would happen. Okay Walter there is no need weeping over spilt milk. My only regret is that my planned marriage to Rosemary is dash off."

Chapter Ten

Wearily Peter got up from his desk pushed his chair backwards and walked to the window. Whenever Peter was pensive, he always walked to the window and leered down on the road, on the cars moving and those parked as if he would get the answer to his problem down there.

What a lost, this is really the end of the road for me. I don't think I will get any help from anywhere to try anything. Everyone is going to fear me now. An educated professional beggar. I cannot try anything that can make me succeed and become financially independent. Problems pile on top of another every day. I want to start a living, things disintegrate and fall apart. Some canny freaky bums wait on me like vultures wait for a sick animal to fall dead before they tear the flesh in bits. I am betrothed to Rosemary. Without money now, how will I maintain her when she comes in? I had thought I was going to earn some money from these tusks, and indeed this was a lot of money two million shillings, that was a fortune. Say if we got that money and went back with it couldn't I have doubled the same in the second trip. God why have you abandoned me? Peter thought and felt warm tears irritating his eyes. Peter thought back about his hay days he used to spend with his dead wife Rose how they used to go out in the evenings and in the night clubs, cinema, he thought of the sudden death of his father and the loss of their properties then the untimely death of his wife in the motor accidents in which all his happiness went. He regretted why he didn't die in the same accident. *I would have rested by now if we both of us died in accident. Why? Why? Didn't I.* Peter thought. The telephone buzzing on his table made him turn round and looked at it and looked away. There was a pause for about a minute and the telephone buzzed again. Peter wearily walked to his desk and nonchalantly picked the receiver and said "Hello." His own voice sounded strange to his ears it sounded like an owl hooting. Beatrice noticed the gawkiness of the sound of his voice. She knew that something was wrong but she could not ask him on the line.

"Andrew is here he wants to talk to you."

"Okay. Peter said cutely and immediately cradled the receiver. The door opened and Andrew walked in like someone who already was told about sad new which has befallen a dear friend and he was coming to condole the same.

Peter sat back on the chair and looked at his finger nails like a chiropodist diagnosing a fungal infection of the nail fearing to look at Andrew in the face. He looked up and saw the anxious look on his face. He knew that Walter must have told Andrew the news about their loss.

"Hello Andrew you are welcome. Sit down". Peter said waving him on a settee and he got up and walked and sat next to him.

"How is the day?" Peter asked Andrew.

"It has been fine and yours?" Andrew asked and looked at Peter suspiciously. Peter sighed and looked at Andrew grinning. Generally, it was a fine days but until yesterday afternoon when I got the worst sock of my life." Peter said and looked away towards the window. He acted as if he wanted to walk up and stand by the window but instead he set back on the settee and clasped his hands on top of his head. Has Walter not told you about what happened?"

"He did. In fact, I came here for that. It is so sad Peter that you suffered so much to bring those tusks in and you risked so many things. Your jobs, your prestige, your prides and your futures were all in jeopardy if those police men got you. It was sheer luck that you came away clean. I am terribly sorry for what happened. I was optimistic that what you brought was going to be a foundation to your financial recovery but now this son-of-bitch has swindled all what should have rightly be yours. Anyway Peter you have had so many shocks worse than this. I am sure of that but you bore them and you are still alive. I am encouraging you not to despair. There are days to weep and days to laugh in our lives. You are, if I may say, reached the days when everything you want to do to buoyant you financially, are like a sinker looped round your neck with additional one being added to make you drawn. Well Peter it's no good to fall into despondency. When you do that, you will have the fear to try anything new. Because you will always be nervous to try anything so that even if you were going to succeed. But because of lack of self-confidence, you could easily tip the fulcrum of success and you see the whole thing tumbling in ruins. As long as I am still alive Peter, I will try with every bit of my ability to help you. I understand you as much as you understand me. We grew most of our lives together is schools and Universities and now when we are old men we still fill the bond binding us together setting even harder and harder that nothing can decay the bondage. It's only you and me who can destroy it. Walter is a nice friend except that I wish he could correct his habit of trusting people at sight. I am sure if he didn't over trust that Omony you would have not lost those tusks. But as I said we shall talk to him and advise him to correct that flimsy habit."

"Thank you very much for your sympathetic fraternal advice which has enlivened my lugubrious heart. Indeed, as I told you this has been the biggest blow to me since my happy days. The other failures I have encounter did not devastate me like this. Surely even if I convince myself that all will be alright next where is the capital and where will it originate from? I haven't a nickel in my purse now. Now how do I start from nothing? Every time when things flop like this I am on your neck or Walter but surely I feel shy to incessantly burdened you two. Well you have a family and…….

"I have a wife if that is what you mean by a family."

"Yes of course you have a family of two, husband and a wife."

"Accepted." Andrew said submissively.

"Yes, as I was saying, you and Walter, although he is still lavishly leading single life he might one day say he has seen enough of women therefore he must settle down and begin to lead a decent responsible life with a wife and children may be. If that is going to happen, which is indubitable of course, what am I going to do if that time catches me like this. You are not going to look after your families and me. I don't want that to happen." Peter said wring his fingers.

"That is the spirit I want you to have, endeavoring spirit. Uganda these days does not need despondency. If you despair, then you will regret it yourself. I think tonight the three of us, you, Walter and I will go out possibly to Kololo night club where we could spend the evening and forget that loss. You won't see the boy again. Even if you saw him he might not be able to refund a dim to you and Walter. Nonetheless, you cannot take any legal suit against Omony.

"That much, Walter and I know and we have no intention of trying to find him."

"That is what I would strongly advise, because it will expose you negatively. Andrew said looking at Peter.

Peter walked to his desk and said "let me just singe these letters the rest I will do tomorrow." Peter said.

"You can never finish these office works."Andrew remarked.

"No. You do what you can for the day. After all what does one get from it these days we paper men. Work and get the so call salary which should rightly be call allowances being given to the civil servants for national service not as salaries." Peter said disdainfully, and quickly singed the letters, closed the file he was working on and clipped his pen on the breast pocket of his shirt, took his basket and came back to where Andrew had already got up on his feet and was pacing the floor to and fro waiting for him. He took his coat from the hook on the door and slid in it and they walked out to the Secretary office. Beatrice was very busy on the typing machine typing letters Peter had dictated during the day. She glanced at them for a moment before she turned to her short hand note book.

"You still have a lot to type?" Peter asked Beatrice affirmatively. Beatrice glanced at her wrist watch and saw that if was forty-five more minutes to five o'clock before the offices closed.

"Are you accusing us that we are leaving offices before time?" Andrew said while looking at Beatrice when he saw her checking the time on her wrist watch.

"Oh no Sir I just wanted to know how much time I have to at least finish these few files."

"You'll finish them tomorrow. I am not in the mood to do any work." Peter said

"Well just let me finish this letter." Beatrice insisted.

"Okay assiduous servants of Uganda." Andrew said and caressed Beatrice on the shoulder before he walked out after Peter.

Peter always shared their office vehicle with Beatrice both in the mornings and evenings. But that evening, because Andrew has invited him for the evening he let the driver used it to take Beatrice home.

"When you're done the driver can take you home. I am going to ride places with Andrew and he will take me home." Peter told Beatrice.

"I wish you good time and see you tomorrow." Beatrice said while typing without looking at them.

It was striking nine thirty p.m. when Walter swung his Citroen in the round about in front of Andrew's house and braked making the car dance on the wheel like a see-saw before he lowered the rear of the car right to the grown. He walked out and knocked on the door.

"Hello Grace how are you?" Walter said as Grace opened the door wider for him to come in.

"I am fine thank you come in and join us."She invited him in. Walter walked in and saw his two friends Peter and Andrew seated at the balcony around a table with four chairs. A bottle of John Walker and four glasses stood on the table. Walter took the chair near Peter leaving the one near Andrew for his wife Grace.

"Huu! They have already set the flag waving. Look at that one gargling the stuff like his mouth wash." Walter said pointing at Andrew.

"You are always on my neck I don't know why?" Andrew returned the joke and they all laughed.

"Sit down buddy."Andrew said getting up with a glass of whisky in his left hand while he extending his right hand for a handshake with Walter. I Love *Johnny* and I am glad Grace loves him too.

Walter sat down next to Pete who had sat with his glass in hand looking bored with drink and said. "Why are you coiling up here like a snail in the shell and as quiet as a stone?" Walter asked resting his hand on f Peter's thigh. "Are you still mourning our loss? Drown your worry in *Johnny whisky* here man. He is going to wave his wand in front of your face and you won't know what happened to you today." Walter added. They all laughed and Walter continued,

"So how are you all?" He asked as Grace walked in with anther bottle of *Johnny Walker whisky* in a tray.

"We are fine thank you." The two men answered in chorus.

"Hey are we having it all in this joint?" I thought we were going some places. Walter remarked as he flashed the whisky in his glass and saw Grace walking in with another full bottle of Johnny Walker in the tray. She came and stood the bottle on the table and popped it open.

"This is just a warm up don't worry." Andrew responded.

"A warm up, and to have more in this den of you?" Walter added with laugher.

"We know your weakness." Peter put in. You call this a den because we are almost mono-sex here now except Grace who is even useless to you." Peter put in cynically

"Shssss. Shut up you. Do not let Grace know I am........." Walter said to Peter.

"Who doesn't know you Walter in the whole of Kampala that you are a sex maniac? Even in Kisenyi, Kibuli, Makerere Kivulo, and all those places of freaks and bums you get your car parked there during odd hours what do you go to do in such places?" Andrew asked.

"Have you personally seen my car in those places?" Walter asked Andrew

"Yes."

"Fine. There you have answered your own question what did you yourself go to do there when I was also there? Checking on me? Walter said and they all laughed as Grace walked in again.

"Is Grace coming with us?" Walter teased Andrew.

"She will begin to sleep there. She sleeps very early you know especially after she has tasted *Jonny*."

"Then you will drive her home when she begins to sleep or you carry her on your lap ."Walter continued to tease Andrew

"Waste of fuel." Andrew said as they took their seats at table.

It was after supper when Andrew and his friends decided to go out to take Peter to Kololo night club to make him forget about the money swindled from them. On the contrary Peter was not in the mood in spite him participating in jokes. His mind kept slipping back thinking about how he was going to make money to make him bring Rosemary to his house. Even that chance of marrying a girl who resembles his late wife Rose was as remote as the sun is to the earth. He didn't see any possibility of marrying her any more. *These girls in Uganda these days, none of them bother to think of a man who cannot buy for her the latest women fashion on show. And here I am thinking of a girl who has gone with tycoons of all kinds? She has tasted all the luxuries from there and she fell for me probably because of my title, the Permanent Secretary without money even those wheelbarrow boys in Owino market are better than me financially. I do not know what next. May be I should write a letter to her cancelling the planed marriage.* Peter thought. The thoughts made him soberer the more whisky he drank. They had just finished the one bottle of John Walker Grace had brought before supper when Grace came and sat down near Peter and asked Peter who sat with his hand between his thighs his glass of whisky stood on a stool near him.

"You don't look happy as your friends why?"

"Oh no I am quite alright". Peter said stirring clumsily from the chair.

"I think we must be going". Andrew said addressing himself to Grace.

"Okay gentlemen I only come to wish you good night I am going to sleep. These days I sleep too much." Grace said and sneered at them before she walked away to the bed room.

"Go and put your baby to sleep first before we go out. It looks she needs some milk." Walter told Andrew. Quietly Andrew walked after Grace in the bedroom. He found her sliding into her see through night dress. He fondled her on her buttocks. She made no response. He grasped her from under the night dress and turned her towards him she turn nonchalantly and stared at him not even blinking her eyes. She was colder than the inside of a deep freezer.

He tried to kiss her. She never moved nor did she open her lips to welcome his. Turn her head slightly away and push him gently away from her. Let me go to sleep. I don't want to interrupt your outing." She said and entered under the blanket.

"I am sorry darling I did mean to hurt you. I was only joking."

"Well I am not talking about anything. You haven't hurt me and you were joking because you apologized when you said it. You see Andrew, do not think that I am to blame for this misfortune we have in this home. You haven't bothered to check yourself medically to prove you are alright and a real man. I have done so. The gynecologist at Mulago believes I am alright. He advised me to tell you to go for a checkup but you didn't go. I know you want to prove you are alright by marrying again. I am not against your belief you go ahead bring her but I tell you, you won't impregnate whoever that girl will be. I was sympathizing with your condition and bearing with you what I believe is your problems not mine. Do you think I am happy to see us two only in this house for years? I am sure if I was an unfaithful woman I would have cheated on you and now I would be as pregnant as jiggers to hatch for you children who do not belong to you. You would of course only realize they are not yours if they resemble their daddies. Do not think because you pour your useless fluid there in me every night that you are productive? That is just there to make you get the pleasure of a man and not to produce. I am sorry Andrew. I have to be frank with you. You are putting yourself into shame, a big one. I pray you bring that girl in. I am not going to hate her. I will stay and live with her so long as you two want me in this house anyway. If you should decide I pack and close the door behind me I will do it but I tell you, you will not impregnate that girl unless someone does it for you. And here you are proudly insulting me in front of your friend that I sleep in public! Since when and how many times did I do that since we got married Andrew? You tell me?" Grace said sitting up from her bed her eyes sparking with tears.

"I am sorry darling forgives me." Andrew said putting his hand on her shoulder.

"Do not touch me". She said as tears slopped from her eyes streaming down her checks. *Bringing me back home is a waste of fuel.* Good night I don't want to talk to you. Go and enjoy yourself." Grace said and wriggled under the blanket and she continued to sob. Wearily Andrew got up from the bed and stood akimbo over her and watched her sob in the blanket. He sighed meditatively and walked out to the aisle leading to the sitting room. The sounds of his foot fall walking out of their bed room tick-tok: tick-Tok: sounded like that of a man walking out of a ward in which he has left his sweet heart critically ill on life support Oxygen, told Peter and Walter that things didn't go well with him. Slowly Andrew dragged himself to the sitting room and slammed himself on the sofa he was sitting on and sighed again.

"Hey what is up your sleeves?" You look a stranger in your own house the baby didn't fall asleep fast? You didn't play for her the lulling record?" Walter joke and they all smiled. It looked as if the care free Walter was the only one who was enjoying the situation in which they were that evening. Peter was still brooding over the loss of the ivories and Andrew sudden change of mood was an indication of bad blood between him and Grace.

"You are a lunatic." Peter commented.

"Lunatics do not know the difference between good and bad they are very happy all the time. That is my advice to you in Uganda today. If you are very sensitive about your environment all the time you will look worse than those malnourish kids in the malnourished clinic in Mulago.

"It seems we might not go to the night club tonight Peter said."

"Why? Because I sound and smell whisky?" Walter asked with laughter. And added "You not go me go."

"You swallow that fluid and we go". Andrew said looking at Peter who still had a mouthful of whiskey in his glass.

On their way to the night club, Peter and Walter were surprised when Andrew told them to pass by the residential place of Beatrice the secretary of Peter to pick for himself a girl who lives in same block for the night.

"Is that why you left Grace behind? I knew you were roughed by your baby who refused to sleep when you went to put her to sleep." Walter commented.

"I need a….."

"Change." Walter completed it for Andrew

"You are not my spoke person."

"I could have as well be." Walter said as he pulled the car to a stop at Block C where Andrew has advised.

The girl to be picked was Clare Namusoke. Clare was a nice short girl about a few centimeters shorter than Andrew. As soon as Walter brought the car to a stop, Andrew jumped out and ran up the steps to Clare's apartment. He raped on the door and Immediately Clare flung the door open. She was already dressed and seated on the bed waiting impatiently.

"Ready to go?" Andrew asked Clare who stood in the door way holding the door with her left hand.

"Sure. I am ready, been waiting for you in the last thirty minutes." Clare said looking at her dress.

"You are smart and look delicious." Andrew remarked

"Just for You." Clare remarked.

"What a sweet fragrant scent. It has overrun the smell of the whisky which had filled the car." Peter commented as Andrew and Clare climbed in.

"That is why I like them. When I roll them on I transfer their scent on me and keep sniffing my body for hours." Walter joked.

Walter and Peter sat in the front seat while Clare and Andrew sat at the back. Under normal circumstances Andrew and Clare would have been squeezing and kissing each other but that evening because of the axiomatic remarked Grace made to him, before he left the bed room, made him frigid. Walter parked his Citroen at the far end of parking ground and Peter and Walter walked out of the car leaving Clare and Andrew behind.

"What is the matter darling? You are not happy with me tonight?" Clare complained.

"Of course you know I am happy, would I have gone for you if I wasn't? I have a slight sore throat and I feel I should not infect you as well." Andrew lied.

"Oh sorry you are sick when did it start?"

"Yesterday."

"But this afternoon you were not that way you gave me quite a passionate kiss and you promised me more tonight hadn't you realize you were sick?"

"Stop asking many questions I am sick in the throat full stop. I love you and you know it. I want to take care of your health in the way I love you. Andrew said and they got out of the car slammed the door shut and walked after Walter and Peter. The open air bar was sparingly populated. Peter and Walter took a long big table for six. Walter thought the two of them might get a girl each so with Andrew already occupied it left him and Peter to fill the remaining chairs. But Peter wasn't very keen in picking on a girl to night he knew there was going to be a lot of taxation in the job. Firstly, if he took a girl, she would definitely not spend the night with him for nothing and he did not have the fees. Secondly, in the morning she will need breakfast with him. And the type of breakfast he always took would make even a girl from the slum not to go in his house again. Milk less, sugarless tea with cassava were not good combination for a girl who has been used to rich milked tea with well-buttered bread may be with some omelet and sausages from some tycoon of Kampala who carry *No problem* wallet packed tight with bank notes. These men lavishly spend their money to impress the girls without feeling any financial pinch. Peter thirdly worried about the lack of good furniture in his house, No TV no radio, no basic means of entertainment in the house to show the world his status. The furniture Government loaned to him to furnished his house were old and worn out. Lack of fund in the Ministry of Works and better furniture made it impossible to replace Peter's dilapidated sets he got some time back. He had applied for new ones but the reply he got was '*no funds, no furniture*'. Beside all those, the lack of proper bathing soap, modern cosmetic skin lotion, and toothpaste in his house worried him. *I can't risk it I will not bother to pick on any girl.* Peter thought as he drank more Nile Special beer. The myriads of thought rooming in his head displaced the alcohol he was ingesting making him more sober than the Bishop on an altar.

The band was playing a tango number after 3 a.m. Most couples were sitting down resting only a few were dancing. Walter was on the stage. He loved tango number most, he was good at it. "I like tango better than any style of dance because it brings you closest with your partner and you really feel the warmth of her breasts on your chest, and as you slid your legs between hers, you feel how she fidget in your arm her breath changes and you feel the stroke of the breath on your face, with a bit of alcohol in the head you could only look for a dark corner." Walter said when he came back to take his seat. He took a glass of beer he had on the table and drank from it. As they talked, a lanky, swarthy young man opening his thirty walked out from the inner bar through the open door passing the table where Andrew and his friend sat. He paused for a moment and turned to look at Andrew.

"Hey uncle so you are here?" The young man said, walked back and shook hands with Andrew. He pulled an empty chair next to Andrew and sat down.

"I have been sitting here with my friends since yesterday at 10 p.m. How his Grace you?" The young man asked Andrew.

"She is not feeling very well". Andrew lied.

"Sorry to hear that what is wrong with her?"

"A bit of headache. I am sure she will be alright tomorrow." Andrew said.

"How is the evening with you? Are you alright here?" The boy said looking round at the empty bottles of beer on the table. Perhaps I should give you one each if you don't mind". The boy said and unzipped a wallet popularly known by Ugandan as *No problem* and pulled out two thousand shillings note and gave them to Andrew.

"You organize the drink for your friends." He said and hurriedly got up walked towards the public toilet. Andrew received the money and said "Thank you very much."

Peter glance at the boy and shook his head. When the boy had walked away Peter thought. *How can a young man like this carry so much money in the public places like this? When will I make money to enable me to buy beers for friends as I use to do before the misfortune stroke me?* Peter thought. The young man soon came back from the toilet and sat again near Andrew.

"Perhaps I should let you know each other". Andrew said and set up. "This is Clare" he said moving his hands toward Clare who had sat beside him, without detail and this is Peter my good friends and the one at the far end of the table is Walter. We have been friend since our childhood days. This boy you see here is Ucamgiu is the son of my sister." Andrew introduced them.

"Nice to meet you lady and gentlemen." Ucamgiu said bowing towards Clare , Peter and Walter respectively.

"You are most welcome Ucamgiu". Walter said as he shook hands with him.

"Thank you very much". Ucamgiu said with his primary six type of English and got up and shook hands with the others before he came back to take his seat. Ucamgiu was well dressed in a three piece navy blue trivia suit. Though he looked kingly in his suit, but for the occasion, where he was, in the dancing hall, where most men were casually dressed, made him looked odd.

The young man must be one of those who fell in to wealth by accident. Look at how he is dressed in a warm crowed dancing hall. His English actually confirms his standards. He must have learned that English on the job somewhere before he got his wealth. Peter thought as he looked at Ucamgiu seated next to him trying to converse with Andrew in English. The shyness he exhibited while talking to them revealed his inferiority complex he was suffering in the company of Andrew and his friends.

"When did you come to Kampala?" Andrew asked Ucamgiu.

"A week ago?"

"A week ago! And where were you staying all this time without calling on us?" Andrew complained.

"I was living in Apollo Hotel." Ucamgiu replied wringing his fingers shyly. Apollo Hotel is one of the most expensive classic hotels meant for milliners.

"Isn't it expensive to stay in Apollo hotel for such a long period time?"

"No. I like it there because it's safer there than anywhere else in Kampala these days."

"Well, you men with money stay anywhere. But I ...."

"Where is the money Uncle?" Ucamgiu interrupted Andrew

"How is your business getting on I gather you have started to cross the border?" Andrew asked.

"Well, I am picking up slowly." Ucamgiu replied

"Is that why you are here?"

"Yes".

"I see."

"How easy is it to get the metals there?"

"Very easy."

"Is it?"

"Yes. All you need is, to know someone to lead you to where the real stuff can be found. Because there are some crooks there who sell fake stones even metals, sometimes filling from old stoves and if you do not know, you buy fake ores exorbitantly only to regret afterwards." Ucamgiu explained.

"What is that metal you are talking about?" Peter asked getting interested. Andrew crooked laughter and said. "It's one of those precious stones people are actively making wealth from, these days in our place. Free money with little labours and risk attached. If you get the market, you need only capital and you will be walking the world with *no problem wallet* like Ucamgiu here, and look a man worth millions like him." Andrew said causing laughter among them.

"Oh no Uncle. I don't look like that. Is it because of this lousy suit I am in?" Ucamgiu complained

"You call that lousy, when some of us are unable to afford used second hand suit from market?" Peter said. Walter had pick Clare for a cha-cha-cha number the band was playing leaving Andrew Peter and Ucamgiu only at table.

"I wonder why I did not think of this deal before. It is quite a healthy one. But as I said there is some risk involved but not as much as you would expect from the tusks anyway. This one is quite handy. You could easily slip it in your pockets and no one will know you are carrying ores worth million on you. But those lousy elephant tusks, there are no convenient way of carrying them without being seen or suspected. Well I think we need to try this Peter. It might be the last resort. If it fails, then I really don't know what we can do to generate more money for us. I have a feeling that we will succeed. Ucamgiu should be able to help us. Don't you think so Ucamgiu?" Andrew asked looking at him.

"Oh well that's no problem at all." Ucamgiu agreed.

"That is why you carry *no problem wallet*". Peter commented getting amused at the discussion. The beer he had been drinking since dusk had refused to take effect on him but because of this new discovery of survival and the recovery of his financial difficulty and the possibility of marrying Rosemary, Peter got excited and the excitement seemed to have made him drunk instantly. He felt his mind reeling with the hope of getting of his financial mess this time. He took the glass of beer he had on the table and drank the beer excitedly his eyes glowing with optimism.

Ucamgiu was a primary seven dropped out. He tried the primary seven examinations seven times and each time he tried, he did worse than the previous year. His father Ucamgiu senior decided against sending him to school because he considered it a waste of money and time. Instead he sent him to stay with his brother Mark Oyugi in Kampala with the hope that he could get some casual jobs in the city. Ucamgiu stayed with Mark helping him with all house work. It took him long before he found a job with an Indian as a shop attendant selling radios. Ucamgiu worked well for the Indian. The Indian trusted him because of his good honest character. When the regime change took place in Uganda the Indian was forced out of Uganda. The Indians for whom Ucamgiu worked was, a British citizen. The Indian eventually left, leaving each and everything in the shop in the hand of Ucamgiu. Ucamgiu at first didn't know what to do with the business. He wanted to sell all the shop and the radios in it and leave the place. But Mark quickly came to him and advised him not to sell the shop. Mark helped Ucamgiu to transfer the shop in his name. When all were done Ucamgiu settled down in his shop and started to make money. He kept it up until the regime State Research boys sighted him as one of the most progressive Alur business men in Kampala.

They attacked him falsely accusing him of being antigovernment element, supporter of the exiles fighting government. Ucamgiu was lucky he escaped and fled to his Uncle's home land in Parombo in

Nebbi District. Without job and money Ucamgiu found life in the village appalling. He was used to town life, food, electricity but those in the village were impossible. Digging was impossible. He thought of all the possibility to make money but there was none. He was semi illiterate. To get a decent job in Uganda was impossible. The best he could get was to go back to his old job shop attendant or become a house boy of some tycoon in Parombo. He didn't like the idea nor to think about it. He thought of all the luxuries he was enjoying in Kampala and the wealthy he left behind it made him hate the regime with all its Hench-men. In spite of the fact that it was that regime which had elevated him to the status he lost. Simon Ucamgiu did not despair. He sat at home with his ears, eyes and nose hearing, seeing and smelling the possible site where money could be located. A few years past Ucamgiu was almost giving up hope of succeeding again in life. His only dress he fled in when he ran away for his dear life from the regime's State Research boys, had worn out and they were threadbare. He became true Ucamgiu they knew in the village before he took up the job of shop attendant in Kampala. But to those who knew him in Kampala, he was a stranger. His friends knew him as chief of Tycoon Ucamgiu. The man who used to drive no other car smaller than a Mercedes Benzes or a Citroen these were his only cars of preference. The Peugeot estates were business cars. People ate and drank in his home like the home of the President. Whenever one call on Ucamgiu private residence one never left without drinking or eating grilled pork, beef, or chicken. They were always there. That left his place a hunting ground for women and girls as high as the University girls. That life made him very popular in the City. Ucamgiu was the pioneer of the people who started the name of the wallet popularly known as *"no problem wallet."* Ucamgiu thought about all these and knew he was sunk. He confined himself to home. Worries were killing him faster. Then a thought occurred to him: why, an illegal gold mine was discovered somewhere in Zaire just a few miles only from Uganda boarder at Parombo! Ucamgiu heard about it and saw some of the ore mined from the illegal mine. But being semi illiterate as he was Ucamgiu didn't know the value and the used of the ore. People were selling it illegally to Kampala and elsewhere and making tremendous money out of it. Ucamgiu never bothered. He only sat and thought of his past. He thought it was dame risky to try to show himself again in Kampala where heis the most wanted man in the City. He stayed put and ignored the illegal gold trade going on around him. But one day a friend of his, one of his sympathizers came to him and advised him to try. Ucamgiu could not imagine going to Kampala with the illegal commodities in his pocket and being netted at the check points which were lined up from Pakwach up to Kampala which he wrongly assumed were meant to catch him. The men falsely accused him of being the sole supporter of the rebels fighting to oust the Government. He knew if they lay their hands on him, they were not going to rush it up with bullets but do it slowly at their leisure, until he was pieces of meat. When he was in Kampala, he had heard of how the regime thugs tortured and murdered the traitorous suspects. The story always made his hair stand on end. He couldn't imagine going under the same process of death. He turned down the advice of his friends. It was until he heard that the man who hatch problem for him became the hunted by the regime and he became the victim of death, that Ucamgiu took up interest in the illegal gold deal but he had no money to start with. The same friend who had advised him earlier to try the business loaned him the money to start off. Ucamgiu with the know-how of business at his fingertips didn't take long to rise up again. Only a year after that, he was back to normal life almost. The first things he did were to dress himself up to enable him to look the smart Ucamgiu who used to own fleets of cars in Kampala before he was forced to run to the village for his dear life by the State Security. Ucamgiu kept up with his illegal gold trade and regained almost all what he had lost.

The night when he met Andrew and his friends in Kololo night club, he had just finished selling off his two kilograms of gold he had smuggled in Kampala. He got a good sum of money from it. The one hundred thousand shillings he had carried in his *No problem* wallet was just to celebrate with his friends the death of the man who drove him out off his business in Kampala.

Andrew, although was an intimate friends of Peter, was an Alur from Parombo a tribe in West Nile of Uganda. He met Peter and Walter during their early secondary education in Nyapea College in West Nile. The three were great friends in the College and when they completed, they all put their first choices for the Advanced Level (A-Levels) education in St. Mary College Kisubi. They were taken and after their A-Levels examinations, they were all admitted to Makerere University. Walter and Andrew decided to read Commerce and Accountancy while Peter read Education.

Parombo is a small commercial village in North-Western Uganda situated only six miles off Zaire boarder. By the virtue of its position, the village steamed with all sorts of commodities smuggled in by indigenous citizens of the two States. Meanwhile Nyaraburu in Zaire, was another small satellite business hob of Parombo, was much better developed than Parombo. The two sister villages in the two countries served as the smuggling deports for goods originating from Uganda and Zaire respectively. The smuggling were done across the border in broad day light, through the secret paths passing in bushes up the steep rocky hills like *"Meda nyuka"* (literally meaning give me more porridge to give me energy to climb this hill) and "*Alor mana*" (also meaning I have to sit down and move on my buttocks with my testicles rolling on the ground as one descends steep hills). Occasionally the soldiers in Zaire commonly known as *Solda or Arad* intercepts the smuggler but the term for release were always decided there and them between the smuggler and the *Solda*. Parting with few Zairian currencies will most of the time exonerated the smuggler. The most precious good smuggled into Uganda from Zaire was Gold. Trade in gold left very many school going children in the two countries to dropout of schools. These boys were immensely rich. They had everything a rich man wants. Because that was their life line, they set up their own governing board to control the movement of the precious gold in Parombo. They knew the staunch smugglers of the gold from Zaire and they made sure that they sell the gold their governing board only. They had monopolized the trade so much that, they exercise their monopoly by setting up their own security body that kept Parombo village under strict surveillance. They set up their own gold administration of Parombo village so that Parombo became an autonomous mini gold state within Uganda. The pioneer in gold trade extended their wings and put up business in all town of the West Nile districts used as gold depots.

Ucamgiu explained all these vice and virtue of the gold trade to Peter and Andrew. They listened with keen interest especially Peter, who according to him, wanted to jump on the job instantly. He knew if he fails to lay his hands on money this time with Ucamgiu, then he would never ever see money again in the way he had it before the misfortune landed the devastating hummer blow on his head. But although Peter axiomatically believed Ucamgiu that all would be well his main obstacle remained, and that was the capital. How and from where was he going to raise the capital to start him off? It remained the same old story. He must fall back to Andrew and Walter for loan to get him some few Toller of gold from Parombo. Ucamgiu had told them that a Toller of gold cost thirty-five thousand Uganda Shillings and that sum of the money, would have been alright to him had Omony not run away with his two million shillings. Peter found himself clenching his fist. He wished he could lay his hands on Omony he would squeezed life out of him like squeezing water out of a sodden sponge.

Andrew explained to Ucamgiu the long relationship between him and his two friends Walter and Peter dwelling more on Peter and his misfortune and his attempt he had been making to start life afresh.

"He has tried, Ucamgiu I don't deny that."Andrew said and added," he did all sorts of things a man of his status should not be doing." Andrew said and sipped the beer in his glass. Can you imagine him going down the Goods Shade in the Kampala Railways Station to sell charcoal, carry bags of beans in the village to sell? Of late he was nearly arrested because of smuggling elephant tusks from Gulu. He laboured to bring those tusks here with the hope that it would bring him something only to lose the whole effort in the hand of untrustworthy boy who ran away with all the money he had earned from the tusks. We first heard of the information this morning. Now Ucamgiu", Andrew said turning to Ucamgiu. As you know, I trust you and these two gentlemen, Peter and Walter and I are no other persons but three persons in one. That is what we are. You do well to one you have done to all of us. You provoke one of us you provoke all. So you see, Ucamgiu these are your true uncles. Now that they have known you, do not be afraid of them, do not be shy to meet them, they are me. All you need to know are their places of residence and work and you could sleep anywhere with us when you come over. You have indicated here that there is no problem in getting the gold so long as we follow your foot step. I agree that there shouldn't be any mistake if we do that. Those tycoons who have turned Parombo into their own state will not hinder us. I know most of them. I could go home and they will all shake like leaves in the wind and fall in front of me on their knees. They are those young boys who acquired wealth just by the virtue of the gold trade." Andrew explained to Ucamgiu.

The band had played three consecutive disco numbers which kept most people who love dancing twisting, rocking and swinging their limbs hilariously. Even those who were only warming the chairs in the night club, kept busy nodding their heads and drumming their feet on the floor. Walter had been on the floor with a girl he met in the dancing hall throughout the three disco numbers and the girl was tired. She wanted a rest. Walter also wanted a rest. So they returned to their respective tables.

"Next number." Walter proposed.

"With pleasure." The girl replied as she sat down on her chair. Walter would have invited the girl to join them but he hadn't made up his mind whether to pick on her or another one. Well, the tango number was on again. The girl was flirting around eyeing at Walter insinuating to come and pick her up again so that they go at it. Walter saw it and knew she could be the catch for the night. Not bad looking. He immediately jumped across the floor and picked her as she was impatiently waiting for him to come and extend his hands. They lasciviously hooked themselves together. With alcohol in her head, coupled with the tight grip Walter had on her waist, the girl was left maximally stimulated. She put her head flat on Walter's shoulder and accentuated his sexual impulse by breathing near his ears romantically. Ravishingly Walter squeezed her on his chest and danced occasionally falling out of step. When the number was over, the girl, who was almost falling asleep on his chest, stirred and looked at him in the eyes insinuatingly.

Walter was good at reading the faces of his captives.

"Shall we go?" Walter asked her.

"Where?" She asked sheepishly

"Home of course." Walter answered with a trembling voice

"Not now." She said and looked at him persuasively.

"Of course I know that."

"Will you come with me to our table?"

"If there is a room for me."

"There is. Even if there is none, I will create one for you. Come-on let's go. Walter said dragging her by the hand to their table. They walked to the table where they found Ucamgiu was supplying beers to Andrew and his friends.

"Hi your beer is here." Ucamgiu said to Walter when he saw him walking hand in hand with the girl he has just picked from the dancing hall.

"Shall I get something for her and what does she take." Ucamgiu said showing his financial might.

"Oh no don't worry about her. She is my guest I will take care of her. Walter replied proudly to impress the girl that he has the money to care for her. Peter looked at Ucamgiu and Walter picked the bottle of beer in front of him and drank from it, thinking *when will I regain my financial status?*

Chapter Eleven

The life band at the night club played until five in the morning. All this period, Peter and Andrew kept discussing and planning with Ucamgiu, his new youthful friend, how to try his hand at the gold deal in West Nile again. The excitement, made Peter who never mixed brand of alcohol, drunk all tribes of lager and whisky Ucamgiu was able to bring at their table. This was not his course of action in the past, when he was able to sponsor himself and Rose to the social centers in and around Kampala. But this time when he had to be taken and offered drinks, he had almost no choice but to take whatever the pocket of the sponsor can afford. Walter who had spent most of his time dancing was less drunk than any of his friends and so was Clare who just contented herself with little sips of Nile Lager Special. But Peter and Andrew were sodden with the mixture of the alcoholic booze they had drunk. Peter was immobilized completely by the drinks. He had to be walked by Walter into the car while Andrew staggered alone and climbed to the back seat of the car, slammed the door and almost went to sleep immediately.

"Where do I take him to your flat or to his home?" Walter asked Clare who stood near the open door of the car leering at Andrew snoring in the car with his head sagging on the back rest of seat of the car his hand thrown limply beside him.

"Take him to his home. He is useless to me tonight." Clare said disdainfully. Walter laughed and patter her on the back but Clare with her carnal desired worked up was near to tears. She didn't smile nor showed any interest in Walter's joke.

"Okay you go back and keep my chick there I will drive them home first and come for you two. Do not pick on another one." Walter said teasing Clare.

"She turned and eyed him insinuatingly. Walter the sex manic quickly interpreted the meaning of the look and regretted she was his friend's girl and secondly he has already picked on the girl he was taking for the night whose name he didn't even know. Walter never bothered to know their names anyway all of them were *Miss* or *madam*. Clare enviously walked back to the table where the girl of Walter was seated empting her Nile Lager Special bottle in the glass, complacent with everything in her vicinity.

"They are too drunk." The girl of Walter said, as Clare sat down and crossed her legs under the table.

"Yes they are" Clare replied nonchalantly.

"I hope they are not going to end up in a dice or against an electrical pole."

"Walter is alright." Clare answered cutely. The girl noticed the uneasy note in the voice of Clare and decided not to talk anymore about the departed men. She knew as a woman what it meant when one has her carnal desired worked up by alcohol coupled with a man's caresses. Nothing can subdue it but the rod Hers was on the build-up she was almost sure she will have it only if Walter came back which she was of course sure he would because of Clare who was still there. *Who will return her home if he doesn't come back?* She thought.

Walter distributed the drunken men to their respective homes. He took Peter last. He walked him into his bedroom. Stripped the coat and removed his shirt and left him lying in his pair of trousers.

He pulled the blanket over him and left him snoring, breathing the alcohol laden breath which saturated the air in the bed room. The heat generated by the blanket and the alcohol, generated sweat and Peter tossed the blanket from his body and lay on top of the bed without any covering.

The early morning sun rays reddening the Eastern horizon with thick dark stratus clouds above it, pierced through the tartar curtain at the windows to his bedroom, fell on his glistening face left by the sweat which poured from his body at night. Peter opened his eyes slowly and woke up. It was seven O'clock one hour after his usual waking hour at six. Peter stirred clumsily with a heavy hangover of alcohol. He found his head too heavy to be lifted up from the pillow, his limps too feeble to lift up his aching body. He tried to sit up in bed but he couldn't. He fell on his back on the bed and almost went to sleep again but the overflowing bladder forced him to put in more effort. He struggled on his feet and got up supporting himself with the wall he toddled to the toilet. He hated the smell of his own breath which smelt as if he had swallowed rotten eggs. He gaggled some cold water to rinse his mouth but it smelt worse than before. How he wished he had some tooth paste he would have used it to reduce the bad smell in the mouth. But the charcoal mixed with salt he was using for tooth paste did not improve the situation. Annoyed because of lack of tooth paste, Peter toddled back into the bedroom and sat on the bed holding his head in both hands. As he sat he nauseated and felt like vomiting at the smell of his own mouth. He fell on his back on the bed and started snoring almost immediately.

Daniel, his house boy walked in to the house using the behind door as he always did. The absence of Peter in the bath room surprised him. He always got him up by seven bathing or cleaning himself up in the morning but that day the stillness of the house sent a cool chill along his spinal which made him fidget. *Has anything serious happened to him or is he ill*, Daniel thought as he stealthy walked toward his bedroom. The snoring sound from his bedroom which sounded like distance roars of a lion , told him that he was in, but still sleeping. Daniel thought it was strange because Peter never behaved like that. *Could he be ill?* He thought as he peeped into the bedroom through the door left a jar. He saw him lying in his pair of trousers on his back on top of the bed. His left arm flung on the pillow while the right hand was folded on his chest. The alcoholic stanch from his room told Daniel that he must have had too much the previous night. *But he has never suffered from hangover, why today?* Daniel thought as he stealthy closed the door behind him and walked away to the kitchen.

Poor man, I hope he doesn't become alcoholic. His problem seems to build up day after day. This is the problem with the schooled. They always have that pride which drive them to think that they must always live luxuriously whereas people like us, what do we care for, food, sleep and drops of drink here and there. Worse still these days with the hangover of new regime the situation in the country has been reversed. The so called intellectuals, the learned, the schooled are the people who are walking on foot on the roads while the illiterate or the semi-literate are the one flying on international business trips abroad and they have dominated all business sector in Uganda these days. Their pot bellies make them look men with brains but they are thick-skinned clowns. This has caused most of the professional to emulate them with the hope that they would succeed like them. Their failures are frustrating them and will make all of them drunks. I pity this Uganda of ours. Clinics have sprung up everywhere in towns as hospital equipment and drugs in the hospital disappear and end up in them. At school private teaching are rampant because teachers see no way of surviving on their merger salaries they get out of the schools. As results they register in numbers of schools beside their parent schools where they spend little time and attention to the pupils making the results of the final examinations appalling compared to what used to happen in the past, when they able to live within their salaries. They cannot sell chalks of course. Veterinary Doctors treat your cows when you give them tokens. Police always complain of lack of transport to attend to criminal cases reported to them but the vehicles are made available only when you have bribed, or fed them. At the road check points although you are as innocent like a new born baby sometimes you are embarrassed because you have no dough to give to the soldiers. Everyone is busy grabbing from each other. What a life? I don't know if we shall correct ourselves. Daniel kept thinking as he made breakfast for Peter.

When Walter dropped the girl he picked from the night club the previous night at her home in the morning, at 7.30 he drove to his office first and put a call to Clare. He wanted to check on her how she spent the previous night.

"Hello Electricity Board office. Can I help you?" Clare answered the call. Clare worked as the Secretary to the Manager of Electricity Board of Uganda.

"Good morning Clare. How was your night?" Walter voice came on the line.

"What an unlucky day today to receive the first call from you." Clare remarked and continued, "I wish you don't remind me about it. I felt like dragging him out of the car and clawing him all over the body. He got me worked up throughout the evening and I was expecting him home only to see the fool unable to raise an arm up. It's sad to have a drunken man in bed." Clare said.

"Walter laughed and said, "I am sorry about that," before he hung up and put another call to Peter's office. Beatrice received his called and informed him that Peter wasn't in at that time.

"No he hasn't shown up since morning."

"I know why, we returned late from the night club last night." Walter remarked.

"Yes that is what the driver said."

"I will go home to check on him. He might be in need of help." Walter said and hung up.

Walter immediately walked out his office and drove straight to Peter's home. He knocked on the door and immediately turned the knob open and walked in. He found Daniel laying the table for breakfast for Peter.

"Good morning Daniel." Walter greeted the old man

"Good morning Walter and welcome I am sure you have come to check on Peter." Daniel said affirmatively.

"Yes I Have."

"Still in bed seems he has had too much yesterday. Never seen him like that before." Daniel said

"Sometime it's inevitable to go outside the norm especially when you meet new exciting friends." Walter remark as he walked in the bedroom of Peter.

"Hey you wake up." Walter said lifting him up by the hand. Without talking, Peter sat up on the bed and clasped his head in his hand. He stared down on the floor without looking up at Walter. Eventually he opened his eyes slowly and saw Walter standing over him in his bedroom.

"How is it?" Walter asked smiling at him while looking round the room. The house was saturated with the smell of alcohol only. "Wake up and wash up." Walter said shaking him on the shoulder.

"Oh dear, I don't think I will be able to stand up. I am still badly off." Peter complained.

"Well I came to check on you." If you are not able to get up you rest."

"I think I must. What is the time now?" Peter asked.

"It's nearly lunch time. It's 12.30 p.m." Walter remarked.

"Ho my God!" Peter sighed and without further word fell on the bed on his back clasping his head in his hands. "I am badly off. I mixed too much last night. Tell Beatrice I am not feeling well. I'll be alright tomorrow."

"I will do that." Walter said and walked out of the bedroom closing the door behind him. He walked to the dining hall of Peter. The late breakfast of cooked cassava flask of hot water, coffee tin and a bowel of sugar, still stood on the old dining table surrounded by six dining chairs with torn cushions. Walter stopped briefly to look at the set up and walked to the sitting room where Daniel was mobbing the floor with some rugs using water from the basin.

"He is not well enough to get up yet." Walter said as he neared the old man squatting on the floor mobbing.

"No he isn't." Daniel agreed

"I do not think you need to make lunch for him."

"He hasn't given me anything to cook either."

"Well then you-------- does he normally give you what to cook for every meal?"

"Yes Sir."

"That means you need something for supper. You'd better come with me to town and get something for your supper." Walter said and walked out of the room to where he had parked his car. Daniel put away the mobbing rugs and followed him with his shopping basket in his hand and they were off to town.

The day was crawling to 3 p.m. When Peter woke up from bed, he felt drowsy and weak but well enough to get out of bed.

The dizziness had left him but the splitting headache still persisted. He got up and walked to the bath room and with his mixture of charcoal and salt which he used for tooth paste; he brushed his teeth and bathed. He walked out of the bath toweled himself, dressed and walked out into the dining room. He found whatever Daniel had laid for his breakfast still stood on the table. Peter was hungry enough to eat anything. He sat at table and began to munch the cassava washing it down with the dry coffee. He had just finished drinking his coffee when Daniel loaded with the food basket packed with meat, baking floor, cabbages onions, tomatoes, sugar and cooking fat walked in through the back door his usual entrance. Peter heard him come in and walked out to meet him and apologies for what happened.

"Good afternoon sir" Daniel greeted Peter

"Good afternoon. Oh! Where are you from and who gave you all these? Peter asked looking at the basket on the table.

"Walter bought them for us."

"He did?

"Yes sir"

"It is very kind of him." Peter said embarrassed, and walked back to the sitting room. He sat down and took the newspaper *The eyes of the nation* the driver had delivered home and began to read it. Then he remembered his encounter with Simon Ucamgiu. They were to meet at 8 a.m. in the morning the next day to discuss the detail plan of how to move to Parombo. How grateful he was, that the appointment was not that day. He felt relieved and briefly folded **The** *eyes of the nation* and sat staring emptily at the door.

The sound of the motor car of Andrew driving in interrupted his thought. Andrew drove round the roundabout in front of Peter's door parked and walked out to the house. Peter got up and walked to the door to welcome him.

"Hello Andrew. Good afternoon. Peter said opening the door as Andrew walked in.

"Hello Peter good afternoon. How are you now? Walter told me that you were not well at all in the morning."

"No I wasn't, but I am improving. It's my head, still aching like hell. I hope I will be alright soon.

"Take some aspirin or Parasol it might do you some good."

"I have done so just now. I'm waiting for the reaction." Peter said and laid down on the long sofa set he was sitting on, resting his head on the arm of the chair.

"How was the office?" Peter asked yawning.

"It was fine. Simon called on me at about 10 a.m. in the morning. He is meeting you tomorrow at 8 am."

"Ah I will be there for him."

"I think you should because he is going back tomorrow."

There was a pause between them and Peter said. "I certainly had too much last night. I didn't know how I got home. I only found myself in the bed. I hope I didn't misbehave when we were in the bar?" Peter asked Andrew.

"You are asking the wrong man. I could have been worst. I can't tell that. Walter might since he was the one who brought us home."

"You mean you were also knocked out?"

"Seriously," Andrew said and they both laughed.

"Then what happened to Clare?"Peter asked turning his face towards Andrew.

"Walter took her home. She was behaving funny this morning." Andrew said

"Well that is understandable. You kept her expectant for the whole night did you expect her to come and kiss you for that? It will all blow out and you will start a new life." Peter consoled Andrew.

"It might not be Peter, she was very hurt last night."

Peter kept quiet while thinking. *What do you lose if she jilts? After all you are married man.*

There was a pause between them and Peter sneered and said, "Her relationship with you was even interfering with your marriage life at home. Take it easy. Grace is a lovely woman. Why don't you content yourself with her?" Peter advised serious.

"Because she has not given me a child."

Peter laughed and said, "You blame her wholly?" Andrew kept quiet, but Peter said, "If I were you I wouldn't mind sticking on a barren lovely woman like Grace." Peter said. Andrew shyly said, "Okay Peter, I am glad you have sobered up, I am going home to rest. I I will think about your advice."

"You should really." Peter agreed.

"Well from me good evening, see you tomorrow." Andrew said and got up from the chair. Peter also got up and walked with him to where he had parked his car. They shook hands and Andrew drove off to his home.

The following day Peter woke up early and went through his routine and soon the vehicle was ready to take him to work. That morning the drive drove Beatrice first to office and after he came for Peter. That was because of what happened the previous day. Beatrice was at her desk busy typing when Peter walked in.

"Hello sir good morning" she greeted him stopping to type briefly

"Good morning Beatrice how are you?"

"I am quite fine thank you. And how are you today? Beatrice asked

"Much better, thanks. I apologized for what happened yesterday."Peter replied and began to walk to his office.

Beatrice only smiled and continued with her work.

At 10 a.m Ucamgiu driving the latest model of Mercedes he had just acquired reached the gate to the Ministry of Education and the gate keeper who had sat on a stool near the gate walked to open for him. Ucamgiu drove in and park in the slots for visitors. He climbed down from the car and walked back to the gatekeeper and asked to see The Permanent Secretary Peter. The gatekeeper brought for him the record book where every visitor was required to register his or her details and the name of the officer they want to see. He put the book open on a table for Ucamgiu.

"What am I suppose to do?" Ucamgiu asked

"You are supposed to fill in the details as indicated in the headings in the columns in the book." The gatekeeper replied.

Ucamgiu hesitated for a moment and smirked, bend down and took the pen which was in the open book, flicked it three times in the air as if to wake it up for the job and began to scribble his name. The gatekeeper was a University Graduate with Bachelor degree in Business Administration. He tried to get employment for the last four years but could not find any. Tired of looking for the job he settled as a gatekeeper at the Ministry of Education. He looked at Ucamgiu with a lot of amazement. *Who is this man so expensively dressed driving such an expensive car but can hardly write his name? His look is deceptive, one would think he is well educated but I am not sure if he....* Ucamgiu interrupted his thought when he asked the gatekeeper what to write in the Column written on top *'reasons for seeing the officer'.*

"Why did you come to see the Permanent Secretary? Looking for scholarship, Job, or are you relatives come on personal reason?"

"Personal."

"So write it there." The gatekeeper said with a sneer.

After Ucamgiu completed filling in his details, he put the pen in the book and the gatekeeper gave him his number tag and showed him where Peter's office was. The gatekeeper came back and sat on his stool and took the record book and began to see Ucamgiu detail. He could hardly make sense of anything he scribbled in the book. He shook his head and though, *Uganda my beloved country everything is upside done because of this privatization policy the regime has adopted. This man could be the son of one of those lucky ones who have been allocated the privatized institutions which used to collect revenue for the Government and provide employment to University graduates like us but now the revenue is collected by the individual families. And that is why idiots like these look the way they look.*

The fragrant body sprays Ucamgiu wore, the immaculate dark suit and the well polished black shoes made him look a man with money. He entered the Secretary Office and stood in front of Beatrice. The fragrant scent in the office told Beatrice that someone has entered the office. She stopped typing and looked at Ucamgiu.

"You are welcome Sir." Beatrice said.

"I want to see Peter." Ucamgiu retorted ignoring the courtesy of Beatrice or he did not know the courteousness. Beatrice looked at him surprised and asked him to sit down at the visitor's seats. With his brown leather brief case in his left hand, Ucamgiu went and sat down.

"What is your name Sir?" Beatrice asked

"Simon Ucamgiu." Ucamgiu answered curtly.

Beatrice lifted the receiver of the phone and talked to Peter, "There is a Mr. Simon Ucamgiu here who wants to see you." Beatrice said when she heard Peter Voice on the line. Peter was expecting Ucamgiu.

"Let him come in." Peter said impatiently.

"Okay you can go and see Peter" Beatrice said addressing Ucamgiu.

Peter welcomed Ucamgiu and the two sat discussing the modalities of the pros and the corns' of the gold business. In end of their discussion, Ucamgiu accepted to give Peter loan of five hundred thousand shillings to start him in the gold deal. With humility Peter accepted the offer and promised Ucamgiu that if all went well he was going to refund him immediately.

"No problem". Ucamgiu told him. "You take your time sir, only when you will be alright you could let me have the money back. In any case it's no point talking about the refund now. We haven't succeeded even once. You know this gold trade is very tricky. Some people say that there are some traditional beliefs in it which if not done, you might not even see it, in-spite the fact that you might be having the money for it. So let us succeed first then you begin to talk of when to refund me." Ucamgiu advised Peter.

Peter was left chastened. He knew from the introduction of Andrew, Ucamgiu is a very young semi illiterate young man who, if Uganda was in its normal set up of the past, wouldn't have been giving loan to him instead it would have been him the old man the Permanent Secretary to loan him the money. He nearly refused the loan but when he thought of his financial position and the number of times Andrew and Walter bore his financial burden he humbled himself and accepted the voluntary help from the young man.

"I think I will leave tomorrow and my main task will be to locate the gold. You could start off with about five *tolla* and that should cost you about the money I have given you.

Peter sighed and sat up on the chair, *well, I hope the game sticks this time. It looks as if I have my back on the financial wall. There might not be any outlet* Peter thought and stared at Ucamgiu seated in front of him.

As if he was reading his mind, Ucamgiu said "I will try to help you Peter, do not be despondent. I will go and when I am ready I will send you a telegram or ring and when this is done you will take off with whatever means is convenient to you and you will meet me in a place I will tell you."

"Thank you very much." Peter said.

"I must be going." Ucamgiu said and got up carrying his brief case in his right hand. Peter also got up and walked Ucamgiu through the Secretary Office to his car. They shook hands and Peter wished him safe journey.

Peter impatiently waited to hear from Ucamgiu for two and half weeks. *What has happened to him? Has he met with some difficulties or has he just forgotten all about the deal. Ugandans these days most do not keep promises. They have too many things in their hands.* Peter thought as he got up from his table. He stood up with a file opened in front of him he read what was on the file he was dealing with and shrugged. *I'll deal with this tomorrow I'm fed up. I must go home and see what there is to cook for supper* he thought and closed the file and tossed it in a tray marked pending. Immediately the telephone on his desk buzzed. He scooped the receiver and talked in the mouth piece.

"Hello"

"Hold on for Andrew". Beatrice said curtly and connected the two gentlemen.

"Hello Andrew how are you this evening?"

"I'm fine thank you and you?"

"I am bored with this paper work". Peter said yawning.

"You really sound bored. You need something to excite you?"

"I do. I thought Simon was going to get in touch with us soon that I go out for a break from this boring routine of mine."

"That is in fact why I rang you. I have just got a telegram from home I don't know where the telegram delayed. We should have received it last week on Saturday, because it was received in Kampala Post office last Saturday according to the date stamp on the telegram. Simon was expecting you in Pakwach this week between Monday and Wednesday hoping that we got the telegram on Friday or Saturday. Now I don't know what to do. But I think you should go all the same. I sent him a telegram telling him to keep on checking on you daily at the Railway Station at Pakwach for at least five days beginning from the day he fixed to meet you. What I would like to suggest finally is, we are going to send him another telegram today saying that you are on the way and he should expect you at Pakwach Railway Station within this week. I think that will be alright with you?" Andrew asked.

"It will be okay". Peter agreed.

"Fine then I will send him the telegram now." Andrew confirmed and hung up. Peter cradled his receiver and stood starring at the phone meditatively. *I really do not understand why nothing works out right with me. Supposing I go and find that Simon has not received our telegram and he is out or he is on his way here. Won't that be a waste of money and time?* Peter thought and walked out of the office into the Secretary Office where he found Beatrice and Clare dabbing her face with a handkerchief and doing her hair while looking into a small round mirror in her hand. Clare had passed to see Beatrice to share with her what happened between Andrew and her the previous night at Kololo night club

"You look gorgeous."Peter commented her and stopped near her."

"Thank you sir." Clare said, slipped the mirror and the handkerchief in the hand bag and snapped the bag closed. She got up flicked off some of the specks of particles of her hair on her shoulder and walked out towards the door. Peter opened the door and held it opened for her. "Thank you sir." she said and walked out in front of Peter swaying her meaty buttocks in her cream colour skirt. The *tuk, tuk* sounds of her cream colour high heels shoes which matched the colour of the skirt confirmed the weight of the buttocks on the legs. She had a transparent white blouse without a bra so that her pin pointed succulent breasts danced freely on her chest. She looked to be out for an evening with a guy.

"Going home straight?"Peter asked suspiciously

"No I am still in town. Clare answered with a smile looking behind at Peter. She knew Peter was going to relate all these to Andrew

"Andrew is meeting us down there." Peter said.

"I am sorry I won't wait for him tell him I have gone my way home." Clare said and stood looking expectantly towards the gate. After a short while a dark middle age man driving a dark blue Mercedes Benzes UXA 335 entered the gate and pulled up near them. The man jumped out and opened the door for Clare. Clare fell in the comfortable co-driver seat of the car swinging her legs as the shirt pulled up exposing the brown meaty thighs. The man closed the door. They exchanged greetings and they drove off. Peter stood there with his basket looking after them as they sped away towards the Nile Manson, one of the entertainment center for well to do people only. Prices of eats and drinks in the Nile Manson were much higher than those in the open markets. Peter noted the model of the Mercedes Benzes as 280 automatic plate number UXA 335 one of the latest arrival in the country. *Well, that is it. That is what it means. Wet hair, wet face and wet everything moves in such luxury. Can you dare talk to such a girl well knowing that you either walk it or use a taxi or even a commuter train to take you home? She will just laugh at you and call you a clown, a punk.* Peter thought as Andrews' Peugeot pulled up to take him and Beatrice home. That day their departmental vehicle was in the garage. The two men first drove Beatrice to her flat before they continued to Peter's home.

"I know that boy if that is the Benzes which picked her up." Andrew said after Peter had narrated to him all what happened before he came.

"He is one of the primary seven drop out" Andrew said.

"You don't mean it!" Peter exclaimed.

"What else can I say to make you believe me? I know that boy very well. He comes from Lira in Lango he is Omara Tom. He does not even have a primary six certificate. If you hear his English, you may think he is just a chauffeur of some millionaires but he is the millionaire himself. The vernacular accent is too much in his English, which he speaks without tenses, verbs, or subject." Andrew said as he swung his car along the gate to Peter's home and parked.

"Do not let Clare worry you Peter. If anything I am more directly connected to her than you. After your advice I am beginning to have a second thought about her also. It's good my relationship with her didn't affect Grace much. She knew that it would not hold that was why she was very confident and she never made trouble." Andrew said.

"I am glad you are beginning to see the fact of life." Peter said and walk in the gate as Andrew drove away.

With one hand in his trouser pocket, the other holding the palm leaves basket he used for carrying his books, Peter walked to the house with his head stooped down, Peter looked down on the ground meditatively as he walked in the house. He knocked on the door and Daniel opened for him and he walked in. He looked round the house to see how badly his house was furnished with some old fashion furniture from the Ministry of Works most of which had lost their cushion covers. The back rest of some of the chairs were badly torn so that the materials used for packing, loosely hang out. One of the settees had lost its legs, so stones were being used to prop it up instead of the wooden legs. The carpet which was once a beautiful oriental mat was then torn with so many charred sports on it. Peter sighed and tossed his basket on one of the dilapidating chairs and threw himself on another one wearily.

The new chairs, in the furniture shop in Kampala, were just too costly for him to think of one new set. Anything to do with money was farfetched from him as the sun is from the earth. With all these thoughts worrying Peter, Daniel put his dry coffee in front of him with some boiled cassava, in an old plastic plate. *I don't know what impression Rosemary has made out of my situation when she last visited. If it is, as Walter puts it then I have no hope of marrying her. But she was happy with me and she didn't show any sign of remorse.* Peter thought as he drank his evening coffee.

Rosemary had one time made what she called fact-finding visit to Peter residence in Kampala. Rosemary was a simple quiet girl but very adamant in decision making. She takes things easily the way they come. When Rosemary made her visit to Peter she was shocked to find what she found in the house of Peter. The most sensitive parts of a house for a house wife where her pride lies are the sitting room, and the kitchen which were miserably stocked. Rosemary sympathetically looked at the condition of the chairs and the carpet in the sitting room, the look of the cutleries in the kitchen, made her to decide that unless something could be done immediately, their planned marriage should be called off but she didn't disclose her resolution to Peter. Instead she assured him that they would marry as planned. Peter with that conviction was left with no doubt that Rosemary was the only girl in Uganda decent enough who did not ran after luxury as all other decent looking girl in Uganda today.

As Rosemary rode in the bus back to Gulu she seriously reconsidered marrying Peter the Permanent Secretary Ministry of Education. The thought of the hard spring mattress they slept on, and the pinches the metallic springs made on her ribs that she bore in the two nights she stayed with Peter, made her think of not going back to the same house again. She could not imagine being called the wife of a Permanent Secretary who serves visitors with dry tea or coffee in plastic cup without saucers and not evens a tray to carry them in. The chairs in the living room were not worth being in the house of a man of his status. She thought about all these and finally made up her mind that to be fair to herself she should leave him alone.

Chapter Twelve

Although Peter had been to Pakwach several times during his school days in Nyapea College, he knew very little about the small villages surrounding Pakwach. The thought of going there and failing to meet Simon at the Railway Station worried him. Andrew had sketched for him the directions to the home in case that happened. The desire to get money to rehabilitate him was much more than the fact that he might get stranded in Pakwach. *I am an old dying man. I do not think I need to worry about what is going to happen there. I will, with the help of the people there, find out Simon even if I do not meet him at the Railway Station* Peter thought as he boarded the train bound for Gulu on Sunday from Kampala main Railways Station.

The journey was boring and less interesting because this time he was travelling alone without Walter. Peter spent most of his time reading a magazine, **Africa Now**. He had bought it at the Railways Station in Kampala before he left for Gulu. One of the most interesting articles in the magazine which probably caused Peter to buy it was about the *"Economy of Uganda Today" was one of the articles in the table of content*. He wanted to get himself informed about the current fact expressed internationally about Uganda's economy. To Peter the fact expressed by the *Africa Magazine* 'snow special economic correspondent were all false. Shoeman, the author of the article praised the recovery program of Uganda and the financial stand of Uganda as promising. Peter could not see any single sense in it. *How, when prices of commodities are increasing every day. Roads, schools and hospitals, Government institutions are collapsing. Taxation of all kinds are climbing up; Civil Servants who have no access to Government facilities to aid their incomes are just unable to live on their salaries and* **this stupid white man** *tells us that the economy of the country is sound and promising? I hate to read such lies* Peter thought as he jolted and swayed from side to side in his compartment as the train rattled away to Gulu. The night rolled in. It was turning 8 p.m. When the train hooted and pulled at Jinja Railways Station four hours since it left Kampala. Peter had been browsing through the magazine occasionally his reading was seriously interrupted by the thought of how he was personally going to recover from his financial setback. *I have tried all the possible ways where many Ugandans have gained their success and are still succeeding but me the moment I get into the system it goes dead. What am I going to do? If I fail, this one with Simon then I will believe I have no good luck.* Peter thought as he walked out of the train to a café for a warm cup of coffee. The train left Jinja at 8.45 for Tororo. With no one to converse with, Peter slept most of the way. It was the banging of the coaches of the train chanting at Tororo Railways station at 1 a.m that woke Peter up from his sleep.

Where are we now? He mumbled and rolled down the window glass. He leered through the window and the number of people plus the many stagnant bogies and coaches told him that it was Tororo. The typical local music issuing from the kiosk at the station confirmed that he was in Tororo. The train from Gulu and that from Kampala normally cross at Tororo. And this depended entirely on how the two trains moved. Peter knew that there was going to be a long delay there so he walked and sat at the place where he once sat with Walter when they had gone to Gulu in search of the elephant tusks. The memory was a sickening one especially when he traced how he moved from Gulu with the tusks up to Kampala and then into Uganda House and how finally Omony swindled them and disappeared mysteriously. He felt like crying but no tears came except his stomach whizzed and chanted as if he was going to have diarrhea. He got up and walked to the kiosk, bought for himself another mug of coffee with a cake and sat on one of the lower steps of the kiosk and began to eat the cake. The train from Gulu reached Tororo very late at 5.a.m. 2 hours behind schedule. The passages disembarking at Tororo and those in transit who wanted some coffee at the kiosk jumped from the train and rushed to the window some with their mugs and flask while other rushed to secure the empty *Kimbo* or Cowboy mugs which were once used for packing cooking fats but now properly cut and shaped by the kiosk for serving the passengers. Almost immediately the bell rang indicating that the train bound for Gulu was leaving. The train hooted a warning and the passengers on transit climbed their coaches and they left.

Peter went in. It wasn't easy to fall asleep again he stayed awake until dawn. He kept thinking about Rosemary what future there is with her. *If I don't succeed it might as well be okay to stay alone like this. Bring her in will double my problems worse still if we get children. I will see what will come out of my visit to Parambo this time. I can't depend on friends to support me and my wife.* Peter thought. With the jolting and the swaying of the train Peter was lulled to sleep again.

The train got to Gulu at 6 p.m. the following day after the twenty four hour journey. It was raining cats and dogs when the train pulled at the station. Peter leered through the window and saw people darting out in the rain rushing for shelters on the verandah of the Station. Peter took his basket containing a bed sheet and a few sanitary items, the only luggage he had and skipped for a shelter at the Station. During their first visit to Gulu they had made very good friendship with the Gulu Station Master. When they got to Gulu, the desires to talk to Rosemary overwhelmed all other thoughts. Peter walked to the Station Master's Office and knocked on it.

"Come in". Peter heard a voice from within the office calling. Peter opened the door and slowly walked in.

"Hello Peter it's you again? It's nice to see you after a decade of months." The Station Master said and got up to shake hands with him.

"Nice to see you too, John." Peter said and grasped his fatty hand in his. He felt the smoothness of his fat fingers which contrasted sharply to his cold boney hard fingers.

"Sit down Sir."John said waving him to an office chair next to his desk. Peter sat down and put his basket down on the floor.

"How was Kampala?"

"it was alright." Peter replied curtly.

"Yeah we are also here fine with plenty of rain. Peasant farmers are complaining now that it's too much. It's spoiling their crops especially cotton. Secondly they do not have time to weed them." John informed Peter of the weather situation in Acholi as a whole.

"And yet we have very little rain in Kampala. It should be shinning here now." Peter remarked.

"Quite true, the seasons seemed to have changed a bit".

"I hope the 1961 story won't repeat itself when it rained from April 1961 to April 1962"

"I hope not."

"May I use your phone I want to telephone somebody in town?"

"Sure. Why not?" John said and pushed the telephone set to Peter.

Peter dialed the post office and asked to be connected to the house of the cousin of Rosemary the number she gave him for any call.

"Will you give me Gulu 205?" Peter said when he got through to the post office.

"Call you back." The man at the switch board answered.

Peter replaced the receiver on the cradle of the phone.

Presently the telephone buzzed and Peter lifted it with a thumb heart wishing he would get Rosemary herself on the line. But to his disappointment a lady voice came on the line.

"Lukwiya's house can I help you?"

"Good evening Madam." Peter said.

"Good evening sir can I help you?"

"Yes please. May I talk to Rosemary?"

"May I know who is speaking? She isn't in she's still on duty any message?"

"I am Peter. Tell her that I rung and I am on my way to Pakwach. I will call on her on my way to Kampala.

"Very well sir I will deliver the message."

"Fine." Peter said and hung up.

"Oh well she isn't in, still on duty." Peter said to the Station Master who was busy writing something in a book. He lifted up his head and said "Where does the person work?"John asked

"Wilobo Inn."

"Try 304Q." John suggested.

Peter contacted the post office again and asked for 304Q this time it took longer to come indicating that the line might have been engaged.

"Hello Wilobo inn. Can I help you?" Peter recognized the voice as that of Lilly the girl Walter slept with during their elephant tusks mission

"Hello Lilly how is the Inn".

"Who are you?

"Peter, you don't recall my voice."

"Oh no I almost thought you are the one. But I could bring myself to believe it."

"It's me."

"Where are you speaking from?"

"Gulu Railway Station."

"What are you doing there? Stranded, looking for accommodation, come on. Come up. There are plenty of rooms here."

"I know but how do I get there. Is it not rainy in town? Here it's pouring like a falls and there is no taxi to bring me up. The rain water is nearly washing the train off the rail." Peter joked.

"That's how we have been living for the last ten or so months."

"It's terrible."

"Yes it is."

'Is Rosemary around?"

"Sure yes she is right here."

"May I talk to her?"

"Sure why not."Lilly said and called for Rosemary who was reading a novel.

"Who is it"?

"Peter of course who else." Lilly said with excitement and Peter was hearing them talk.

"Tell him I am very busy."

"What do you mean Rosemary?' Lilly said. You can't refuse to talk to Peter can you? Lilly asserted staring at Rosemary."Reluctantly Rosemary got up and came on the line.

"Hello good evening." Rosemary spoke in a voice with no interest. Peter didn't know where to start after he had heard the two ladies arguments and the way Rosemary greeted him.

"Oh Rosemary it – it nice to hear your voice after so long honey."

"Some to me." Rosemary said nonchalantly. Peter felt the coldness in Rosemary voice like a knife through his heart.

"What is wrong Rosemary?"

"Many things are wrong."

"Such as?"

"I can't tell you now." Rosemary said emphatically.

"Oh dear, am I speaking to you Rosemary and I am Peter the Permanent Secretary you have betrothed to.

"I know you are the one and I am the one."

"And why are you talking to me like that?"

"That's how I talk sometime. You will excuse me sir I am a bit busy I can't talk to you longer than this."

"My goodness what is the change all about? What have I done Rosemary?"

"Nothing."

"Then why?"

"I will tell you later."

"When?"

"When we have the time."

"I am going to Pakwach now by the 8 a.m. train. I hope to spend a couple of days there. I am going to call on you on my way back and you tell me what is happening."

"Wish you a nice journey." Rosemary said and the line went dead.

"Rosemary." Peter called as she cradled down her receiver.

Peter sat with his receiver in his hand not believing the turn up of event. He stared fixatedly on the wall not even seeing anything but Rose his dead wife in his house, in the hotel, and elsewhere wherever they went together. Cold sweat slowly oozed from his skin in that cold night. Slowly with a trembling hand he replaced his receiver down.

The station master had walked out when Peter started to talk to Lilly and since then Peter was left alone in the office. The sweat beading on his fore head increase and coalesced into stream of sweat streaking down his face. Peter wiped off the sweat and with a hollow stomach he got up and thinking of walking out of the office. Immediately the Station Master walked in.

"You want to go? John asked Peter.

"Yes, I want to sit outside."

"Is it alright to sit outside? John asked studying the face of Peter which looked as someone who has just received the news that his wife was dead.

With a thick voice Peter replied," sure it is."

"Umm I see. It's cold outside and where are you spending the night?"

"It is not very cold and moreover I am bound for Pakwach by 8 p.m. train."Peter said controlling his emotion.

"Anything wrong sir?" The Station Master insisted when he saw the worrisome look on Peter's face.

"Nothing." Peter said forcing a weary smile which died out faster than it came. He bit his lips and swallowed his annoyance. *Why? What happened? Is this the same story of Clare and Andrew? I am sure Walter is damn right. It's very sad to take any of these girls of today seriously. Now look this one has jilted me. Why? I don't know if not because of my financial status. God I have wasted my love for nothing and now I am suffering the loss of her. Why did she consent and gave herself so much to me?* Peter thought.

The train bound for Pakwach arrived promptly and it pulled out at exactly 8:15p.m. The absence of the first class coach on Gulu Pakwach line compelled Peter to book in the economy class with all other persons. The train hooted and rolled out of Gulu Railway Station after all passengers bound for Pakwach line had boarded. The night was sleepless for Pete partly because of the noises and the congestion in the economic class. Peter thought about Rosemary. *Why? And what happened?* Were the two questions which Peter sullenly brooded over trying to find their answers? He couldn't find anything wrong he personally did or said to Rosemary. All he knew was lack of money. *I can't help it, if that is what love means these days. I have no money and I don't deserve the love of any girl. She could be right, say I fail to succeed in these entire struggle will she still marry me. How? And what will I do with her. I will hear what she will tell me when we meet.* Peter kept thinking as the train crossed the Pakwach Bridge over the Nile.

The train pulled to a stopped at Pakwach Railways Station at 12 noon and the passengers started to disembark from the train. Peter walked out and looked round for Ucamgiu. He wasn't there. Peter with his basket in one hand and the other hand in the pocket walked the whole length of the Railway Station searching for Ucamgiu. He reached the last end of the station Ucamgiu wasn't there. All other passengers looked happy and knew where he or she was going except Peter who was dispiritedly walking looking a stranger who needed a guide.

"*Come what may. I will find my way to Ucamgiu.* Peter swore as he pulled out the sketched map Andrew gave him. Kitwe Primary school on old Nebbi road leading to Ucamgiu home was not shown on the map Andrew sketched for Peter. *Could this be the road? There is no other old Nebbi road.* Peter whispered to himself after he had walked the whole length of Pakawach town. Andrew didn't detail the direction because he was certain his telegram would get to Ucamgiu before Peter got to Pakwach and therefore Ucamgiu would definitely meet Peter at the station as planned. The only distance he indicated was that from Kitwe Primary School to Panyigoro which was only six miles to Ucamgiu home. Peter looked at his watch it was ten past one o'clock. *Well I think I can make it.* Although Peter was a senior Government Officer he used to go walking with Rose and at times they went jogging. Beside, since the breakdown of all their departmental vehicles Peter walked most of the time to the department. He wasn't scared of the six miles walk indicated on the sketch. Although Peter knew Pakwach fairly well because he used to pass there when he was going to his school in Nyapea he did not know the old Nebbi Road. Peter eventually walked away carrying his basket containing his bed sheets and half bottle of Lira Lira gin. As he walked, he met an old man walking on a stick. *Perhaps I should find out from this old man where Old Nebi road is.* Peter thought.

"Good afternoon Mzee." Peter greeted the old man.

"Good afternoon my son." The old man politely replied leaning on his walking stick.

"I am looking for Old Nebbi road." Peter inquired

"Hi my son you are new to Pakwach? The old man wondered. "Nebbi road is that dust road opposite the Catholic Church in front at the end of this small village town." The old man replied not bother for the answer for the question he asked Peter.

Peter thanked the old man and was soon out of town. At quart to 2:00 p.m.Peter got to Pajubi Primary School about four miles from Pakwach town. According to the sketched map that Andrew gave him, he thought the Kitwe Primary, which is supposed to be near the home of Ucamgiu must be only one to two miles away. He walked and walked the sun sank and sank but there was no Kitwe Primary School in site. The thought about Rosemary jilting him made him angry and he walked fast to reach Ucamgiu and collect his gold to go and show her probably that would make her smile. The bright hot sun was cooling down at 4:00 p.m. without any school in sight leave alone Kitwe Primary. *Have I missed the road? But there is no other road beside this.* Peter thought and was again forced to ask another old man he met riding on a old bicycle which was squeaking each time the old man peddled, to ascertain if he was not off track.

"Good afternoon Mzee" Peter said.

"Good afternoon."The old man said and stopped. Peter crossed to shake hand with him as customary courtesy. The old man extended his hand and shook with him.

"How are you the old man asked him?"

"I am fine thank you. How far is Kitwe Primary school from here? Peter asked

"The old man quizzically looked at him and asked. "You are going there?"

"Yes I am." Peter answer

"It is not far. But it could be between three and four miles away."

"What! Peter exclaimed and sighed.

"I guess so because from here to Paroketo Primary school is about a mile and from Paroketo Primary school to Kitwe is about two or three miles."

"My God, I don't know if I will make it Peter said despondently."

"You are new to this place?"

"Yes."

"You are visiting someone there?"

"Ucamgiu Simon a friend of mine leaves near that place. Okay Mzee, thank you I must trudge on. Peter said and did not want to spend more time talking to the old man since he was kind enough to let him know that he still had more walking to make.

The road to Panyigoro was very sandy and difficult to walk on because the faster you walk the more you slide back. After a long weary walk Peter got to Paroketo Primary school and short walk later brought him to Kitwe Primary school. He was happy that after one mile he would be resting his feet at Ucamgiu's home. According to the description of Andrew the home should be very near the road with a big mango tree in the compound.

Peter got home at 7.p.m.Ucamgiu had just returned from the gold mine. He was over excited when he saw Peter.

"I was not expecting you anywhere here."Ucamgiu said as he shook hands andhugged Peter.

"Come in and sit down."Ucamgiu said and took away his basket from him.

"You are welcome sir."Ucamgiu said.

"Thank you very much."

"I went to check on you at Pakwach for three consecutive days but didn't get you and I thought you were busy to come so I gave it up."

"You haven't got our telegram?" Peter asked.

"No, you sent me one?"

"Yes. Andrew sent you one before I left Kampala to tell you that you come for me today."

"No I haven't seen any mail from Andrew. Break down of services in the country that is all. There is no one in the whole country who is devoted to his work.

"How is it here" Peter asked.

"Lots of rain."

"Yeah I have been seeing it along the way." There was a paused between them and Ucamgiu said, "You know when I didn't get you at the station for three days I decided to sell away what I was keeping for you to a buyer who came from Kampala. You know with this gold we do not hold on it for a long time. We mine and sell it immediately most of the time at the mine."

"Oh dear you did." Peter said desperately.

"Yes."

"That means presently there is nothing with you?"

"No. But don't worry we will get something from my friends in Parombo. We shall drive there in the morning and talk to them." Ucamgiu said reassuringly.

"If that is the case then it's alright." Peter said doubtingly.

Parombo, a small town about six miles from Uganda-Zaire boarder, was the center for all sorts of trade in all commodities smuggled in and out of the two countries. Gold took the lead. The prominent dealer in this trade had formed what they termed *Gold Association of Parombo* and set up their spy ring within the trading center to watch and report to them suspicious strangers in the town who may be looking for gold. If confirmed, the skin-head boys, recruited for surveillance by these men, were set on their heels. They always track their victims until they are either left dead or half dead with all the money robbed. Ucamgiu was not known by the Gold Association of Parombo he wasn't a member. But Aromborac his cousin brother was General Secretary of the Gold Association of

Parombo, one of the high ranking members of the Gold association of Parombo. It was Aromborac who introduced Ucamgiu in the gold trade. When Ucamgiu applied to join membership, of Parombo gold association his application was rejected on the ground that he was a Panyagrarian and could not be a member and he wasn't allowed to trade in Parombo. Secondly the fee of one million shilling to join the Association was too much for Ucamgiu at the time of application. This money was a monthly contribution. The Parombo Gold Association used it for purchasing gold from Zaire and for transport to Kampala, and occasionally to Dubai. Part of the money was for paying the skin-head boys and to buy up their ways in case they got in the hand of the law of any of the two States and finally their spies.

Ucamgiu knew about the Parombo gold association. When he got to Parombo they were approached by the spies of the Association because his Land Cruiser had a registration number foreign to Parombo Millionaire. Ucamgiu knew what they were up to. They came and walked round the Land Cruiser looked at him and Peter and walked away. When the spy boys left Ucamgiu advised Peter that they sit and wait in the Parombo Paradise bar to see what was coming up. Paradise bar was the meeting joint for the members of Gold the Association of Parombo but anyone was allowed to drink in it.

When Ucamgiu and Peter walked out of the Land Cruiser and were in the Paradise bar, two Lorries came and parked one in front of Ucamgiu Land Cruiser and the other behind so that it was not going to be possible for Ucamgiu to take out his Land Cruiser. The Proprietor of the Paradise bar was the President General of Parombo Gold Association, Kertho. Tall slim man, Kertho was avaricious and ruthless. He alone has the right to admit in new application of the membership of the Association because he was the pioneer of the trade and he started the Association himself. Unaware of what was taking place outside the bar after their two bottles of Skol Lager, a Zairian beer, Peter and Ucamgiu rose to go but only to see their Land Cruiser sandwiched bumper to bumper between two Tata Lorries. Ucamgiu knew at once that there was something in the air. He looked at Peter who was beginning to complain why the two lorry drivers park so provocatively like that. Ucamgiu took Peter by the hand and walked away after he had locked the Land Cruiser and rolled the window glass up. The boys who circulated around them before they went to the bar again came back and started strolling behind them. Peter with the beer tickling, him, wanted to find out who parked those Lorries.

"Don't make a fuss about that," Ucamgiu said calmly.

"Why should they do that?"

"I will tell you." Ucamgiu said as the boys close up on them.

"We have to report to the police."

"They won't help you Peter."

"What the hell are you talking about? Someone parked blocking me like this and the police can't do anything about it? What traffic law do you have here? Peter seethed. One of the boys tailing them was at the ear shot he come nearer as if he didn't know what was happening. He listened to Peter complaining and swearing that he would let the police know about it. He quietly walked away and told his friends what Peter said. They all laughed and said, "let him try his luck he's really a stranger to this town he doesn't know we are the police men of this town. All these police stations are there for the Government not for President General of Parombo Gold Association Kertho. We have our own autonomous government here. "Government within a Government." The boys said. Ucamgiu was more attentive to the talk of the boys than to what Peter was uttering.

After a long wait without the drivers of the two Lorries in sight, Ucamgiu decided to contact his cousin Aromborac for assistance. Aromborac, as one of the many Milliners of Parombo escaped illiteracy by having seven years of Primary seductions but which he could pass seven times. He was one of the pioneers in gold smuggling from Parombo with Kertho. Kertho introduced him in it being his nephew. The two were great friends and whatever one said the other obeyed immediately.

Ucamgiu told Peter that they should walk to Aromborac hotel situated about a quarter of a mile off the town. Peter reluctantly agreed to walk to Aromborac place in his hotel office. When they got to the hotel they found Aromborac with one of his staff, a young man, a graduate who had just completed his Bachelor of Commerce degree from Makerere University, two other boys with elementary accountancy and bookkeeping from Uganda College of Commerce in a meeting and the stenographer also from Uganda Commerce was busy on the typewriter. The accountant was explaining something to Aromborac who did not seem to appreciate the explanation. Ucamgiu and Peter stealthily sat on chairs for visitors and waited for them to finish with their discussion. When Aromborac finish with meeting he lifted up his head and saw his cousin Ucamgiu.

Hi Ucamgiu that is you? Nice to see you." Aromborac said with excitement got up from his chair and came to meet them. He shook hand with them and sat down looking suspiciously at Peter. Ucamgiu noticed the uneasy glances Aromborac was making at Peter and said, "Peter meet my Uncle Aromborac. He is the owner of this hotel." Peter nodded his head and said hello and kept quiet. Ucamgiu later turned to Aromborac and said this is Peter a great friend of Andrew."

Peter was not happy about what happened in town so that after that brief introduction he sat quietly without any interest in what Ucamgiu and Aromborac were talking although it was concerning their Land Cruiser in town.

"I did not know it was you. We had to embarrass the owner of the car so as to know who he is or they are." Aromborac said.

Peter absent minded turned to look at Aromborac and asked, "You are talking about what happened in town?"

"Yes" Ucamgiu said.

"Why was that done anyway?" Peter asked exasperated.

"You have just heard what I said that we did it to make us know the owner of the car. We received a report that a strange Land Cruiser with two occupants was in town and that the owners were drinking in Paradise bar. Their motive here is not known. So to make you talk to us we blocked your ways with the two Lorries."

"Was there no other polite way of making us talk to you?" Peter asked again.

"I didn't do it but I ordered for it to be done." Aromborac said proudly with a smile exposing his golden canine tooth. Peter sighed and looked at Ucamgiu. Aromborac smiled again and looked at the upset face of Peter. He knew he was annoyed at the information.

"What if we take you to the police for that matter?" Peter continued to attack Aromborac

"You think there is any police man in this town for us beside the secret police we have here. Those you see in uniform who carry numbers on their chest like motor cars have nothing to do with us. They can't raise a finger at me." Aromborac warned.

"Why did you not explain this to him when you came in?" Aromborac asked and turned to Ucamgiu and continued. "This town is small and unique in its own way. I am explaining this to you because my nephew is here with you." He said and touched the back of the hand of Ucamgiu who sat closer to him. "And I want you to get it right. You could report this anywhere but you will never get at me in steady I will get you and you may never.....Aromborac said and let his words float. "I am not threatening but try and you will regret it." Aromborac warned Peter. The real facts that the wealthy men and women in Uganda today commit any crime and buy themselves out of it, wasn't new to Peter. He knew Aromborac was talking with lots of experience which if he overlooked he could be in trouble.

"So as I was telling you Aromborac said cleared his throat and went on, Parombo is a unique town in Uganda. We have two sets of governments here; the first is for all Ugandans; the second government for this place is, The Gold Association of Parombo. Similarly we have two types of securities, these are men and women looking after our interest namely the skinheads and they are the most powerful and they are everywhere more than the police you are talking about. Their bosses are in the two types of governments systems. So what do you think a constable in Uganda police can do if I roar? We shut their mouths occasionally with some bundle of notes and that is that. You open a case against any of us we walk in and put the bundle in front of court Clerk and the file will never be seen again not even a record for it. You see the power of second government we have here of very brainy men. They have made sure they got all of the leading men in the first government so that all below them take our commands without question. The Magistrate, the police commanders, the prison and the army commanders just to mention but a few are with us so you see making a noise against us is suicidal. The whole town will laugh at you. So when you come to Parombo know this brief hard fact I have explained to you, watch the ground you are stepping before you sink. Aromborac explained to Peter.

"Why do you have to treat strangers like that?" Peter again put in

"Not because they are strangers, but because news has gone through out Uganda that Parombo has heaps of gold and that is not a joke. The place has it." Aromborac said and pulled out a box full gold and showed it to Peter. We are people without job, without formal education, to enable us to get jobs in town like you people. And above all we are lazy to dig so our only source of money is this precious metal. We want to confined this to ourselves and strangers from outside shouldn't taste it s' sweetness. It is sweeter than honey. Those whom we brought in the system from outside are all members whom we think give us vital protection from the central government as I have already explained to you. Without that, no one was going to come in our circle because, first of all the monthly contribution to run the second government is too much for anyone to think of joining us. One million shilling per month can you afford it?"Aromborac asked Peter.

Peter disdainfully looked at Aromborac and cursed himself why he was born in this world, a man with hardly any education talk so proudly to him because he has the money?"He nearly refused to answer his question but when Aromborac repeated the question,

"Can you afford that monthly contribution?"

"No sir," Peter said sarcastically and looked out of the window.

"Well there you are. So we want to monopolies this market here. No one will take a grain of gold from here without being spotted by us. We are few in this town we know each other. Any stranger in this town is picked up easily like a magnet pick up an iron filling in sand. Our boys have been allocated areas to work at and they know all the sand there. Any new face is always communicated to me or to the boss Kertho. Your case this morning got to my office first and I communicated it to the boss. If you were on foot we were going to set our boys after you until they netted you. But as they reported that you had a Land Cruiser parked outside the bar, we said fine, block their escape two. Lorries should be sent to do the job. One lorry from Parombo highway and the other from Pajok road and your Land Cruiser was completely sandwiched no clever driver could ever maneuver that Land Cruiser out. We at the same time reported to the police the Magistrate and to the all concern that we have netted big fish. So you can see for yourself, if you went to the Police you were going to be entertained with lots of statement writing until late in the night when we would call the drivers of the two Lorries. The police would complain to the driver that it was a bad traffic offence meanwhile they are behind everything. And at night you might book a room with me here or decide to go to other Parombo bar and there are our boys and girls at you service. You could be looted dry and we don't follow up such cases because the notices at the back of the receipt say so. *While attempt could be made to assist, the management of the hotel is not held responsible for any loss or damage of the visitor's property.* Our girls are smart at that. They can pick your wallet when you are seeing but you won't know they are the ones who picked it. I do not have much to add to you I do not know whether you have been here before but from your look you are a true stranger in this town". Aromborac concluded and looked at Peter who sat quietly in front of his desk.

"Can you release our Land Cruiser then?" Peter asked.

"We will, but the authority must come from the boss Kertho. He is the only one who has the right to bind and unbind any problem."

"I am sorry Aromborac that I didn't explain this to Peter. I thought we were going to reach you before we met such incidence." Ucamgiu apologized.

Chapter Thirteen

"Um" Aromborac suckled. You must be joking. Our boys are lined up from the sign post, *'welcome to Parombo town'* in all directions up to this town center. You just can't enter the town without being noticed. We want, and I think, we have succeeded to monopolies this gold trade here. Those which get out through Nebbi, Goli and other places are not our problem. We are mainly concerned with this place, Parombo." Aromborac said emphatically.

"Now that you controlled everything I wonder if Peter could purchase the same. He wants to try his luck with it. He is great friend of Andrew as I have already told you.

"Which Andrew is this you are mentioning from time to time?"

"Andrew Obwona."

"You mean the son of Marcelino."

"That's him."

"I know him quiet well, he works with Transocean doesn't he?"

"Yes an accountant."

"Chief accountant Peter corrected." getting enliven

"Is he?" Aromborac asked.

"Yes". Peter replied.

"Why don't I employ him here other than him wasting time in Kampala getting that merger salary from the company?"

Peter sneer at the boastful comment from Aromborac. *I wish Andrew was here I don't know what he would have said to this man.*

They, the educated have become the house boys and house girls of the illiterate simply because they have the money? Andrew had vowed that he would rather die poor than to insult his Masters 'Degree in Accountancy and go to work for those types of boys. Peter thought.

"I will mention that to Andrew that you like to employ him when I get to Kampala." Peter said sarcastically.

"Please I will be very happy to receive him here. Tell him I will double his salary. I am sure he will like it home here. We could even sink him in the system and he will find how sweet it is to be at home with such big money." Aromborac continued to brag.

"Thank you Uncle for the detail explanation of you set up here in Parombo, and the precautionary measures required when in Parombo. We appreciate the explanation. However, I would like to put my request before you Uncle for assistance......."

"What is this?" Aromborac interrupted him.

"I was down in Kampala only about a month ago where I met Peter in the company of Andrew who introduced him to me and his other friend...." Ucamgiu paused

"Walter." Peter completed it for Ucamgiu who was forgetting the name of Walter.

"Peter has been rather unfortunate in the past. He lost his father, properties and his wife almost at the same time. Andrew and his friend Walter have all along been assisting Peter financially. And you know with the present situation in the country Civil Servants work just for feedings. Their salaries are not enough to carry them through the month. As a result, it has been impossible for Peter to replace any of his property stolen. After our discussions, I was sympathetic to his condition and offered to help by loaning him some money to start this trade. Before I left for Kampala I had about seven *tolla* in the house which, I was sure of letting him have it. But when I came back I was force to sell it away because there was some delay on their part. He has just come. Our local miners in Panyagoro have not collected a lot because of the rain. I thought maybe you could be having something which we could buy to let him go back with that is why we are here."Ucamgiu explained.

"Aromborac sneered, and said I guessed you understood what I was telling you earlier on. I said our policy is monopoly over gold in Parombo, no grain of gold from here shall be sold to anyone outside the association. To tell you the truth we have them, I have some, I have it right here." He said and pulled out the box of gold out again but this is an oath taken by all the members that no gold from Parombo under any circumstance and condition be sold by member to anyone outside the government of Parombo Gold Association. We buy every gold in the market we send our sale men out to sell them when they come back we sit and share the profit accordingly and the capital is used to purchase more gold. That is how we are living. Every amount of gold in my custody is known and they could want to check on me anytime so you see I can't help you, though I would have gladly sold you as much as your money could buy."

"What if you get for us one of your boys who buy the gold for you and we buy the gold before it is put in your stock." Ucamgiu asked.

"I can't. Because; firstly, I will be breaking the oath I have already explained. Secondly, the boys we send everywhere do not look for the strangers only, they also make general report how many kilo of gold crossed the border into Parombo and at the end of the day the amount of gold in stock is checked. And this could be dangerous to me. If I lose my joint, it means I do not get any gold from here and powerful as they are, they may even lose me. The boys are working very hard in all ways they even counter check themselves that is why they earn their ten thousand shilling per month. The gold salaries make them work very honestly. You can't bribe any of them.

"Is there no way you can help us now?"

"From here yes." But I could direct you to a friend in Nebbi who could help you. I am sure he will have something for you to buy.

"May be you could release our car and we try him."

"I will but first I must talk to the boss about it."

Aromborac lifted the receiver of the phone put it on the ear and dialed a number and waited.

"Hello good afternoon Kertho here. Yes, I wanted to talk to you about the development of the netted men how is it going on?" A voce came loud on the phone and continued, "Why have you not yet brought them to me?"

"That's why I am ringing you. They.........................

"You mean they escaped." Kertho fumed.

"Hold your top on Sir. The men came to me by themselves they are right here in front of me."

"Very well, very well, that's fine. How did they know you?"

"Its' my cousin Ucamgiu from Panyagoro he had just come to say hello to me and he was on his way to Nebbi with his friend."

"Well the duty of the boys is to screen any suspicious element in this town. Your relatives or mine if they come to Parombo must be screen all the same." Kertho said.

"I am not denying that and I am not accusing the boys from reporting them to us after all that is what they are being paid and secondly how would they have known they are my relatives, there are no special engravers on their forehead to show that."

"What next then with them."

"I told you they are going to Nebbi and they want to go."

"Please bring them to my house first before they go. They can take a short cut to Nebbi through Pagwata and to Padel and to Nebbi."

"If it's your choice I will bring them." Aromborac said and hung up the line.

"He sighed and sat with his elbows on the table his palms paired together. And said, "The boss wants us at his place before you go."

"Why? what for? Peter interjected.

"I don't know but I think it's just a matter of proof. He wants to prove that you are the one and still with me."

"He doesn't trust you?" Peter asked

"Administrative order of the Association. No arrested person should be released secretly. All released must be witnessed by at least two members of the Association preferably the Chief, Kertho ought to be included." Aromborac said and pressed a button on his desk. Immediately two men in overalls come in quietly and stood in front of Aromborac as straight as candle sticks with their arm folded on their chest they listened to the command to be given.

"Go and remove the Lorries and I do not want any fly to touch that car before I get there. "You hear me."

"Yes sir." The men answer in chorus.

"Okay get moving." Aromborac order and the men showed them their backs.

"We shall go in my Land Rover to town; you pick yours, and drive following me to see the boss.

The drive to Pagwata the home of Kertho was a tedious one because of the bad road worsened by the rain which had just poured. It made the sandy road very slippery. In spite of their four wheel drive vehicles, skidded and nearly got stuck where the slur of the sand was thick. After about thirty minutes, they got to the home of

Kertho. The homestead of Kertho was on the hills of Pagwata and it looked like a concentration camp. There were about one hundred grass thatched huts scattered everywhere in the compound on the hill. These were the porters' residence. The headmen had small rectangular brick wall hut with corrugated iron sheets roof built for them planted among the grass thatched huts. Two big houses built in a "T" shape stood side by side some distance away from the ring of the huts and these were the residence of Kertho. The chauffer of Aromborac who was leading the way in the Land Cruiser 120Y came and parked in a parking slot mark Secretary General. All parking slot were labeled.

Ucamgiu did not know where to put his Land Cruiser420Z.

He looked round and decided to park anywhere in the compound away from the labeled slots.

"Well if I am not guided what do I do?" Ucamgiu said with disgust and walked out of the car slam his door as Peter got out sneering.

"The world is really very unfair. I don't know why we should be held at ransomed like this, just to please some punks." Ucamgiu said annoyed. Peter did not reply to his comment but walked quietly as they near the big house where Aromborac had entered. Inwardly Peter thought, *but you are both the same.* Peter and Ucamgiu came and stopped at the door waiting to be invited in. At last a young lady walked out and invited them in. They entered and were waved to sit down on a sofa set.

Money is power. Peter thought as he sank deeper and deeper in the chair. A slim tall man, wearing a dark Chinese suit, a pair of golden framed spectacles on his face with a turban on the head and smoking a pipe held between his lips walked in and sat on a swinging chair with high back rest, upon which was a leopard skin. Two young ladies came and sat on the floor near him. The man greeted Ucamgiu and Peter, nonchalantly and turned to talking to the ladies at his feet with the pipe held between his lips. Big wardrobe with dressing mirror in front of it stood in front of him in the sitting room. Another low dressing table stood near the wardrobe. Peter survey the house and concluded that it was the type of furnishing you got from a man who does not know the use of what he buy sand where to put them in a house. He just buys because there is still space in the house. The sitting room was large enough to be used for disco. There were four huge sets of sofa sets lined up against the walls. Thick heavy decorated carpets covered the floor completely. A book shelf without books stood at the corner of the house near the door. There were four wall clocks one on each walls so that wherever you sat there was a clock ticking in front of you. Below each clock there sat a colour television and next to the television nearer the main entrance to the house there was a disco deck with huge loudspeakers which stool like shields, beside the deck. There were radios Panasonic make in all corners of the walls in the sitting room. His photographs, half naked in pants, hang everywhere on the walls. Skins and horns of animals which would have been used properly in the hands of a man who knows their use, strewn the wall so that one got the impression of a museum. Peter shook his head thinking *it's dangerous to be rich with no education. Look at this man putting wardrobe and dressings mirror in the sitting room all these televisions and radios what for.*

When Kertho finish smoking, he gave the pipe to one of the ladies who went out and emptied the ashes while the other lady remaining in, refilled another empty pipe on the table with the sweet mart tobacco on the table.

"Are these the men? Kertho asked Aromborac who was sitting next to him.

"Yes they are."

"Give them drink he said to one of the ladies." I know they drink because they were found in our bar."

"Aromborac laughed but Peter and Ucamgiu only sneer. The beer Skol Lugar was brought and they drank. Peter nudged Ucamgiu on the ribs with his elbow and indicated with node of his head that they should leave. Ucamgiu realized it and return the node. When their beer was finished Ucamgiu excused themselves that they wanted to go.

"You can't go away now there is still some more drink and he has not talked to you. Aromborac said.

"But we must get to Nebbi." Peter protested.

"It's now late you can't go anywhere not that you will not reach but because you will not get that man in. He is out in the evening most of the time. Therefore, I advise you to go tomorrow in the morning." Aromborac said.

Peter did not know what to do. The whole day wasted for nothing. He was tensed with anger. He rolled the back of his head on the chair from side to side. He fell like walking out of the house.

With no respect for the three men in the living room Kertho continued to romance with the ladies waiting on him. However, after he noticed impatience look on the faces of Peter and Ucamgiu, Kertho suddenly said.

"So you are Ucamgiu the cousin of Aromborac.

"Yes I am," Ucamgiu said stiffening to attention.

"You don't need to fear anymore. He told me all about why you came here. That, your friend Peter, is in need of what we are trying to control for ourselves here. I am sorry you can't get it from here. No one except the members only can. I would advise you in the same manner you go to Nebbi that man he has introduced to you will help you. We do not have any controlled over that place and we do not intend to do so. We have some interest there alright but not the gold market. Ours is here in Parombo. You had to be screen this morning because any stranger in this town is properly studied. We do not and will never apologies to anyone who has been inconvenienced or embarrassed through this kind of act. We have taken percussion not to embarrass the government officials who come here on duty so long as they do not come to interfere with our trade, we will have sympathy for such fellows. We do not hide any fact we tell the truth about us. The government knows about us but what can they do? Any proof that we have gold? Will any local security man sling a speck of dust in our eyes? If he does, then he has run his head against a brick wall. If he breaks his neck, then it his fault." Kertho said and turned to one of the lady at his feet.

"Give them some more drink, these are our guest tonight." Kertho ordered. The woman got up, walked out and again come with two bottle of Skol Lager in a tray. She removed the empties from their tables and replaced with the full bottles in front of Ucamgiu and Peter. Peter wasn't happy at the imprisonment imposed on them. He definitely wanted to leave that house as soon as possible. The drinks which were being served to them was a delay tactic so that they could do any harm on them at night. Peter nudged Ucamgiu again. Ucamgiu threw his ears to him. "Why can't we spend the night somewhere else do you think it's safe for us to sleep here?" Peter asked.

"I don't know I will ask Aromborac." After their talk Aromborac advised them to stay on because Kertho is a very dangerous character.

"He has never ever hurt anyone at his home. And secondly here is one hundred percent safe but if you try to defy his order, or request, he will let you go, but do not be surprised to find yourself in hospital tomorrow, that is if you survive the accident. He has ways of operations. I think you spend the night here and tomorrow at 8.a.m. you will go and meet Watmon in Nebbi. I am sure if you get him, you will get all you need. You won't have enough money to buy his stock.

"How are we going to be sure he won't dispatch his men after us tomorrow?"

"There is no reason why he should. Whenever Kertho treats you well in his house it is very unlikely he will hurt you immediately but when you fall out with him in future then you become a target.

It was at 11:45a.m when Peter and Ucamgiu got to Nebbi after a difficult drive through the muddy steep road. They drove straight to Tourist Inn where Watmon was supposed to be.

Ucamgiu parked the car in the parking lot and they both walked to the reception desk where a dark plumb girl sat behind the counter. She was knitting the table cloth when the men arrived.

"Hello good morning." She said and gave them a smile which would make any soft hearted man sympathizer with her creation. She made Peter turn his face away in protest. It was like a bitch snarling at a dog on heat.

"Hello good morning." Ucamgiu said resting his fore arms on the counter

"Is-what do you call him? Ucamgiu tried to recall the name .... Watmon booked in your here?"

"No he works here but never sleeps here." The girl replied

"Where is his home do you know?"

"It is just across the road, behind that shop." She said pointing to a shop mark

Nebbi whole sale and retail shop Box 1 Nebbi. "But I don't think he is in. He was off duty yesterday and he was talking of going to

Zaire. He might have gone. His wife should be at home." The girl advised

Ucamgiu and Peter shook their heads in disgust and walked across the road with no hope of meeting Watmon. As they expected, the wife of Watmon told them that her husband went to Zaire but she was expecting him back that afternoon. The two disgruntled men walked back to the car with their head too heavy to be lifted up. Peter went and stopped near the car, folded his arms on top of the bonnet of the car, and rested his face on his arm not interested in anything anymore.

I am sunk there is no way for me bye – bye Rosemary I have no money to feed you and dress you. All my attempts are in vain. Peter thought and he fell like weeping.

"What next?" Peter said to Ucamgiu who had entered the Land Cruiser and sat with his head resting on steering wheel.

Ucamgiu stirred clumsily and clasped his hand on top of his head and said

"I think we have to wait for him meanwhile we look around in this place. I have some friends here who might give us the lead."

"Where do you normally get yours from?"

"The man who brings them for me has gone back to Zaire for more I hope he is coming back next week. It takes a complete one week or two to make such journeys. But I think we should give Watmon a chance." Ucamgiu said disappointingly.

"If you decide we wait for him then let's wait." Peter remarked worriedly.

"We should, if he is on duty tomorrow, then he should at least return tonight for duty. Ucamgiu explained and continued to urge Peter to go to Goli. "Come in and we go to Goli to see a friend there. If we get him, I am sure he should be able to advise us."Ucamgiu suggested desperately looking embarrassed from what he said to Andrew and Peter in Kampala. Goli is another boarder town between Uganda and Zaire. The town is more popular for food and fabrics commodities from Uganda and Zaire respectively than for Gold.

Peter and Ucamgiu got to Goli and they found his friend in. He was very busy with the customers buying from his shop. He welcomed them and sat them near him on a flat form for customers. After some trivial talks, Ucamgiu enquired about the gold from his friend.

"I wish you came an hour ago." There was a man who was selling it here very cheaply. He must have gone back to Zaire. Let's see if we can locate him." Peter was no longer interested in anything like gold he sat in the Land Cruiser waiting for Ucamgiu and his friend. After about thirty minutes Ucamgiu and the friend came back, Ucamgiu looking more desperate than before.

"What happened?" Peter asked smiling at Ucamgiu

"We got him but he has just sold it. I just can't explain it now."

"It looks a wild goose chase we are in." Peter said laughing unbelievingly.

"May be but I think there is room still to try. My friend says there is a teacher in that school who deals in the same. He is coming to take us to the place. Ucamgiu said

"Try your lucks for me; I have lost the world and everything in it. I have no hope now to succeed in anything. Peter said despondently.

"Do not give up the struggle. Carry on until the end of your life."

"What is the use to struggle without a twinkle of success like this? Frustration after frustration. No. Never, not with me anymore." Peter said and threw his head backward on the seat of the Land Cruiser.

Ucamgiu climbed in and they drove off to the school. They got to the school and went to the school headmaster to enquire about the teacher.

"I am sorry we haven't seen this man in the school for the last one week. Ucamgiu was tempted to introduce Peter as Permanent Secretary to Ministry of Education but he refrained from it since he was then, on smuggling job not education.

"He doesn't teach these days?" Peter asked forgetting that he is also out of office in Kampala.

"The headmaster suckled and look round at them first as if to detect who he was talking too. "He works except that he is a man with a large family and he has to move round to get something to assist the salary we primary teacher gets. I won't like to call it a salary. Because women selling in the markets have better income than we primary teachers. We have similar problems but his is more." The Headmaster said defensively.

"Oh well I think that is understandable." Peter said with a shrug.

"Let's go back." Peter added. "We are burning the fuel running around for nothing. Why don't we go back to Nebbi and I go away tomorrow? I am wasting time here. Let me go back to Kampala and face the truth of life." Peter said dejectedly. Ucamgiu understood the message conveyed by Peter. He fell he must do something to make Peter come out with. *Why? Everywhere we went, sold, not there.* Ucamgiu thought as they drove in silence back to Nebbi. They went and check on Watmon if he had returned from Zaire. They found him at home. "Yes my wife told me that you were here and that you have left."

"We left and went to Goli." Ucamgiu said and introduce the topic to him that they were sent to him by his uncle Aromborac to help them buy the gold.

"Oh dear you are unfortunate. I wish you told my wife why you were looking for me. I would have certainly kept what I came with this afternoon. Aromborac is my great friend. I will be going back to Zaire again at the week end. I left my supplier mining." Watmon explained. Peter was not interested in anything other than to travel back to Kampala. After Nebbi they went to spend the night at Ucamgiu home in Panyagoro.

In the morning, after their breakfast of fried fish filets with milk tea, buttered bread, orange juice in the glass jar, eggs omelet, pot of honey, and sugar bowel completed the layup of the breakfast table Ucamgiu offered for Peter. The plates, forks, table knives at table were all marked *Smith Company Limited, United Kingdom*. Peter looked at the setup which reminded him of his lost wife and their properties. The set up of Ucamgiu house was a great contrast to that of Kertho. He was more civilized.

"It's time I should leave." Peter said to Ucamgiu after their breakfast.

"I am sorry Peter for all these. I apologize………"

"No need to apologize. You have tried, and done your best, but we were unfortunate. Because of this, I am handing back to your money you loaned me?" Peter said and was beginning to pull the bundle of money from underneath of his basket which stood near him.

"No-No-No Peter." Ucamgiu said and reached out for his arms holding them down in the basket. "Please," he said, "although I used the word loan when I was handing the money to you, I have actually given the money to you." Ucamgiu said while holding the arm of Peter down in the basket. Ucamgiu let his arms go when Peter slowly started to let go the bundle. Peter sat up and stared at Ucamgiu unbelievingly.

"I have no words to express my gratitude except to say thank you and may God continue to bless you."

"Thank you Peter for the kind words." Ucamgiu acknowledged

It was 10 am when Ucamgiu drove Peter to the Railways Station at Pakwach. Before they got to the station, Peter asked Ucamgiu to stop over at a local distillery which distilled the local gin for consumption of the local people. Peter had seen the distillery on his way to Ucamgiu. Peter bought two bottles of a liter each of the gin. After that they continued to the Railways Station. After buying his ticket for Kampala via Gulu the two men came and sat on one of the Platform for Passengers waiting for the train from Gulu to come and make a return Journey back to Gulu and Kampala. In a few moments the train rolled in and turned in the rails for Gulu. Ucamgiu escorted Peter to the train. Before he boarded, Peter hug Ucamgiu and said "It is not your fault. You did your best but things didn't work out. Thank a lot for all you have done. Let's not divert the will of God forcibly." He shook the hand of Ucamgiu and departed in tears.

The train rolled off for Gulu at 2.p.m. along the way Peter thought of his worthlessness. His wife Rose left him without a child what does this mean a blessing or a curse? Who will ever think of him when he dies? With these thoughts in mind Peter made up his mind to approach Rosemary in Gulu before he proceeded to Kampala. The train delayed in the several sub stations between Pakwach and Gulu Picking passages and loading and offloading cargoes and got to Gulu 6.pm. The train to Kampala was scheduled to depart at 8p.m. therefore Peter had two hours of waiting in Gulu railways station. *Why not, let me call on Rosemary at Wilobo inn and talk to her face to face and let her tell me what are in her mind within these hours.* Peter thought as he disembarked from the train with his only basket in his hand.

Peter got to Wilobo Inn. The reception desk at Wilobo inn was quiet there was no one? Peter look at his watch it was only 6. 45p.m not yet supper time for the Wilobo workers. *May be they are busy somewhere in the rooms.* Peter thought. He walked and sat in the waiting launch. After a few minutes he heard a door squeaked and opened. A tall young man in the uniform for the Wilobo Inn walked out with the hotel register in his hand. He went behind the counter and sat down on the chair. Peter moved to him and greeted him. The boy replied his greeting and stooped to write in the book. Immediately a well groomed man walked out of a room came and threw his keys to the boy and walked out saying "I am late." Peter turned and looked at the man and thought he was impolite and arrogant by tossing the key at the boy. Nevertheless, the boy took the man's keys quietly hooked it on the nail bearing the number of the key and came back to Peter.

"Yes please I would like to see Rosemary or Lilly?

"Sorry Sir. They are both off duty today. They are attending the engagement party of Rosemary to that man you saw rushing out."

What? Peter asked with a sharp grating voice it sounded like the noise you hear when a stylus slides through a record rotating on deck. Peter could not believe his ears

"Why, is it a surprise to you?" The boy asked when he noted a disappointment in Peter.

"You know Rosemary is................ Peter said a let his word die way. "I don't believe it. Where is the party taking place?"

"It's supposed to be in a hall in Paacholi inn. You want to go there?"

"No I don't think so. Because, I know a party like that, not anyone is allowed. Beside you must have a card or coupon inviting you for the party." Peter said and looked round and saw that the creamed colour Mercedes Benzes which was parked at the door was gone. *It must be the car of the man who is going to tie knots with Rosemary.* Peter thought and wearily walked out of the gate. He stood and looked left and right and saw a flat stone at the gate. To gain strength to walk to the Railways Station Peter sat down on the stone with the head stoop down. Recalling what Ucamgiu told him while in his office, *you know this gold trade is very tricky There are some traditional beliefs in it which if not done, you might not even see it, in-spite of the fact that you might be having the money for it. So let us succeed first then you begin to talk of when to refund me. Could this be why we failed? If it involved witchcraft, then I am out of the game. I have never done it and I will not. I rather die poor.*

Then he remembered the bottles of the gin he bought from Pakwach. He pulled one out and opened it. From the mouth of the bottle, Peter took a mouth full and swallowed. It was strong and sent his brain cells in motion. He repeated the process thrice, *what am I going to do in this world?* Peter thought as he continued to drink from the bottle. He thought of Rosemary being squeezed by the guy who walked passed them at the counter on his way to their introduction party and shrugged. *I have no money to maintain her. Money speaks.* Without realizing what he was doing Peter had emptied the one litter of gin and blew his seeks and said *this is enough for now let me walk back to the railways station. This will make me sleep most of the way.* Peter thought, got up from the stone, tossed the empty of the gin on top the rubbish in the bin which stood near the gate and staggered towards the road to find his way to the Railway Station.

The sun had set and a bit cloudy. As Pete staggered and tried to walk across the road, he under estimated the distance and the speed at which the army jeep AU 234 was travelling towards him. Within few minutes, the vehicle hit him and threw him at road side dead. The body of Peter was identified by the Police using his Ministry Identity card found in his pocket. "The Permanent Secretary Ministry of Education, Peter Lapyem! No! It can't be.

What was he doing in Gulu and alone?" The police officer in charge of Gulu police station exclaimed, as he examined the blood stained Peter official identity card. His blood stained basket with the content intact was also delivered together with his smashed body to the police mortuary.

The following day the head line in the state own newspaper *"the eye of the nation"* carried the sad new about the death of Peter throughout East Africa. "**The Permanent Secretary Ministry of Education Peter Lapyem was knocked dead by a speeding army Vehicle in the northern town of Gulu.** Christine the sister of Peter in Nairobi got the newspaper in their office in the afternoon, the usual time they always get the paper. And when she saw the head line she read it about four times trembling without accepting the news. Then she saw darkness covering her and she collapsed hitting her forehead on the sharp edge of the corner of the table before she felled hitting the back of her head on the floor. Moses Mushilla, Christine's boss was busy in his office which was adjacent to her office. He was startled by the noise coming from her office. He rushed out to find out what happened only to see her lying under the table with one leg still resting on her chair. He did not need to ask what happened. The head line in the newspaper *"the eye of the nation "*which she left on the table spoke by itself. Moses quickly organized transport and she was rushed to Kenyatta hospital where she was pronounced dead.

Moses was aware of Christine family background. He knew that the only surviving relative was her brother Peter Lapyem who was also now dead. His close friends Andrew and Walter from whom he could have inquired for help were hospitalized after they received the shocking news early in the morning as they walked to their offices. The two were all treated for shocks from which they recovered after one week of hospitalization. Because of that Moses thought it was worthless to try to return Christine body to Uganda so with the help of the Trans Oceans staff Christine remain was given temporarily burial in Nairobi cemetery.

The Ministry of Education was thrown into shock and depression. Everyone did not understand why Peter travelled to Gulu without the departmental vehicle even if He was on private business. Similarly, the Ministry records showed that his immediate next of kin was his dead sister Christine. It was at this moment that Walter and Andrew were discharged from the Hospital. The two approached the Ministry of Education and expressed their willingness to traveled to Gulu and arrange for the burial of Peter. A few staff members from the Ministry Headquarter including Beatrice, accompanied Walter and Andrew to Gulu.

Since the death and the burial of his wife Rose Peter never paid attention to their home in the village. As the result the fruits and shade trees they planted with Rose grew into wild bushes. Grass grew everywhere even on the house tops. The graves of his parents and Rose were severely damaged by roots of trees so that they cracked badly. It was hard to find the way home. Because of these sorrowful state of the home, when they received the body of Peter from the police mortuary, Walter and Andrew decided to bury Peter in Gulu cemetery.

www.ingramcontent.com/pod-product-compliance
Lightning Source LLC
Chambersburg PA
CBHW071734190726
48292CB00003B/750